About the Author

Ellie Boman grew up in Northern Minnesota in the US, and got her bachelor's degree in teaching Spanish from the University of Minnesota. Later, she got her master's degree in education from St. Mary's University in Southern Minnesota. She has been lucky enough to teach high school Spanish for many years. She lives in a small town in Minnesota, and her husband and she loves to travel, spend time with their families, going to sports events, and enjoying Lake Superior.

47 Seconds

Ellie Boman

47 Seconds

Olympia Publishers
London

www.olympiapublishers.com
OLYMPIA PAPERBACK EDITION

Copyright © Ellie Boman 2023

The right of Ellie Boman to be identified as author of
this work has been asserted in accordance with sections 77 and 78 of the
Copyright, Designs and Patents Act 1988.

All Rights Reserved

No reproduction, copy or transmission of this publication
may be made without written permission.
No paragraph of this publication may be reproduced,
copied or transmitted save with the written permission of the publisher, or in
accordance with the provisions
of the Copyright Act 1956 (as amended).

Any person who commits any unauthorized act in relation to
this publication may be liable to criminal
prosecution and civil claims for damage.

A CIP catalogue record for this title is
available from the British Library.

ISBN: 978-1-80074-926-9

This is a work of fiction.
Names, characters, places and incidents originate from the writer's
imagination. Any resemblance to actual persons, living or dead, is purely
coincidental.

First Published in 2023

Olympia Publishers
Tallis House
2 Tallis Street
London
EC4Y 0AB

Printed in Great Britain

Dedication

I dedicate this book to my son who knows why. I love you.

"Fact: Every forty-seven seconds a psychopath is born."
Kent A. Kiehl, Ph.D.

Part One

1

Did she really hear someone up ahead of her? She stood perfectly still to see if she still heard the crunch of the leaves. She heard nothing. "I must be imagining it," she thought. "No one is up ahead of me in the bushes. I'm so paranoid, and I watch too much Discovery ID." Her thoughts raced. Her boyfriend called The ID Network "The Bad Decision Network" Every story showed someone making a really poor choice:

"I know he's addicted to heroin, but I love him."

"He was convicted of second-degree murder, but he did his time, and I love him."

Seriously, what could go wrong? It was her favorite channel. Now, her senses were heightened. This felt real. She could even smell him. It was a weird smell of cheap after shave and sweat. She tried to pinpoint the cologne smell. What was it? Maybe her dad wore it.

Suddenly, the smell appeared in front of her. He couldn't have been more than five feet, eight inches tall. There was a bad energy surrounding him. He wore a beanie hat that sailors and hipsters wore. Chloe thought he looked too old to be wearing one. If her roommate, Shelley, was with her, they would mock this sweaty dude in a beanie with cheap cologne. He was wearing a sweater. It wasn't exactly a Cosby sweater, but it was close. "Boomer," she thought. "Total boomer." He wasn't exactly a typical scary guy, but he had scary eyes. They were large pools of brown. They looked through her. It felt like she was looking at a man with no soul. She wondered how crazy he'd look if she had her glasses on. He was a bit blurry, but she saw his eyes. She felt those eyes. "This is great," Chloe thought. "I'm going to get raped because I'm vain. I wanted to look cute while I cheered on Alex in the play." She and Alex met three weeks ago and had been inseparable since. She thought he could be the one. He had the cutest smile, and he was so kind to her. He opened her door, he watched the ground as they walked so he could point out potential danger like pot holes and glass, he never lied, and he was funny. He loved acting and he had the best singing voice. She adored him. He was one of the brothers in "Joseph and the Amazing Technicolor Dream Coat." Chloe knew every word to every song of that play.

She heard him sing, "Those Canaan days... we used to know... where have they gone?... Where did... they go?" It was so much fun to watch him make the part his. It didn't hurt that she loved this play. All her roommates and friends were busy and couldn't come with her. She even asked people she didn't really like, but she knew them from class. They all had exams coming up and papers due. Midterms were fast approaching. She didn't blame them, but right now, she would have felt a lot safer if she was with someone.

She looked at the ground and tried to just walk past that part of the bushes. Whenever strange men approached her, she looked at the ground. She thought maybe if they thought she didn't notice them, they'd leave her alone. So far, it had worked like a charm.

"Anna?" he asked.

"No," she said. "It's Chloe. Anna is one of my roommates." If he knew her, how bad could he be? "Why didn't I wear my glasses? Did I really think I was so much cuter without them? I'd have been able to see this guy from further away with my glasses on." She berated herself in her head. Instead, she walked closer to him, and that smell got worse, and his eyes were more clear.

"Oh, hey, Chloe. It's me, Jim."

She didn't know a Jim, but she didn't want to look stupid, so she just said, "Hi, Jim.'

She got even closer to him to see if she could recognize him. She searched her mind for anyone Anna had introduced her to named Jim. She came up empty. Because he knew Anna, Chloe wasn't afraid of this guy any more. It was a little weird that he wanted to stay in the shadow and wouldn't walk toward her, too. Chloe didn't want to be rude, so she went to shake his hand.

She was almost close enough, when she recognized him.

"Hi, what are you…" she didn't finish her sentence when he grabbed her and turned her around.

Her back was to his front.

Shit. Good thing I didn't say his name, she thought. Maybe he wouldn't kill her if she didn't know who he is. He wouldn't have to worry about her turning him in.

"Chloe, if you scream, I will kill you. Do you understand?"

Chloe nodded. He had his arm wrapped around her neck with his hand on her mouth. She couldn't have screamed if she wanted to.

Chloe tried to spin out of his grip. He was remarkably strong. He didn't seem little any more. He pushed her away from him, and she fell onto the ground. She felt deep pressure on her head, and everything went black. When she woke up, She was naked, hand cuffed, and in the back seat of his car. She had no idea where we were or where he was taking her. She thought better of asking. She thought talking at all could send this crazy fucker right over the edge. He was teetering next to that edge and could go over it at any moment. Her head was killing her. But the worst pain was in her chest. Chloe was so completely scared that she felt a panic attack coming. She occasionally had them after her mom died, and her dad left Chloe and her brother, Matt, at their grandparents' house. Luckily, her grandparents were young, healthy, and wanted nothing more than to be with their daughter's children. Chloe knew she was loved, but her panic attacks got her once in a while still. She knew to just think about breathing. As she did that, she calmed down and could breathe normally again.

She looked at him, and he looked absolutely crazed. He hit her in the head again with a big piece of metal he brought from his car. It had a big hook on the end of it. Was it a tire iron? With that, she passed out again. When she woke up, she saw that they were up in the hills of Duluth W. She guessed they were somewhere on the skyline parkway. She looked around hoping to see a car with a couple of love birds in it, but even the make out crowd was gone. They were completely alone. This was not good. "Good morning, princess," he said. When he grinned at her, she could see he was missing one of his teeth in the front. She wanted to pass out again, but she was pretty lucid. If he hit her like that again, she didn't think she would survive it. "Get out of the car," he said.

She was still naked and handcuffed, but she managed to get out of the back seat.

"The cuffs are really tight," she said. She saw that tactic used before on her favorite channel. That woman was able to wiggle out of the cuffs after he loosened them up.

"You're fine," he said.

So much for that plan, Chloe thought. All she had left was to make herself a person to this asshole. Right now, she was an object, a plaything. She was something that belonged to him, and that gave him power. She would have to compliment him and tell him about her family so he could see her as a human being. "Please don't hurt me," she begged. "You're so strong that I bet you can have anything you want. I promise, I won't tell anyone what happened. Maybe some day we can hang out without all this. My grandma always says you never know who your best friend or love could be. Even a rocky start like this could be overcome," she said. The total nonsense she spewed to him was not well received. He ignored her. His eyes were blank, and he was totally focused on the task at hand for him. She would at least be raped, she knew. There was no way out of this.

He pulled her further into a wooded area. The moon was full, so she could see everything, but so could he. And it wasn't blurry to him.

He pushed her down on the ground when he decided they were far enough into the woods. She had no way to block her fall, and she fell face first into the mud.

He untied her feet, but there were tree stumps. He tied each leg to a tree stump.

"Oh my God," she thought. "He's been here before. He knew those tree stumps were there." He was so repulsive. He smelled so terrible she could hardly stand it. The sweat was pouring off him now. Chloe just wanted her mom or her grandma. She wanted a hug. She wanted someone to tell her it would be okay. She wanted to scream and cry and fight this little bastard who was gearing up to rape her. What gave him the right to take her body in this way? Rape, at least, had an end game. Chloe was shooting for an end game. She just wanted to survive.

He rattled his zipper up and down, up and down. He looked at Chloe and laughed this sick laugh with his tongue sticking out as if to say, "You know you want it. Look how sexy I am." She thought he was repulsive.

He undressed. He raped her endlessly. He couldn't finish. Chloe wanted to yell at him that it wasn't her fault. She didn't ask for this.

Oh God, this hurt. She was so embarrassed. No one should be able to take her body without her permission. As long as he didn't take her life, she would be okay. She could was strong, she told herself. Where there's life, there's hope.

She couldn't look at him. She turned her head to the side. By this time, he didn't care. He was slapping, biting and punching her. He pulled out his knife and ran it along her body. Chloe felt the knife go in once, then her mind transported her to a different place. She was not part of what was happening to her body at that point. The white hot pain of the stabbing disappeared. It was such a relief. She couldn't smell him or feel him. Her brain and body separated. She could see her mom in her mind. She was sitting at the kitchen table with her calculator and her bill box as she called it. She told Chloe to sit with her. She just stared at her mom. Couldn't she see what was happening?

"Don't worry, Honey. Everything is going to be okay. You will be very happy after today. He is not real. Keep looking at me, honey. I made Special K bars. Here honey, eat one of these. They were your favorite when you were little," her ghost mom said. Chloe tasted the bar. It was chewy and crunchy at the same time with a quarter inch of chocolate as the frosting. They were so good. She almost forgot that she was being raped and probably murdered down below in the real world.

"But Mom, how am I seeing you? You've been gone for ten years. I've missed you every day. Am I dead?" Chloe asked.

"Not yet, honey. But keep focused on me, and you won't be

afraid any more. You have nothing to be afraid of. Everything is perfect here. Nana and Papa are here. They miss you so much. They'll be at the gate to greet you. Don't be afraid."

"What about Grandma and Grandpa? Will they be okay if I go?" Chloe asked.

"Grandma and Grandpa will join us here when it's their time. They will be fine, honey. Matt will take good care of them. Don't be afraid," Mom said.

"I'm not scared, Mom. I can't wait to be with you all."

Just then, her abductor slapped her hard across the face. The slap brought her immediately back to her body.

"Tell me you love it. Tell me you want me."

Chloe whispered, "I love it."

"Say it like you mean it," he said.

She refused. She just saw her mom, and she knew she was going die. She would deny him what he came here for. She wouldn't be his puppet. That threw him, and his temper flared. It would have terrified her if she wasn't just with her mom.

He strangled her as he raped her. When she started to panic, she heard her mom speak to her. Her mom showed her Heaven so she could see everyone, too. She could see peace that was moments away.

"Focus on me, baby. It's almost over. This coward will get what's coming to him, and you will be happy with us," the ghost of Mom said.

Chloe knew she was dying. She felt her energy drain. She felt so tired. So tired. She couldn't get air, and she had fought so hard. She could die knowing she fought. But she couldn't keep this up. He was too strong. She was on her back, and he was on top of her. He had one hand on her neck while he thrust into her. With every last bit of energy she had, she scratched the hell out of him wherever her cuffed hands could reach. There was no way to explain that away if someone saw them. He had finger nail marks all down the side of his chest and legs, and Chloe knew she had his DNA under her finger nails.

Everything started to go dark. It was such relief. She wanted to die now. She was ready to go. She quit fighting. He was still squeezing and grunting as Chloe drifted further and further away and closer and closer to her mom, Nana, and Papa.

2

"No, Olivia! I do not want to go out tonight! I have to work in the morning!" I told my roommate. We called her Liv. She'd been begging me to go to Import Night at our favorite dance bar. It still had disco lights on the dance floor although it was 1989. We loved that place. It was called The White Elephant, and they had theme nights and cheap beer. Import night was our favorite, although we stuck pretty much to American Beer. That wasn't on sale, but it was cheap, tasted like water, and I could drink several and not be drunk.

"Izzy, you work at eleven. That's almost not even morning any more," she struck back.

"I know, but still. I have homework, and I don't have the ambition to get ready."

"David called and he'll do your hair if you go out with us."

Dammit. She knew the right buttons to push. I wasn't passing up David doing my hair. He was the best! He was the only one I knew who could tame my curls. His big ambitions were to own a salon and be a stylist to the stars. I had no doubt he would be. He was all personality, he was smart, and he was good at what he did. I may have been a bit biased because he was like my brother. He didn't offer up his services very often.

"Why does David want me to go out so bad that he'll do my hair? He only offers that up when he really wants me to go."

"Brian will be there tonight, he needs his wing girl, and I need her, too. Tyler will be there."

"Liv, I thought you were done with him," I said. "He's such an asshole. He's dating that Linda girl. He's such a dick."

"Izzy, stop. They're not actually dating, and he called and asked if we'd be there tonight, and I said we would. Please come out tonight."

"So I get to be wing girl for both of you?"

"Yeah, pretty much, but I'll DD. David will do your hair, you be there for back up for us if Brian and Tyler are shitty tonight. Shelley will probably be there, too, so if David needs you, and I need you, David can have you, and Shel will be my wing girl."

"This is complicated, but yeah, I'll go."

The cool thing about Tyler liking Liv, when he felt like it, was that he was the DJ, and he knew what songs we danced to. While I strongly disliked Olivia being so devoted to someone who kind of liked her when he wanted to get laid, I liked the music. Liv would have to figure the rest out for herself. She, obviously, wasn't listening to me. So, when we walked in the bar, Express Yourself, by Madonna played the minute we found a table and put down our jackets.

"I'll be your wing girl in five minutes, you two! We have to dance to Madonna," I said.

"Agreed," said David.

Liv was already half way to the dance floor. She knew the rules! If Madonna or Prince played, we danced together no matter who we were talking to. We could have been talking to a John Stamos look alike, and we had to stop everything and dance. No matter what. It was 1989, and the bars still played our music. We always had a blast.

I loved Madonna. I loved that she was unapologetic about her personality, her style, her vision, her attitude, all of it. She just was. And her music was my favorite music to lose myself in.

I'd forget about having to wear my Perkins polyester the next day, or the presentation I had to give in my Lit. class. I'd close my eyes and move my body. I loved to dance.

The next song was danceable, but not our favorite. I could take or leave Whitney Houston. She did not call us to the dance floor like Madonna, Prince or Morris Day, who gave us ten seconds to get to the dance floor.

We went up to the bar to get a beer, and the bar tender set out three Coors Lights and handed them to us. "Is it bad that the bartender at the White Elephant knows what we drink? Does that make us regulars?" I asked.

"Yeah, pretty sure we are regulars since we haven't missed a Friday all school year," David said. We all laughed and found our table.

"Izzy, did you pay for this round?"

"Nope, I thought you did."

"David, was it you?" I asked.

"I thought you bought them," he said.

"Who in the hell bought these beers?" I asked.

When I looked up, I saw him staring at me. I knew he was the one who bought the beer. I told Liv and David, and told them not to look. Of course, they both looked.

"He's hot," Liv said. "He's staring pretty hard at you, Iz. Go say hi."

"No, he kind of creeps me out. Plus I'm wing girl tonight."

"I release you of wing duty. David, what about you?" Liv looked, and David was long gone talking to Brian in the corner. "Tyler is about to take a break anyway, just look at me occasionally to make sure I'm not having a meltdown," she said.

I'd never been looked at quite that intensely before. I had to go say hello. I was totally drawn to this stranger with the beautiful brown eyes, jet black hair that fell to his collar, and the sexy way he stood looking at me as though he knew I would make my way over there. I could feel his vibe and confidence a long way away. I couldn't decide if he was cheesy or sexy. I had to get to the bottom of that dilemma.

I approached his table holding my beer. "Thank you for the beer," I said.

"Wasn't me," he said.

"What? I was sure it was you because you're the only one looking at me like that."

"Like what?" he asked.

"With bedroom eyes," I said. I couldn't believe my own confidence. It wasn't like me to say something like that, but this guy was sexy in that mysterious Harlequin story way. I half expected his name to be Fabio and have him live a quiet, pained existence in Montana somewhere on a cattle ranch. It was either that or he was a brooding English professor. Still pained, quiet, shy, had an obsession with Sherry and Bach, and was ridiculously good in bed. Either scenario would take me years to really know what pained him, did his mother die? Did his father desert him? Did his little brother suffer from Leukemia? Did he see someone murdered? What caused the sadness? I would get to the bottom of it. My mind always made up stories about people, and I would see how close I came to correct.

"Bedroom eyes, huh? What constitutes bedroom eyes?" he asked.

"Well, your eyes follow me. I feel a little exposed because you look at me like you think you know me." I was really going out on a limb here with this guy. I held nothing back. I told him what I thought, and why I thought it. I never did that. It felt liberating. I didn't really care if I was way off base or not. If he was looking intently at a girl next to me, and I didn't see her, this would be a funny story. David would die laughing.

"Now, I feel exposed," he said.

"Why?" I asked.

"Because I was thinking about you in my bedroom," he said. "But I was also picturing you sitting with me at dinner or a ball game or on the couch watching television."

"Really? Why? You don't even know me."

"You have a quality that I like. I can tell by looking at you that you are open and honest, and obviously beautiful. I want to know you."

"I'd like to get to know you, too," I said.

He went to the bar and bought us a couple more beers, and we started to talk like we had known each other forever. He talked far more than I thought he would, and when he did, he was funny. I thanked God that I let Liv and David talk me into going out with them tonight.

He was both cheesy and sexy. That, actually, was my favorite combination. Cheesy in that he'd tell me anything even if it was stupid, and the sexy part is obvious. His stare almost burned through me. No one had ever looked at me like that before. If this guy didn't call me, that was it, I was never dating again. Ever. I meant it this time. I'd be an old, lonely, dog lady. I wasn't into cats. I didn't even know his name until we wrote down our numbers for each other.

Michael: 517-448-9896. It didn't matter what his phone number was. I'd never call him. I was old school. If a guy didn't call me, that was it. We didn't speak again. I prayed that wouldn't happen here. I liked him a ridiculous amount. It made no sense. I didn't even know him. I knew how I felt, though.

Liv drove us all home although all three of us were sober. It wasn't that kind of night. Liv was devastated because Tyler wanted to tell her about Linda in person. That was why he asked us to come. What an asshole. The way he announced that to her just hurt her feelings and fed his ego. She swore she was done with him this time. Tyler thought they should sleep together one last time to say good bye. I was so proud of Olivia. She told him to fuck off, and that she actually came to tell him about the new man she was dating. And he would never see her naked again. Tyler would be a little shocked that Liv was so adamant. He assumed he could do whatever he wanted to her, and she'd always be there for him no matter what. God, I hoped she followed through.

David was in love, he said. I didn't think much of it because he fell "in love" with everyone he dated. I didn't speak. I didn't want to jinx it. I was fairly certain Michael wouldn't call anyway. Wasn't that the way it worked? When I wanted them to call, they didn't. When I didn't want them to call, I couldn't get them to leave me alone.

We sang "I Will Survive" all the way home at the top of our lungs. Singing that song helped us feel tough. We needed a little toughness. They didn't even ask about Michael. The phone was ringing when Liv and I walked in the door. It was either Michael or Tyler. No one else would call at three a.m. It was Michael.

"Hey beautiful," he said.

I blushed and said, "Hey, hot stranger."

"I don't think we're strangers any more," he said.

"I guess we are not."

"Want to have dinner with me tonight?" he asked. "It's already tomorrow."

"I would love that. I get off work at eight, though."

"That's fine," he said. "I'll cook for us, if that's okay with you."

"That's great, but I can't get there until about nine."

"You're worth the wait," he said, and I beamed into the phone. Liv was staring at me. She was happy for me but wanted me to be careful. He gave me his address and said he'd see me tonight.

"I can't wait," I said. Wow. Where did that come from? I was supposed to be playing it cool, but I couldn't do it. I was one hundred percent taken by him. There was no turning back for me. That was it. Michael was it. I was in love before I had dinner with him that night. I floated through my shift at work, and all the waitresses teased me.

"Earth to Izzy… table three needs water." Mary, the shift manager said.

"Leave her alone, she's in love," Connie said. Connie waited tables there for years, and I loved her. She always had my back. I had hers too, for what that was worth.

"Huh?" I asked. While they were talking, I was busy trying to remember what Michael's eyes looked like exactly, and what he said his favorite food was. I think it was spaghetti, but I couldn't remember for sure. So, I missed the entire exchange between Mary and Connie.

"See, I told you," Connie said, and she patted my head like a toddler.

I should shape up so I didn't lose my job. Michael could turn out to be a big loser. Most of them did.

The rest of my shift, I focused on my customers, and the time went much faster. My tips were better, too. We had our usual dinner rush that started at four. The Midwest had notoriously early dining habits. But we went to bed early and got up early and worked hard. That was my response to my Latinx friend who

27

mocked our eating habits regularly. Things slowed down about seven, and Mary cut me a little early. I got my side work done, and got home before I was even supposed to get off work. I decided not to call Michael to tell him I'd be early. I decided to take a bath and get the syrup and French fry smell out of my hair instead.

I knocked on his door almost exactly at nine. I couldn't help it. I was not cool, and I was punctual. It's who I was. He might as well know that up front. I brought a six pack of beer with me, I didn't really drink wine. I was a college student. I couldn't afford wine, anyway. Boonesfarm was about the extent of my wine-drinking knowledge, too. I knew I liked Boones, but the rest just confused me. Beer, every college student knows. I just grabbed Coor's Light since that's what we both drank last night. There were a million different kinds of beer, too. I didn't know one from the next. I just drank what was cheap or what someone offered me. I wasn't exactly a connoisseur.

Michael looked so cute. He was wearing Levi's and a UMD Bulldogs t-shirt. His eyes still sparkled, and he had a towel over his shoulder. He had a bit of a mess going in the kitchen, but the table was set with candles, and he kissed me long and deep before I even put the beer down. There was no way I was going to be able to eat. We had a beer while the sauce simmered. I did remember right. Spaghetti was his favorite food, and according to him, it was the only thing he knew how to cook.

I choked down a few bites. It was delicious, but I was too wound up to eat. I'd been anticipating this all day. After dinner, we watched "The Twilight Zone" and made out on his couch. At midnight, he still hadn't asked me to stay, so I said that I should go. He didn't fight me on that, so it was the right call. Guys always fought me when I said I should go home. I always heard,

"No, please stay." I was used to that. Guys always wanted to have sex. Maybe Michael was a man and not just a guy. Maybe Michael was different. Maybe I meant something to him. It was possible that he didn't like me enough to have sex, too.

I focused on that. I thought that if he didn't want to sleep with me, he must not like me in that way. We saw each other a lot, but we never had sex. I never spent the night, and he would never come to our place. His rationale for that was that he didn't have a roommate. But he wouldn't even come over when Liv was gone for the weekend. That was kind of weird. Weird in a good way, though.

I had an obsession with Minnesota Twins baseball. It started with thinking Steve Lombardozzi was cute on second base during the 1987 World Series. I have since evolved to like baseball for what it is, and not because a cute guy plays it. Michael loved the Twins. He was more obsessed than I was. That was so great! We talked baseball and went to games. Mostly, however, we watched from his place. We yelled at the TV although they couldn't hear me. Michael said that every time I yelled at the TV.

"They can't hear you, Isabelle!" I thought they needed me, though. I would jinx it if I wasn't yelling at the TV. They needed my support telepathically.

Finally after three months of "dating" he asked me to spend the night. We made love, and it was everything I hoped for and more. He was tender and sweet, and he clung to me like a life raft. He whispered into my ear that he needed me. He didn't tell me he loved me yet, but he did say he needed me. That was enough for me at that moment. I was completely happy. Well, almost completely happy.

One evening, my parents came to town from Stillwater. I told them about Michael, and they wanted to meet this man I talked about incessantly and seemed to be in love with. I confided in my mom that he was the one. He was the man I wanted to marry. She said, "Please, just finish college first." That wasn't the reaction I hoped for. Of course, I'd finish college. That was never in question. I wonder what I'd told her about him that made her hesitant. She never kept her mouth shut where my boyfriends were concerned, and I usually didn't have to guess why she hated them. This time, I was stumped. He was so sweet. He needed me. I was head over heels in love with him. He was it, in my opinion. My search for the right guy was over. I found him. Why did my mom change the subject all the time when I brought him up? Well, when they came to Duluth to see me, they wanted to take the two of us out for dinner. We went to Dusty's Wine Bar, and it was great. I was having the best time, and I thought Michael was making a good impression.

Until he said, "Jim, look at the woman who just walked in. Wow, I keep telling Izzy it's normal for women her age to wear short skirts, and show cleavage. She just won't. Honey, look how hot that girl is. You'd look like that with a push up bra and a low-cut top."

My dad didn't know what to say. My mom pursed her lips so hard that it looked like she'd just tasted something sour. He made it infinitely worse when he brought my mother into it. "Our women are hot, right Jim? Nothing wrong with showing it off." My dad just made a weird throat clearing sound, and I wanted to disappear. I knew that comment was not good. But that was just Michael. He said all those things that popped into people's heads. Most people had the good sense to know their audience and use a filter, but I told myself it was good that he didn't hide anything from me. I don't think my mother agreed with that assessment. I think it showed her that she was right all along.

"Izzy, where's the ladies room here?" she asked.

"I'll show you," I said. I could tell she wanted to talk to me, so I thought I'd let her get it off her chest.

"No, that's okay. You can just tell me," she said. "Finish your meal."

Wow. That didn't happen. My mom was so upset that she couldn't even talk to me. When she came back from the bathroom, she said they should get home to my little brother. Grant was sixteen. The only thing he needed a babysitter for was to keep him from having a party or getting his girlfriend pregnant. I was a little jealous that they liked Ceci without question, and Michael was under a microscope. So he made a stupid comment. So what? He was nervous. I was angry. But I was pissed at my mom. I wasn't mad that Michael said what he did to my dad or to me. I should've been mad about that, in retrospect.

We said goodbye to my parents, and my dad paid the bill. We decided to stay and have one more drink at the bar. My parents couldn't get out of there fast enough. I was humiliated.

"Well, I think it's safe to say that your parents don't like me," he said.

"Well, you did tell me to wear a push up bra and low cut shirt and pointed out the hot girl in the room. Sometimes you really need to know your audience."

He just stared at me. It wasn't a sexy stare like at the White Elephant. This stare was different. It was menacing. I could tell I embarrassed him further. I don't know what made me say what I did. I wasn't mad at him, although I should have been. I was mad at my mom. Why couldn't she just pretend to like him?

"I'm done. Let's go."

I still had over half a beer left, but he didn't care. His beer was gone, and he was ready to go. I didn't want to fight any more, so I followed him.

Michael didn't talk the whole way home. I stole glances at him during the entire ride. His jaw clenched and unclenched, his eyes were almost slits. If I didn't know him better, I'd have thought he was evil. He scared me. He caught me looking at him and sped up. He went faster and faster until I was crying and begging him to slow down. It looked like he got some pleasure out of scaring the hell out of me.

"Michael, please, please slow down. You're going to kill us. It's raining, please. You're scaring me!" I was terrified. I begged, I said I was sorry for such a terrible evening, I said I loved him. I was crying. The rain was pelting the car, and the wind had tree tops bent way over. The only way I saw anything was when the lighting struck. I could vaguely see with the headlights. He had the high beams on which made it impossible to see in the rain. How did he not know this? Everyone in the Midwest knew this. High beams made it harder to see in the rain or snow. I think he knew. I think he was trying to scare me more or make it more exciting for him and to hell with me.

Still nothing from him. His eyes were vacant, but he looked almost happy.

Finally, at my apartment complex, he slammed on the brakes. The pavement was wet, and he damned near hit one of my neighbor's cars. I jumped out of his car and ran for my apartment. I hit the buzzer, and Liv buzzed me in. When I got to the apartment, I latched the deadbolt and put the bar into the sliding glass door that led to the balcony. We shut all the shades. Olivia had no idea what was going on, but she followed my lead. We went into a back bedroom, turned off the lights and lit a candle. I don't know why I felt the need to do that. He obviously knew I was home. I just didn't want him to see our silhouettes. I didn't want to encourage him to stay in the parking lot or try to get in. I wanted him gone. In the bedroom, I told Liv the story of the evening. I shouldn't have. I never should have told her. I knew she would hate him forever now. I couldn't tell anyone else. They'd hate him. I wasn't sure this warranted leaving him completely. Did it? I mean, my mom humiliated him. I don't know why I blamed him. I should have told him that I loved him and that my mom was out of line. Why didn't I just do that?

I told Liv that he was just hurt by my mom, and he needed to calm down. I down played the car ride. I told her it was wet, and I was scared because I couldn't see anything. I told her I don't know why I was so wound up. It wasn't like he'd hurt me or anything. "Isabelle, why are you lying for him? If he just drove a little wild, why are you shaking? You were terrified when you got home."

"I'm not lying," I said. I couldn't look at her.

"Tell me the truth. Right now."

"Okay, Mom," I said. God I hated it when she acted like my mother. "He drove so fast that I thought we were going to die. He was so angry that I couldn't talk to him. It was like he was in a trance. But he came out of it when we got home, and it seemed like he didn't really realize what he just did."

"You might not be scared, Iz, but you should be. I am. He is not allowed here again. I don't trust him."

I understood where she was coming from. It wasn't like he ever came to our place, anyway. Tyler was creeping back into her life, and I didn't like him. How was this so different?

I apologized to her, and I told her that he wouldn't be coming inside. As I said that, we heard something on our balcony, our second floor balcony. Someone was trying to get in our sliding glass door. I thought I was being paranoid putting the bar in and locking that door.

We went back into the bedroom.

"What do we do?" I asked.

"We call the fucking cops is what we do, Isabelle. Are you crazy?"

Liv was right. Why was I waffling back and forth? He got a thrill out of scaring me. I saw it on his face. He was excited by my terror.

"Okay, I'll call the police," I said. I was scared of him, but I was scared to lose him, too. I cannot explain why, but I loved him. I blamed my mom, and I blamed myself for this. If I would have just told him that her behavior was not okay. I should have said that to him. I started to sob. Liv grabbed the phone from my hand and dialed 911.

I could only hear her side of the conversation, but she told the operator that my boyfriend and I had a fight, and he was attempting to break in. The operator made Olivia stay on the phone.

I yelled out to him, "Michael, we called the police. You can't do this. You have to just go home." I was trying to get rid of him, but I was also warning him. I thought he needed to know so he wasn't caught on our balcony.

"Isabelle, so help me God if you are trying to help him, I'm out," Liv said.

"I'm trying to get him the hell off our balcony," I said.

"I know you, Izzy. Your heart is too big. You forgive too easily. Most of the time, that's your best quality. But when it's a guy who's shitting on you, you need to get rid of him. They don't get better. I know Tyler is trying to weasel his way back into my life. The difference is that I don't love him, and he doesn't scare me. Tyler is something to do. That's all I am to him either," she said.

My best friend knew me better than I knew myself. I know I forgive too much, and it ends up hurting me. I get that. But look what I gain by that. I wouldn't have a lot of my experiences if I didn't forgive. And I did love him. I loved the guy I met in the bar. The guy who drove me home, I did not like him. I wanted beer-buying Michael back. I told Liv this, and she hugged me.

"Honey, I don't know how to tell you this, but that guy is gone. He may have seemed sweet hand charming, but after tonight, we know that part of him is fake. The bad part is real.

"How do you know the charming part isn't real and this part is fake?"

"Izzy, no one fakes being mean."

"True."

As I told the story of the evening to the police, I started to regain my ground. I didn't do anything wrong, he did. He made a dumbass comment about my clothes to my dad, and he sped home. He was going to have to apologize to me, and I should not accept the apology. I should cut him loose. The red flag doesn't get much brighter than this. What advice would I give David or Liv? Kick him to the curb would've been what I told them. I would have been right, too. With that, I decided to break up with him regardless of any apology. Then, I cried so hard that I threw up.

Olivia called David. She needed back up on this one. No one could handle my heart break or the craziness of my reaction on their own.

"Honey, this is how domestic abuse starts," he said. "They get you absolutely hooked, then they treat you like shit. Then, you'll do anything to get that first version of him back and blame yourself for that version disappearing to be replaced by this asshole you see in front of you."

"How do you know?" I asked.

"Um, Mitch? Remember Mitch?"

"Oh, yeah. I'm sorry. That was so long ago, and you're fine now, so I kind of forgot about that dick," I said.

"I will never be okay after what he did to me. I will get by, but I'll never be the same."

I knew that David changed after Mitch, but I was used to how he was now. I liked who he was now. He had more of an edge to him than before, but he was also very clued in to behavior and could tell when someone was pretending to be human, and when he was an actual human. He knew a psychopath or a narcissist immediately. I could still be snowed by the charm. He could not.

"Mitch charmed me with fancy dinners, beautiful dates, and expensive gifts. By the time I realized he was a thief, it didn't matter. I was in love. I got tired of the lies, though, and I confronted him. Remember? He beat the living shit out of me, and I apologized. Is this ringing a bell, Izzy? I took it because I "loved him." He was hot and cold with me for the next year and a half. He criticized my hair, my clothes, my brain, my body, my personality until I had nothing left. He beat me until I damned near died. It took a coma to get me away from him. Do you want to go through that, Isabelle?"

"Just because Mitch was a psychopath doesn't mean Michael is, David. God. After Mitch you think everyone is evil."

"You are avoiding the obvious here by yelling at me. I do not think everyone is psycho because of Mitch. I can just see through the bullshit faster because I lived it. I don't want you to live it. But if you need to make the mistakes yourself, so be it. I cannot stop you, but I won't support you. Michael is a textbook narcissist, and I'm willing to bet he has no empathy or conscience."

I was stunned into silence. I hugged David and cried on his shoulder for a long time. Liv sat on the chair opposite us crying too. David looked at her then and said, "As for you, Olivia, Tyler isn't a psycho, but he is an asshole, and you deserve better, too."

"How can you tell the difference between an asshole and a psychopath? How do you know Tyler isn't sadistic and getting off on Livvy's pain?"

"I don't know, I can just tell. A psychopath gets bored easily and will do things like Michael did to you the other night. He'll speed down winding roads in the rain, or he'll need to skydive or rock climb. He'll do extreme sports or take stupid risks. Not all psychopaths are serial killers, ya know. Some are CEO's of Fortune 500 companies. They get their thrills by stepping on people in a work environment. I have read everything I can about psychopaths since Mitch, and all the books say that. I've had a lot of therapy trying to get over it, too. I still go every two weeks, and it has been three years since all this went down."

"I forgot you met Mitch as a freshman. Didn't he pee in your gas tank once?" I asked laughing.

"I peed in his!" The three of us laughed through our tears. I wished I was as strong as David, but I wasn't even close.

"Seriously, Iz, you should dump this bastard before he takes more from you. These fuckers are dangerous, and they're everywhere. He'll take your innocence, your happiness, and your soul."

"Thanks, David," I said. "I hear you, and I'll think about it. I think Michael is lonely and confused, but I don't think he's a psycho. You should see him with his kids."

"Okay, but there's a personality disorder of some kind there, Isabelle. Be careful."

"I will," I said, and I hugged him and told him I loved him.

I was already too far down the rabbit hole. I loved Michael so much, but I knew he was bad for me. I couldn't choose him. After tonight, if I chose him, my parents would hate me, and Liv made it clear that she would not stick around for me to get my heart broken or worse. She thought he was dangerous. Hell, I thought he was going to kill me in that car. I'd never stand by while my friends made that decision either. I had to end it with him if he ever called me again. I couldn't call him.

His quest to win me back began at eight o'clock the next morning. I had to work at ten that morning and had night class after that, but every minute in between my shift and class, he called. If Olivia answered the phone, she told him he was an asshole, and he should go to hell. When I answered, I heard him out, but I stayed strong and said I was done. I didn't want to be done. That was obvious by my puffy eyes and sad face. Mitzi, my manager at Perkins that day sent me home. She said no one wanted to order food from someone who sounded like I did or who had eyes so swollen they were almost closed. I couldn't afford to lose the shift, but Mitzi wouldn't let me stay. She said I was bad for business. She loved me, and I knew she cared and was right. No customer would want their food brought to them by me that day. I went back home, took the phone off the hook, and fell asleep.

I woke up feeling a little stronger. I still couldn't eat, but at least I slept. I was sure I'd make it through my Ed. Psych. class. It was pretty easy, and my professor loved to pick apart Dead Poet's Society for psychological talking points. And he took attendance. I couldn't skip his class. I'd live.

I put the phone back on the hook and went to get in the shower again. I thought a cool shower would help. The second I put the phone back on the hook, it rang.

"Isabelle, please don't hang up," Michael said. "I know you have class in an hour, and I really need to tell you how sorry I am and that I love you."

"Michael, you said this already. It changes nothing. You were an idiot in front of my parents, and you damned near killed us to prove a point. I'm done," I said. I hung up the phone and took it back off the hook. Livvy worked a twelve hour shift at the gas station today, so she didn't care if it was off the hook. But I knew she'd check the machine for a call from Tyler the second she got home. Fuck her. If I couldn't get back together with Michael, she should stay clear of Tyler. Of course, Tyler didn't make her fear for her life. He did, however, make her feel bad about herself because he never could make up his mind between her and Linda. Liv was always trying to figure out what she should change about herself to make him pick her. It was sad.

I took a quick shower, called David quick to assure him that I had not gone back to "the dick" as he called him, and I was doing all right.

I would have no friends left if I went back to Michael. I had to stay strong. They'd kill me, and they wouldn't be excited about talking me through another break up with him which was bound to happen since we were so different. It wasn't like I was destined to marry this guy. I loved him more than I'd ever loved anyone, but we came from different worlds. My best childhood friend, Beth, took that Ed. Psych. Class with me. She kept threatening to drop the class, and I kept threatening to kill her if she did. She took it as an elective toward her psych. degree, and it was mandatory for my education degree. So, we stuck it out together.

We wrote notes back and forth like we did in high school discussing the professor's comb over and grandpa shoes, which boys were hot in the class, who we thought was a psych major and who was an education major, etc. We were probably wrong about everything, and we learned next to nothing, but we were jumping through a hoop with that class anyway. Half a college degree is learning how to read fine print, do what you're told the first time you're asked, and learning how to stand in line with patience. We had to withstand classes that had nothing to do with our degree or that had professors unfit to teach. It was 1989, so we predated the internet and cell phones. We took phones "off the hook" and checked answering machines. We stood in line at Window Seven to register for classes only to find the good classes full. And we weren't so easily bored. Thank God there was no social media because every humiliating detail of life was online now for the world to see. In 1989, we had to actually talk to people.

    Beth and I went to the Lazy Dog Bar for a drink before heading home. I told her all about my day from hell the day before. She was still pining for her high school boyfriend, so I knew she'd be my friend even if I couldn't make this break up stick. She knew what it was like to be in love and have everyone hate your boyfriend. She'd been there. In fact, she'd go back to her ex in a heartbeat. She told him she still loved him when she ran into him one night at the White Elephant. He told her that he'd moved on, and she was devastated. Of course he'd moved on. It had been four years. But I didn't point out the obvious. She knew how long it had been.

    We each had two beers and split an order of chicken wings. I started yawning.

    "We're getting old, girl," I said.

"Fuck that," she said. "You're getting old. I am staying young forever." Then she yawned.

I gave her a look to say I saw that.

"What? Yawns are contagious. If you weren't tired, I'd have started ordering shots."

"Shots are always a bad idea," I said.

"Only when you're old," she said. We were both twenty-two years old. We were not exactly ancient, but I felt like it today. The last couple days were tough. It was just time to go home. I had some homework to do, and I'd have trouble staying awake for that I knew. Neither of us was far from home, so we hugged and told each other we were strong, and we could do this. As we walked outside, he was the first thing I saw. Michael knew Beth and I headed here after class occasionally, and there he was waiting for me as we walked out of the bar.

"Speak of the devil," Beth said. I shushed her, but she was having none of that. She walked up to Michael and told him that if he ever treated me like that again, she'd kill him. He was embarrassed and sort of laughed that he knew. She assured him that she was not kidding.

"Well, Izzy, I'm glad to see you've told everyone about our breakup," he said.

"They're my best friends, so of course I told them."

"Are they more important to you than I am?" he asked.

"Of course not, but you told my dad that you wanted me to dress sluttier and drove like a fucking maniac to my apartment. Oh, and lest we forget, you scaled a wall to climb on our balcony."

"Well, you called the cops on me, and told everyone what a bastard I am, so I think that makes us even," he said.

"Not even close," I said.

"Izzy, I'm sorry. I know I was an asshole last night. I'm so sorry I'm not the man you deserve."

My heart melted a little. I didn't say anything, and I know my face softened. He tried to give me his crooked smile that I couldn't resist. Of course, he knew I found it irresistible. I steeled myself to resist him, though. I couldn't get back together with him yet. If I do get back together with him at all. So, I made no move closer to him, but neither did I walk away.

"Honey, remember, she who hesitates is lost," he said. He had such an arrogant look on his face when he said this. I was so confused by that statement that I didn't care at that moment if I ever spoke to him again. What the hell was he talking about? If he wasn't willing to wait through my hesitation, I did not need him.

"I know exactly where I am," I said. "I'm not lost. You can quote the Bible all you want. Why would you say that? Why are you telling me that if I hesitate, you'll go get someone else? That's not the way to win me back, asshole. That just pisses me off more." I walked away from him and didn't look back.

I put the phone back on the receiver before I left for class in case Tyler called Olivia. She wrote me a note on the table that she went to his place and would be back tomorrow. There were twenty-six messages on the answering machine. Twenty-four of them were from Michael. This was just getting weird. The more he chased me, the less I wanted him. The less I wanted him, the more he chased me. It was a vicious cycle.

I erased the messages, and took the phone off the hook. I talked to him enough today.

That was enough.

Every night that I didn't go out, I went to bed about ten o'clock. I liked to go to bed early so that I could get up early. I loved to talk to Michael at bed time because it felt so much more intimate when I was tired. I was honest and so open when it was bed time. I was attacked the summer of my sophomore in college, and I had trouble sleeping after that. My doctor sent me to therapy and prescribed Ambien to help me sleep. So I was particularly vulnerable. Michael knew all of this, of course. He also knew which buttons to push to make me feel guilty. I didn't stand a chance.

I was half asleep at eleven o'clock that night, and he came over. He shimmied up to our balcony again and lightly knocked. Liv wouldn't be home until morning, so it was okay to let him in.

"Look at you all sexy in that t-shirt. You must've known I'd come over," he said.

"No, Michael, I didn't think this was sexy," I said.

"Well, It is. You are sexy, so everything is sexy on you." "Oh, please. What do you want, Michael?"

"I want you. All I've ever wanted is you. Please don't bail on us."

"Bail? That's what you think I'm doing? Bailing?"

"Yes. If you really wanted to be with me, you'd be with me no matter what. You wouldn't make excuses."

"You don't think trying to kill me is a deal breaker?" I asked.

"Baby, you know I wasn't trying to kill you. This is all these people filling your head with these ideas. This is not you," Michael said.

"What do you mean? You think I'm so easily influenced that I can't think for myself?" I asked.

"That's not what I meant, and you know it. What I meant was, you love more than that. You love me no matter what. Other people are telling you that I'm a loser, and because I was upset, I was trying to "kill you."

"What? No, that's not what happened. And what's with the quotation marks? You did try to kill me. You would've gone down with me, but speeding a hundred miles per hour in the rain down windy roads is someone trying to kill himself and everyone around him."

"Baby, I'd never hurt you. I wasn't driving a hundred miles an hour. You have a creative memory. Your mind is playing tricks on you. You didn't like that I was going faster than you would have, but I did not go a hundred miles per hour. That's crazy. If I was going to kill myself, why would I kill you? If I wanted to kill you, why would I kill myself?"

"But, I looked at the speedometer. It said a hundred and one miles per hour."

"You're remembering that wrong because you were upset. That happens to everyone," he said.

Did it? Did that happen to other people, too? Did I imagine how fast he was going? I didn't think so, but was it possible? Did I create all this in my mind?

"Okay, that might be possible, but what about what you said to my dad?"

"What did I say to your dad?"

"You said that you tried to get me to dress like this girl who walked in in a mini skirt, but I might as well wear sweats everyday with how conservatively I dressed."

"I was kidding! I thought your mom and dad would be proud that you dressed conservatively. I thought what I was saying was complimenting you in their eyes. Apparently, they hate me enough to contradict whatever I say."

In a weird way, that made sense that he would think he was saying what they wanted to hear. He knew my parents still thought of me as a little girl although I was twenty-two. I student taught the next semester. I was so close to my degree that I could almost taste it. I felt tough knowing I'd come so far. I definitely didn't feel like a little girl any more especially after the attack I endured sophomore year. I didn't tell them about the attack, either. I didn't call the police, tell a professor, go to the doctor, nothing. I buried my head in the sand and went on. I pretended or tried to pretend that the attack did not happen. Of course that didn't work well when I couldn't sleep, didn't trust anyone, and wouldn't go anywhere alone at night. If it was getting dark, I was staying put. So maybe what Michael was saying was true. Maybe I was projecting the actions of my attacker onto him. He was my rapist, but that was too hard to come to grips with, so I called him my attacker and left it at that.

Michael stared at me wondering what I was thinking. He just sat quietly. I never saw him do that before or since. Michael was a talker. He needed to bring people to his way of thinking.

As I looked at him, I saw all of his beautiful qualities. I saw the poet. I saw the man who opened my car doors and listened to my theories about everyone and everything. I saw the man who loved me without question. I saw the man I loved without question. Yes, the clothes comment and speeding were red flags, but I couldn't lose him. I loved him too much.

"Izzy, please love me again. I love you so much," he said.

"I'll always love you, Michael," I whispered. Before I knew it, we were making love in my bedroom. Liv would move out immediately if she knew he was here. David would be so disappointed. My parents wouldn't speak to me, but I didn't care at that moment. I loved him.

Two weeks later, he got down on one knee and asked me to marry him with his mother's ring. I said yes. I'd never been so happy or so alone in my life. It was Michael and me against the world, I thought.

3

Amy Roberts felt so guilty. The last thing she told her dad was that she hated him. And now, he was in the hospital having open-heart surgery. Her mom told her that he knew she was just angry, and he knew she loved him. She said the doctors had every hope he'd make a full recovery. She said she'd call when he was out of surgery, but that would be hours from now.

Amy couldn't stand to pace her dorm room any more, so she decided to go for a walk. It was minus ten degrees, but she didn't care. Of course it was cold. It was February in Minnesota. Amy put on her winter coat, Uggs, her U of M hat and Mittens. Her mom made her a scarf last time she went home to Iowa, and so she put that on as well.

Amy was deep in thought as she walked toward Dinkeytown from her apartment. She promised herself that at the end of this academic year, she'd spend the summer at home helping around the farm. She hated the farm, but she loved her family. She was so lonely. She was just devastated that she wasn't home with her dad. She should be in the waiting room, praying, with her family.

Amy decided to pop into a bar for a drink and to warm up. They had good Wi-Fi here, and it was warm. It couldn't be a more collegiate bar. They had Gopher paraphernalia everywhere. The TV's had a "classic" gopher football game on. It was old because it had been awhile since the Gophers were very good. Amy's dad loved that she was a Gopher. He talked Gopher sports with her all the time, so she kept up with all the latest scores and gossip about who was going to be drafted, who was injured, etc...

The man next to her at the bar had a few books about taking M-Cats. She caught him looking at her several times, and finally, he said hello. They chatted for a bit, and he bought her another drink. Amy drank a Tom Collins always. She never varied. She loved the sweetness of the Grenadine and Sprite with the tang of the Gin. He bought her another, and he had another whiskey water.

"Whiskey water? That doesn't sound delicious," Amy said.

"It isn't, but I can drink it slowly," he said.

"I get that," she said. "People keep telling me to switch to Gin and Tonic because it's cheaper and I won't suck them down as fast."

"Nothing wrong with sucking them down fast," he said. He didn't crack a smile, so she didn't know if he meant the double entendre.

"You're studying for the M-Cats?" she asked.

"I'm thinking about it," he said. "I'm just researching them now. I'm a cancer survivor, so I want to pay it forward."

"That's awesome," she said. "So many people forget to be grateful." Herself included she thought. She wondered how her dad was and thought it was time to get back to her room so she could be there for her mom's call about surgery.

Amy told the sexy, kind man that she had to go. He asked if he could give her a ride back to her apartment.

"You don't have to," she said. "I don't live far."

"I want to," he said. "You're very beautiful, Amy."

Well, what girl can resist that? None that Amy knew, so she decided to let him drive her home.

She willingly got in his car, and something hit her hard in the face. She never saw it coming, and didn't know what happened.

When she woke up, she was completely naked and handcuffed and in the front seat. She touched her head and felt dried blood and a big lump where he hit her. It was starting to come back to her. Mr. M-Cats was bringing her home. Where did he go? She gingerly opened her eyes. He was driving, and he looked different. It was probably just her head hurting, but his happy demeanor was totally gone.

"Where are we?" she asked groggily.

"We are definitely somewhere," he said.

She didn't know what to say. This threw her for a loop. She couldn't wrap her head around what was happening.

"Amy, dear, I'm not a cancer survivor studying for M-Cats, in case you haven't figured it out."

"Researching them," she said.

"Ah, yes. Researching the M-Cats. Good memory," he said.

This stranger stared at her. His eyes lost their sparkle and had gone dark. They were blank like there was no soul behind them.

"Look, Amy, I know you don't want anyone else to get hurt over this, but I have your driver's license which gave your address in Iowa. And the card you bought your dad is really touching. Too bad you couldn't be there to watch over him."

"Oh God, he went through my purse," she thought. Would he really go so far as to hurt her family? Was he playing with her? Suddenly, the man pulled over the car. She had no idea where they were. They weren't in the city any more. The head blow had knocked her out, and now she had trouble concentrating.

"Go now, Amy," he said. "Let's see how far you get."

She probably wouldn't have gotten far even if she knew where she was. She had two strikes against her before she started. One was that Amy was strong but not fast. And two, no one had walked on this snow before. It wouldn't be a real trick to track her.

She ran out of his car and headed for the street. Maybe someone would drive by. The man gave Amy twenty seconds of a head start. That didn't seem fair. He had a high powered rifle. Amy was naked, handcuffed, and petrified. "I am the master," he thought. This stupid college kid wasn't even in his league. Unfortunately, in terms of hunting, she was not, but she was fast.

She flagged down a car, and the woman rolled up her window and said, "Drive Steven, there's obviously something wrong with her." Steven apparently agreed because he drove on past. But the next car to pass had an elderly couple in it. Vernon Wells, and his wife of fifty years, Trudy were on their way home from their great-grandson's birthday party. Trudy was used to Vern ignoring her, so she kept talking although he never responded. She didn't realize he'd fallen asleep.

"Vern, really, no mother should buy their child's birthday cake. Ellie wasn't raised that way. Ellie should have made Mark's cake." She went on and on about the store-bought cake to the catered dinner. She said no self-respecting mother would buy the food for a family party. She was expecting Vern to stand up for Ellie like he always did. She looked over at Vern and his head was tilted all the way back and he was snoring. "Vern! Wake up!" Trudy yelled. Vern woke up and shook his head. He looked out the wind shield just in time to see a naked girl with hand cuffs on her wrists trying her best to wave him down. He heard the thump of her body as he ran her over. Vern and Trudy both screamed and Vern turned the wheel hard to the left. His reflexes were off. That left turn was seconds too late. They sailed over the curb and hit a tree hard with the front of their car. The airbags deployed, but Vern and Trudy were eighty-six and eighty-five respectively. They were both killed on impact.

Keagan Nelson just got his license, and he pulled over as soon as he saw the car. Its hood was smashed into the tree and it was steaming. He could see blood on the side window, and heard nothing coming from the car. He called 911 but he didn't stay on the phone long. He left it on, but he ran to the car to check on the elderly couple. He checked both for pulses and didn't find one for either of them. Vern looked a little mangled. Keagan wouldn't be surprised if he had several broken bones because his body was at some odd angles. "Oh man," Keagan thought. "Seriously? This is my first day taking the car out by myself and I come up on this." He was trying to do everything he learned in Drivers Ed. But to be honest, Keagan and his buddies didn't pay that much attention and called it "Driver's Dread." It was so boring. So Keagan honestly was going by instinct. He saw the beautiful young girl. She was naked, hand cuffed and bruised everywhere. She wasn't moving. Keagan found her pulse though. He grabbed his phone and yelled, "Hurry! Hurry please. She has a pulse!"

"Calm down Mr. Nelson, we are almost there. Can you hear our sirens yet?" Keagan started to say no, but in that instant he heard.

"I hear them!" he said. "Oh thank God." He thought about ducking out so he didn't have to be a part of this any more. But Keagan was cursed with a conscience, so he'd do the right thing, he had to. He cursed his mom's little saying that the easy way was never the right way. He never liked that saying. He walked back to the victim and held her hand. He knew he wouldn't want to wait for the ambulance alone. Amy knew she was dying.

She felt her spirit leaving her body. She whispered to Keagan, "Thank you." And then, she joined her grandparents. She would miss her parents and friends, so much, but she was not afraid. She'd never felt so carefree and loved. She went willingly.

4

My parents received the news of our engagement as I knew they would. They put on fake smiles and congratulated us. Michael either wasn't very intuitive or didn't care.

Those smiles were so fake. They had been bracing themselves for this news, I knew. My mom knew me well enough to know that I wasn't easily conned. And yet she saw the con job Michael was pulling here as clear as day. I was oblivious. I thought he must love me if he fought so hard to win me back. She also knew that if she threatened me, in any way, she'd probably never see me again. I was very bull-headed about Michael. I wanted nothing but good news about him before the wedding. I wanted to marry him. My mom saw a man monitoring my every move, and I saw a man protecting me. She saw my personality changing, and I considered myself growing in our relationship. She saw me deferring to him for permission, and I thought of my behavior as including him in my decision making or plans. She saw my feminism dying. I saw it evolving. I did not kid myself into thinking he was the perfect man. He had bills everywhere, and made almost no money. He had three children by two different women. I admired what a great dad he was, and I would have a teaching job before we got married. I thought it meant he loved and trusted me that he'd leave his daughter with me while he took his son fishing or walking in the woods. Oliver was only three years old, and Sophie was only one when I met them. He didn't see his other daughter, Bailey, because his ex-wife really hated the fact that he had a child with another woman, he said.

She couldn't stand it and made all the pictures of Bailey be taken down. She "wouldn't let him" have a relationship with her. I could not believe anyone could be so cruel. Poor Michael. No one understood or loved him. All he needed was be understood and loved unconditionally. I knew we were perfect together no matter what anyone said.

We got married on a beautiful Saturday morning in June 1990. I graduated in May, and we were married in a small church and had a beautiful family picnic following the ceremony. Only our best friends and family were there. My mom looked like her face might break. "What is the matter with you?" I asked. "This is the happiest day of my life except for your face. I know your smile is fake, and so does everyone else."

"I'm sorry, Isabelle Elizabeth, this fake smile is the only one I have. I just watched my daughter marry a psychopath."

"A psychopath? How do you figure?" But I remembered what David said to me all those months ago. There were now two people who found him to be a psychopath.

"Honey, I'm your mother. I feel things in my bones, and I notice everything where my children are concerned. You may think I'm not paying attention, but I am. I cannot acknowledge all these things you tell me because I'll lose my mind. I can't imagine how hard your life will be now that you have that ring on your finger."

"Mom, you worry too much. He loves me. He'd never hurt me," I said with more conviction than I felt. My left hand already felt as though it was too heavy with that ring on my finger. What was the matter with me? I just married the man of my dreams. My mom never liked anyone I dated. I take that back. She liked the ones that I didn't really like a lot. I thought she was just paranoid about losing me, but this was over the top. She thought I married a psychopath is what she said to me on my wedding day. The more I thought about it, the more upset I got. I didn't tell Michael, of course. I didn't want him to hate my mom. Life was hard enough with her hating him. I didn't want the feeling to be mutual.

    We skipped every tradition with our wedding except I wore the dress I always wanted. It was very eighties with puffy sleeves and a crinoline under the skirt to make it a Cinderella skirt. I loved everything about it. What I liked the most was that I bought it, and I didn't need alterations. It cost less than my prom dress because it was just a bit out of style. It wasn't outdated enough to be vintage. So, it was cheap. We got married at eleven am, had a picnic, and were at our honeymoon cabin by six. I thought it was fine that he picked a cabin that came with a canoe. He knew I hated canoes, but he promised we wouldn't portage it this time, and I didn't even have to paddle if I didn't want to. I did love to swim, and I loved cabins on lakes. So it evened out.

5

Two years later, we had the worst heat wave in Minnesota history. It has been ninety-five degrees outside for three weeks. I was about to lose my mind. I live in the North for a reason. I like cool weather. I like sweater and jeans days. With the heat, I had so little energy, but I had to grocery shop before Michael got home. He told me before he left for work that we were out of coffee, milk, and bread. He sarcastically reminded me that I'm on summer vacation. I took the not so subtle hint that I needed to grocery shop.

    I wished I hadn't let him talk me into this house in the middle of nowhere. Going to the store meant a half hour in the car there and another back home. It meant that when I went, I had to stock up so we didn't have to go to town too often. If we ran out of milk, it was a big deal to go get more. I usually didn't mind too much. In the car I felt free. I listened to music and sang like I wrote the songs. I had some time outside of the house, and I could be myself for just a little while. But that day, I felt terrible. I was so tired, and my stomach felt weird. I thought I might throw up. I had a piece of dry toast and watched The Price Is Right before I got the energy and ambition to head to town.

    I got home a couple hours later and collapsed on the couch after I brought the groceries in. I could not make myself put them away. I was so worn out. I watched part of a soap opera and managed to put groceries away during commercial breaks. Once they were put away, I marinated some chicken in a teriyaki sauce and went to sleep on the couch. I woke up two hours later. It was four o'clock, and I had to prep dinner. It dawned on me while I was making a salad that I hadn't had my period yet this month. I was weeks late, and I had no symptoms that it was coming. I could not be pregnant yet. I wasn't ready! I was only twenty-five, and I had only been teaching a couple years. Plus, I knew Michael wanted to wait until we had been married for five years to establish ourselves before we had another child. Right now, having Ollie and Sophie every other weekend was wonderful. That was enough for Michael right now. He said many times that he didn't want to share me more than those days every other weekend that we had the kids. What was I going to do? I thought he'd be so mad at me. "This will be my failure," I thought. "He will think I did it on purpose."

I looked at my pills, and I never even missed a day. Sometimes, under extreme stress, the pill was ineffective. I had been under a lot of stress lately because Michael was not the man I hoped he'd be or that I thought he was. Almost the minute we were on our way to the honeymoon cabin, he started to bitch about my family, about me, about the wedding, etc… He hoped his boss wasn't there because it was, "such a shit show," he said.

I didn't notice a shit show, but apparently, I embarrassed him. I talked too much to my friends who I saw every day. Why did I need to spend so much time with them? Why didn't I pay more attention to his side of the family? Why didn't I insist on liquor being served. Beer looked cheap. The meal was terrible. The chicken was dry and the vegetables were overdone. And on and on. Anything that I picked out was part of the shit show according to him. I knew I made a mistake, and it was too late. Now, I was fairly certain I was pregnant with his child.

I picked up a test the next day when he was at work. I took

the test immediately when I got home. Negative. I was a little sad. I knew that Michael would have to warm to the idea of a baby right away, but he would. He knew I wanted a baby, and this wasn't going to be a total surprise to him. He knew I hadn't been feeling well for a couple weeks. He grilled me about my symptoms a couple days before, and I was fairly certain he was trying to deduce whether or not I was pregnant. Well, this confirmed that I was not. I felt a little lost all day. I made an appointment with my doctor once I knew it wasn't pregnancy making me feel so terrible. She couldn't get me in for a week. I thought I'd probably feel fine by then and could just cancel the appointment.

I didn't feel better though. I felt worse. I desperately wanted my friends. I needed David and Olivia. Liv hadn't spoken to me in two years. And Michael thought homosexuals were sick. I didn't want David to endure that attitude, so I stopped calling him. Why would I do that? It was like punishing David and myself because Michael was a pig. I really wanted to talk through this crazy time with him. I wanted to dissect Michael's personality and talk about my pregnancy with my best friends, but they were gone. My mother never talked to me the same since that night at the restaurant when she met Michael. She couldn't believe I chose him over them. I didn't think I was choosing anyone over anyone. It was my life, and I should be able to date whom I chose. But it was like a competition with her. So they drifted away from me as well. Soon, I was alone. My parents stayed a part of my life, but it wasn't the same. It all felt forced and wrong somehow. I knew my mom hated Michael, so I never wanted to go there or have them over. Michael would belittle them until I didn't want them over anyway. If I suggested having them for dinner, he'd say something to the affect of, "Sure, they can come. Hopefully, your mom won't make you cry this time. They really dislike me. Remember when your mom criticized your cooking?"

Just things that happened in the past were brought up again to make me think maybe I didn't want them over. If I went to their house, Michael wouldn't come with, and I felt like I was on the clock. My parents loved me, and I knew that. I knew that if push came to shove, I could go to them. But on a daily basis, that closeness we had was challenged because they hated my husband. I only saw the negative in them for the longest time. I needed them to just love me, tell me everything would be all right, and accept me exactly how I was. To my parents, that was impossible because they never wanted me to forget where they stood on the Michael front. They could not lie and tell me it was all okay because it wasn't. They loved me too much for that.

Michael had been spending an awful lot of time at the local bar lately. I didn't blame him. I was no fun. I could hardly keep my eyes open and had to take a nap every day. I tried to power through, but I couldn't my body would not let me. One evening after dinner, before he went to the bar, I asked him if he wanted to be nervous and relieved at the same time. I finally told him about the pregnancy test and the negative result.

"Good thing it was negative," he said. "We would have to sell the house."

"That doesn't make sense," I said. "Why would we sell the house if I was pregnant? Didn't we buy this house in order to have room for our family?"

"Yes, but money doesn't grow on trees, Isabelle. We don't have the money to have a kid."

Well, thank God it was negative. I didn't love our house, but I knew he did. I didn't want to lose him or our house. His reaction was not what I expected. I knew he'd be relieved that I wasn't pregnant yet, but I didn't think he'd say we'd have to sell the house. That never crossed my mind. I know babies are expensive, but we'd have to give up a few things if I was pregnant. We wouldn't have to give up the house, I didn't think. Maybe, he could give up smoking or going to the bar nearly every night. I could wait to get my master's degree until later, I could use generic brands of things, I could quit drinking Diet Pepsi. We could both give stuff up. I'd have to, anyway. Diet Pepsi was out of the question if I was pregnant, we could stop eating out. We didn't do that often as it was, but we could stop completely if we couldn't afford it. We needed the house.

As the week went on, I still didn't get my period, and I didn't feel any better. By the time my doctor appointment rolled around, I had to ask Michael to drive me to the appointment. He dropped me off and went to a job site. I was hurt that he wouldn't stay with me, but I knew he was busy. He reminded me of how busy he was all the time in the summer. I felt guilty that I was home, and he worked so hard. I did his paperwork for him to free up some of his time. It was the least I could do, I thought.

My doctor took one look at me and told me I was dehydrated. She sent me over to the hospital for fluids. Luckily, the hospital was across the street because I didn't have the energy to walk much further. My doctor wouldn't even let me do that. She put me in a wheel chair and sent me with an orderly. There was a skywalk system that he used to get me across the street. I didn't know how to get a hold of Michael to tell him I was in the hospital getting fluids. I looked up the number to the business he told me he was doing work for, and they had never heard of him. I was too exhausted to care.

A couple hours later, Michael came running into the

emergency room suite that I was in receiving fluids. They were trying to find a room for me. So far, they were booked, and they thought it would be another hour before a bed opened up for me. I was starting to feel better. I was a little less fatigued, and I felt a little more like myself.

"Baby, I came back, and you weren't there. I've been all over the place looking for you." I didn't believe him. I called and couldn't find him and left a message as to where I was, but I didn't want to fight. I just wanted to get the fluids and let them run their tests. I'd already given them a blood and urine sample, but the doctor wanted to admit me because I was so dangerously low on fluids.

When Michael gave me his bullshit excuse I just let him grab my hand and smiled at him. He was so relieved that I bought it. Maybe that's why he wasn't at the job site he gave me. He decided to come back. He looked so upset that I was hooked to an IV. It really took him aback. I felt sorry for him and wanted to comfort him.

"I'm fine, honey. I'm just a bit dehydrated," I said. "They just want to keep an eye on me while they find out why."

After about an hour of Michael holding my hand and looking worried, the doctor walked in with a huge smile on his face.

"You don't have to stay after all! We know why you're dehydrated and you were throwing up so much. You're pregnant," he said triumphantly.

"But I took a test over a week ago, and it was negative," I said.

"You were probably just a bit too early for the hormone to be detected in the at home test," he said. "According to the first day of your last period, you are only about four weeks along. When you took the test, you were only about three."

I looked at Michael for a reaction. I prayed he didn't say we'd have to sell the house again. I couldn't stand that. Now, I actually was pregnant. If he wanted me to get an abortion, I would have to leave him. I wanted this baby more than anything. My eyes filled with tears.

"You're already the best stepmom, now, you'll be the best mom," he said. "I love you, Izzy. I can't wait for us all to be a family," he said as he put his hand on my stomach. I knew this was a show for the doctor.

"To celebrate, let's go get that dog you always wanted," he said.

"What?"

"You always talked about getting a Corgi, and I found one. It's not a puppy, but she's only two."

I did always want a dog. I didn't care what kind. I did say I thought Corgi's were cute once. I'll give him that. Now wasn't the time for a dog, but he was so proud of himself for thinking of it, that I gave him a hug and thanked him. The doctor beamed. He thought he was looking at the world's happiest couple. He was looking at the biggest bullshitter. This was all show. I'd have to go pick up the dog, and I would do all the work associated with the dog. I didn't care. I couldn't wait to have a little love to snuggle with me while I was home alone. I was alone at night a lot while Michael was at the bar. We'd name her Bailey, and I would love her with everything I had. I didn't care if it was for show. This was the best day of my life.

I always wanted to be a mom, and I was one with Sophie and Ollie. I wanted the whole pregnancy experience, and I wanted a child that I didn't have to share with another mom. I wanted to give Ollie and Sophie a little brother or sister. I couldn't wait. Despite myself, I loved Michael. I still saw that sweet man who cried when I left on a trip to England with students years ago. It broke my heart. I was looking forward to a break from him, the house, chores, etc... And then, I saw his eyes fill with tears on the way to the airport. That did it. If I ever felt like he didn't care about me or like he is a bad man, I think of the ride to the airport that day.

I had to be careful, though. If I only thought of the airport day and underestimated how cruel he could be, I was disappointed every single time. We were going to a wedding reception once, and I thought, "He's been good the last few weeks, so how bad could it be?" He could get wasted, hit on the maid of honor, and lose a tooth when her dad punched him in the face. It could be that bad, and it was exactly that bad. My lesson was to never underestimate him. Ever. If there was alcohol, he'd drink it. If there were women around, he'd hit on someone until one of them took the bait. This was a totally different guy than I married. The guy I married opened my door for me, sent me flowers all the time, called to see how I was, and left me love notes. He wouldn't come to my apartment though, and he never would go to my parent's house. He wouldn't watch what I liked on television, and he sometimes told me that he wanted to be alone. I knew that was a lie after dating him for three years. He hated to be alone. So, his "alone time" was really just time to play the field. I didn't know that then, but I know now. I thought it was cool that we trusted each other enough to be able to say, I just need to sleep or I want a girl's night.

There were signs he was a narcissist, but I didn't even know what to look for back then. The roses, fancy meals, and love notes were love bombs. I'd tell people how great he was. The phone calls were keeping tabs on me, and the rest was him just doing whatever he wanted without a thought about anyone else.

No matter the scenario, he found out how it would benefit him before participating. He wouldn't go to my parent's house unless my brother was going to be there. He loved to pitch get rich quick schemes to him. My brother never, ever bit, but he was nice enough to play along with him. Then, he'd tell me not to let him invest in whatever his idea of the month was. My brother was so cute. He thought I had a say in anything still. I let my family believe that for as long as I could. It became obvious when about ten years into my marriage, I stopped going over to their houses at all. If they did see me, sometimes, I wore turtle necks in the summer and always long sleeves. He liked to choke me while having sex. He wasn't trying to kill me, he was just sick. In any event, it left marks. Sometimes, his eyes went blank when he did this. It was like he had no soul; like there was nothing behind his eyes. That scared me. He had his hands around my neck, and he went blank and wouldn't respond. That was creepy. I begged him to stop doing that. He said okay, but he wanted to tie me up then. I had only ever been with this one man my entire life. I never knew about all this kinky stuff. I'd never even heard of men tying women up unless they were raping them. I was always certain that the strangling wasn't normal either. I always had rope burns on my wrists, thus the long sleeves.

"Michael, if you put your hands on my neck again, I will leave you," I finally said.

"Isabelle, if you ever leave me, I'll kill you," he said.

I knew he meant it. Before this conversation, I was vaguely afraid of him. I knew he had violence in him, but I couldn't explain how I knew. I knew he lied, cheated, stole, and enjoyed watching me struggle or hurt. I didn't like him, and I wasn't quite sure why he scared me. The night in the car was five years ago and nothing like that had happened again. I knew now why I feared him. He made it clear.

6

Michael knew he'd screwed up when he said that to me. The next day, he gave me a card. When I opened it, there were two tickets to Colorado. He knew how I loved the beauty of the Colorado mountains, and the heat was really hard on me these first months of pregnancy. I was so excited. He got us a condo with a pool in Steamboat Springs. He said I could just lay by the pool and read if I wanted to. He would go exploring if he needed to by himself if I wasn't up to it. I was so grateful. I had been so sick, dehydrated, exhausted, and nervous. This was exactly what I needed. Michael could be a jerk, but he really knew me. I was fairly certain he was a narcissist, but that wasn't his fault. And regardless of anything he said or did, he loved me with everything he had in him. He did the best he knew how. Maybe he didn't know how to very well love very well, but it was the best he could do.

    We left for Colorado two weeks before school started. He even found a place that was dog friendly so Buddy could come with. It was the exact vacation I needed. I laid by the pool and read the best book by Stephen King. It was my new favorite next to Salem's Lot that would always be my favorite. It was called Needful Things. It was basically about selling your soul to the devil for stuff. I sold my soul to the devil for a wedding ring just like Brian Rusk sold his for a Sandy Koufax baseball card. I wasn't alone. Other people chose poorly, too. Of course they were fictional. This book was a reminder that only people were truly important, and although it was scary and a thriller, it gave me a new kind of peace. I've always reacted strangely to books in this way. I would have an opposite reaction to most people after reading some of my favorites. Flowers in the Attic made me feel a little sorry for the mom. The grandma was evil, but I wondered what made her that way. I felt sorry for the mom because her mom was evil. I thought that spoke volumes about my personality. I always felt bad for the person people hated. It didn't matter what evil deeds the hateful person committed. I wondered why they would do such things and who hurt them to begin with. I wondered if that would change after living with Michael for many years. I figured that made me both kind and stupid. Mostly stupid. I was naive, and my desire to cheer for the underdog and understand the misunderstood made me vulnerable to a psychopath who needed a beard. I knew that's all I was to Michael. I was a prop so he could think his life was "normal." I should have stayed broken up with him after he tried to kill us that night on the wet, windy road on the way home from dinner. He'd insulted me in front of my parents and instead of being mad, I wondered why he would do that. Then, I remembered he was an abused child, and I felt sorry for him. I think a person with healthy self-esteem would tell him to fuck off right then and there. And she would have stayed gone. I went back and was happy when we got back together. I was mad that people weren't happy for me. Why would anyone be happy for me knowing that I just forgave the guy who insulted me and then tried to kill me. At least he had a total disregard for my life. He maintained he wasn't trying to kill me. He was going over a hundred miles per hour, in the rain, on unfamiliar roads. He ignored my repeated cries to slow down. We so easily could have lost control and hit someone innocently driving at a normal, cautious speed, or run into a tree going a hundred miles per hour.

Michael loved to take me to dinner in fabulous little restaurants he discovered. He found a little restaurant in Steamboat called The Safe House. It's based on the CIA concept of a safe house, and they only tell you the password if you get a reservation. It was like a Speak Easy and was underground. When you're in the Rocky Mountains, you'd think your view would be most important, but he took care of that when he took me for dessert on top of a ski hill at the resort. We had to take the Gondola to get there. The restaurant was amazing. We ate lobster and shrimp at the Safe House We had crab cakes as an appetizer. I'd been craving seafood. Seafood and apples were my craving foods. Sometimes, I craved BBQ chicken as well. But seafood was the only one I didn't indulge. I indulged that night. Then, dessert was so beautiful We split a piece of a five layer chocolate cake and had decaffeinated coffee. Well, I had decaffeinated coffee. He had three Captain Cokes. I was so happy that I didn't care what he drank. It didn't seem to affect him that night, so it didn't matter to me. I wasn't going to wreck this magical night by counting his drinks.

We went back to the hotel, and I got ready for bed. I assumed we'd make love after that perfect night. But he tucked me in and handed me the remote. He asked if I needed anything else before he went down to the bar "for one." It was just as well. I was exhausted as usual. I kissed him back and told him I'd see him later.

I woke up to the shower turning on at four a.m. "What the hell?" I wondered. "Was Michael getting up already? I never even heard him come in." His side of the bed was still neatly made. He didn't come back until now. Why the shower? Did he smell like perfume? I was sure this meant he had sex with someone else.

Still, I didn't want to get into it. He'd never tell me the truth, and now, he'd washed off the evidence if there was any. He could have just smelled like smoke. He still smoked like a chimney, and the smell made me queasy. He knew that. So, I bet that's why he took a shower. No one could go have sex with someone else after the date night we had, could they? I didn't think so.

I pretended that I'd never heard him, and I decided to focus on what I knew. I knew I was having his baby. I knew he brought me to this fabulous resort in Colorado. I knew he didn't complain when I just wanted to read my book and lay by the pool. And we had a perfect date night totally planned by him that night. He just got carried away drinking, I was sure.

The next day, he was wide awake and happy by eight a.m. How did he do that? I'd have been puking and unable to lift my head for days. It was different when you were used to it. He had quite the tolerance built up.

Our flight left at one, so we had breakfast and went to the airport. My hormones were crazy that day. I cried watching the news on the monitor at the airport. There was a wild fire in California, and they interviewed a family who lost their home, the Midwest was still experiencing the worst drought and heatwave in history although it had moved south from Minnesota, and a beautiful young girl's body was found in Steamboat by a hiker. There was nothing but bad news. I decided to open the other book I brought with me instead.

7

My first trimester was torture, but now that I was in my second everything was looking up. School had started a couple weeks before, and I felt human again! I could make it almost all the way to the end of the school day before I needed a nap. Progress.

"How are you feeling, really?" My friend Kris asked. Kris taught English three doors down from me. She taught mostly juniors, and I taught mostly freshmen and sophomores. I just loved her. She always had my back, and I had hers.

"You look tired," Kris said.

"That is code for shitty, and actually, I'm feeling a lot better. My energy lasts until about two-thirty now," I said.

"Progress," she said. We even thought alike.

"Hey, cute pregnant lady! How was your summer?" asked Megan Lilly. She taught Chemistry, and the science rooms were next to the Language rooms, so we all knew each other. Jose Luis Navarro was the Spanish teacher, and he was my favorite co-worker. He was so much fun. He had big parties at the end of each quarter. He made a vat of his salsa, we all brought appetizers, he had a keg on his deck, and we all learned to dance the salsa. It was so much fun. I felt lucky to work with such great people. As a teacher, we are pretty isolated with our students, but we try to "watch the hallway" between classes so we can talk.

As for my students, sometimes I feel like I could write a book on them. They asked me ridiculous questions like "Do Penguins have knees?" I still don't know the answer to this one.

When I asked if they had any questions before the test, one kid raised his hand and asked what I thought my last words would be before I died. Now, I am more specific in my questions.

They are awesome, and they keep me young most of the time. I was not a big fan of the first day of school though. I got very tired of reading my syllabus and telling them how I grade and things like that. But it was necessary, so I spent the day reminding them not to turn work in late, yada, yada, yada.

I wasn't very nice to my family when they warned me against Michael, but I knew they'd take me back in no questions asked if I needed them. Funny how I knew I could count on them in a time of great need, but I'd never attempt to count on them when times were good or if I wasn't in crisis, but could use a little advice. I would never ask for help from them unless I intended to leave him, for good. It would have to be forever. My parents have seen me through a lot, but their patience was very thin when it came to Michael. I didn't blame them, but that made me feel very alone.

Last year my co-workers on my floor asked me to come into the teachers' lounge. They told me about Trivia Night. There were a bunch of them at The White Elephant for Trivia, and they busted Michael with Anna Deadrick. A kid who graduated last year. My former student. That pig. I didn't even know how to address that. She was only nineteen at the oldest. My school friends who confided his… his… whatever it was to me would never understand why I didn't leave. Was it infidelity, was it a predilection for young women, was it psychopathic or narcissistic where he was going to take whatever he wanted just because he could? Now, I'm going to feel completely alone because who could identify with a woman who doesn't leave her alcoholic, abusive, cheating husband? No one would. I would never expect them to. Why didn't I just walk out? God knows I should have. I was too scared of him was the bottom line. I knew I had to play him in order to get out. I had to convince him that me leaving him was his idea. I have to have money squirrelled away, and I needed to have a plan. I couldn't just walk out. He would kill me.

I didn't want confront him when he got home. I was too tired. But I had to say something.

"Michael, stay away from my former students. They are still children for Christ's sake," I said.

"What are you talking about, Izzy? I don't even know your fucking students," he said.

"Anna? Are you going to sit there and tell me that all five of my colleagues who told me they saw you with Anna Deadrick are lying? She's nineteen, Michael. She graduated from high school one year ago. Just stay the fuck away from my students," I said.

"Your pregnancy hormones are out of control, Isabelle. I have nothing to do with this Anna or any other student of yours."

"Okay," I said. In that one word, I hope I conveyed how little I believed him. I just didn't want to fight right then. I was tired. I had nowhere to go. I'd never see Sophie and Oliver again if I left, and I'd have to make up my mind immediately. He obviously had the ability to hurt me. He'd done it before. So, I'd ride this out. I knew he wasn't faithful, but I was afraid to leave him, and I had no one to turn to. I burned every bridge. I would have to start saving so that I could take our child and leave as soon as possible. It wouldn't be easy. He controlled all our money. Thank God I could get cash back from my debit card. I got a little extra every time I went to the grocery store or to Walmart or Target. It would just look like house hold expenses to him. I had done this in the past and used the money for clothes or to put toward getting a manicure or pedicure. Now, I'd use it to escape eventually.

That afternoon, I went to the bank and got a safety deposit box and put my first fifty dollars in.

Now, I had a plan.

8

Barbara Ellis left St. Catherine's Catholic Church at eleven a.m. She was on the committee to fund raise to send missionaries to Guatemala to build a much-needed orphanage. Barb preferred to keep her charities in the area around her house in Superior, WI, but she had a soft spot for orphans and she was the only one in the congregation who spoke Spanish.

So when Father Kruzinski asked her to head the committee, she said she would. Her kids were nearly grown, and she didn't work outside the home, so although she didn't enjoy fund raising and preferred to keep charities local, she said yes. She could not come up with a reason other than she really didn't want to.

After the meeting, she was going to pick up celery, carrots, onions, and chicken breasts. She wanted to make chicken and dumplings for dinner tonight. It was her daughter's favorite and she's felt bad since she didn't make it on to the Varsity Basketball Team. She was a junior, and there were freshmen who made it. Poor Jordyn. She wanted it so bad. But, bless her heart, she didn't quit. She decided to keep playing JV, and her coach asked if she would dress for the Varsity games although she would probably not play. She said she would. She was handling it well, but Barb wasn't. She was worried that Jordyn was hiding her disappointment.

Her mind was fully focused on her grocery list and her daughter. Barb didn't even notice the dark haired man sitting on the bench near her van when he stood up and said, "Hi Pam, how are you?"

Barb was confused because he pulled her out of deep thought. She looked behind her for this Pam he was talking to. There was no one there. It dawned on her he thought she was his friend, Pam.

"Oh, I'm sorry. I think you have the wrong person. My name is not Pam."

"It's my fault," he said.

"I thought you were my friend from High School."

"I'm Paul," he said.

"Barb," Barb said. "Pleasure to meet you."

"Oh no, the pleasure is mine, Barb."

That was creepy and weird thing to say. He stood between herself and her minivan. He just stared at her. He wasn't very tall and he had a man bun. He was grinning at her like an idiot, and he was missing a tooth. It made him look old and creepy. Her guard went up. She couldn't figure out why he just stared at her, so she decided to unlock her car and just go on with her day. As she started to get in her minivan, she felt him push her, and she fell over the center console. Her head landed in the passenger seat, her butt was in the air, and her feet and legs were still on the driver's side. He gave her ass another push and she fell further onto the passenger seat. She climbed the rest of the way in on her own. He was in the driver's seat, and he still grinned at her.

He said, "Keys, please." He put his hand out to her and wiggled his fingers. He had a terrible odor. He was sweating profusely and tried to mask it with cheap after shave that went out years before. Bruit, maybe?

She didn't move. She knew if she gave him her keys she was done for.

Barb had to dig through her purse although she'd just used them. Her hands shook, so she had trouble finding them. This Paul character took her purse and found them almost immediately, but he took her wallet and opened it up.

"Barbara, you're right, you're not Pam."

Barb didn't answer. She stared straight ahead.

"Well, Barb, you live really close to here. You could have walked."

Again, she didn't respond. This freaked her out. This crazy son of a bitch knew her name, age, and address. He had access to her entire life with that wallet.

"I'm guessing Brock is in middle school and Jordyn is in high school?" he asked. He had their pictures out and read the back for their names. She hated hearing his voice say the names of her children.

"What are you planning to do to me?" She asked.

"I'm just planning to have a little fun with you," he said.

She knew what he meant. She was sure she was going to be raped or worse. She had to figure a way out of this. He pulled the minivan out of the church parking lot. She sat in the passenger seat shaking.

"Knock that shit off. You can at least act like you're happy to be with me," he said.

"What shit? The shaking?"

"Of course, the shaking. Knock it the fuck off."

"I'm sorry," she managed to whisper.

"Don't be sorry, just don't fucking do it."

Barb could see the veins in his neck bulge as he screamed at her. His face was beat red. He spit when he yelled at her. She memorized his face and every detail about him in case she figured a way out of this. "At the very least," she thought, "I will scratch the shit out of him and get his DNA under my nails." She had to do something to get him so he didn't do this to anyone else. "He has done this before," Barb thought. She decided to try to make herself human to him. It couldn't hurt.

"My kids are everything to me. You saw their pictures.

They're not grown yet. My mom's name is Elizabeth, my dad is Warren. My dad is a truck driver, my mom is a veterinarian. Neither of them are retired yet. My dad will retire at the end of the year. He wants to volunteer coach little ones, I..."

"Shut the fuck up. Do you think I don't know what you're doing? Do you think I give a shit about your dad's volunteer work? I don't care, bitch. Get it?" Out of the blue, he punched Barbara in the face. His arm came up and hit her so fast that she never saw it coming.

Blood gushed from her lip and nose. She sat stunned in her seat. He was in his own little world. He was absolutely focused on making her his victim. "Is it power he's after?" Barbara wondered. "Does he need to fulfil some disgusting fantasy that combines sex and violence? Is it both?" There was no way to know. He was totally focused on the road. It looked like he was so deep in his own head that he almost forgot she was there. He was completely crazy. He muttered to himself. Barb couldn't make out what he was saying. Previously, when he stopped at a stop light, he pulled a gun out on her. Ahead was a stoplight, and it was busy. There were cars everywhere. If she could get out, he'd never chase her down. She didn't want to leave her wallet. She didn't want him to have her driver's license or her kids' pictures. Her purse was right there on the floor between herself and her attacker. She had to be fast. She unhooked her seatbelt and grabbed her purse faster than she thought possible. She saw him blinking back into the present as she opened the door and jumped out. She screamed as she ran down the busy road she ducked off the road to a wooded street and found a house with a car in the driveway. She knocked. When the guy opened the door, he pulled her inside. She knew her face looked terrible. She could still feel blood dripping down her face. There was no woman in the house. This guy was in his thirties, she guessed. He had kind eyes. He locked the door and shut the shades. Together, they locked the windows. He called 911 and told the operator what happened. They were sending the police. She wanted this guy to stay on the line with her until the police arrived. He took an ice pack out of his freezer and grabbed paper towels He gave them to her, and she wiped the blood off her face as best she could, and put the ice pack on her nose. She heard him tell the 911 operator his name was Dan Greene. Dan wet some more paper towels and put on some latex gloves.

Barb must have look confused to see him grab the gloves. Who just has gloves in their house?

"I'm a nurse, and I paint. That's why I have the gloves," he said. Barb let the breath out that she didn't know she was holding. She was totally unnerved by the fact that he had gloves.

Dan gently washed the dried blood off her face. Her nose and lip had stopped bleeding as long as she left them alone and kept her head still. He held the ice pack gently to her face and talked into his speaker on his phone with the 911 operator.

"They're here. I hear them," Dan said.

"Give them a minute," the operator said. "They're coming around the corner onto your street now. Wait until the knock and identify before you unlock the door."

"Okay."

They knocked heavily on the door and yelled police. They could see the red and blue lights in the driveway.

Dan looked at Barb to make sure she was okay, and he went to answer the door. She was so grateful to this kind stranger who helped save her life. She would never forget his kindness.

9

Eva was born on a cold Tuesday in February. I was impressed. Michael stayed through the whole birth process, and I was in labor for a long time. It was a solid eight hours in the hospital, and about twenty more before he took me to the hospital. I timed little bitty contractions every twenty minutes, then fifteen, then ten, then five... At five, he took me to the hospital. Eight hours later, we had a beautiful baby girl. She was perfect. Even Oliver cried when he saw her. He was a very proud big brother.

So, Michael stayed for the birth, but he left for the child raising. He found every excuse to be out of the house especially when Eva would get sick. Eva and I both had fairly high fevers, and Michael thought that meant he could go to the bar then since we were both sick. I never understood that logic. As sick as I was, I had to do all the parenting of a sick kid. I didn't really mind, but I got frustrated a lot.

I loved seeing Eva with Oliver and Sophie. They all got along so great. They never fought, but I'm sure that had something to do with only seeing each other every other weekend. Either way, it was fun to see. I loved Sophie and Oliver's mom. She and I were the only ones who really understood what it meant to be married to Michael Lewis. Other people thought we were crazy. "Isn't it weird to be friends with your husband's ex?" They'd ask. It really wasn't. We were raising the same kids, we might as well be friends. And we were. Do things ever go according to plan? In my plan, I'd have left years ago. I don't know why I kept telling myself, "Just a little bit longer. I'm almost ready. I have almost enough money." I put it off. I was scared. Beth was the only friend who remained. Michael ran them all off with his rude behavior, criticisms, or disgusting comments. Beth and I had been friends too long for her to ditch me because I couldn't pull the trigger, metaphorically speaking, of course. I kept saving and had nearly two hundred thousand dollars scattered all over. Some was in the safety deposit box, some was with my friend Beth, some was locked in a filing cabinet at work. It was all cash. He could never find out I had it. He'd kill me.

10

Ten years is far too long to sit on a plan. I had to act. Eva was ten. Ollie and Sophie were sixteen and eighteen. Ollie would graduate that spring, and Sophie had two years to go. Their mother promised I'd still see the kids. I could call them whenever I wanted and take them to dinner or whatever. Ollie was going to stay living with his mom next year and attend the

University of MN, Duluth. He figured he could get his generals wherever he wanted and then go the U in Minneapolis to get his degree. He wanted to be an engineer. He always thought like an engineer. At three years old, he was always trying to make things fit right together. I was so happy that he was sticking around for a while at least. When he was ready to move on, he would.

Oliver might have not been ready to go off to college because his dad kept him unsettled.

Michael put a lot of pressure on him and was hot and cold, and hot and cold. One day, Ollie was the greatest son he could have ever asked for, the next, he was useless. We were paying for his car, and his mom paid for his insurance. Michael rubbed it in Ollie's face every chance he got. If Ollie ever disagreed with him about anything, he brought it up. One day, Ollie had a difference of opinion about politics. Michael is a republican and Ollie is a democrat. Michael, however, loves to say he's neither a democrat nor a republican. He researches the person running for office and votes according to that person's views and history. I knew this was total bullshit, and so did Ollie. Ollie thought it was funny. He laughed out loud when Michael extolled the virtues of George Bush and cursed Al Gore during one of their debates.

"What are you laughing at?" Michael asked.

"I just think it's kind of funny that you don't admit that you're a Republican. You think everything Bush says is genius, and that everything Gore says is stupid. You're probably a Republican," Oliver said. Sophie didn't say a word.

Eva laughed with Ollie and said, "Yeah, dad. You're totally a Republican."

"What do you know about it, Eva? You couldn't even tell me what a Republican is. So, shut your fucking mouth."

I wanted to run to her and hug her and tell her father he was an asshole, but that would've made it worse. I would have to wait until he wasn't around before I hugged her and let her vent. Her eyes filled with tears.

Michael wasn't done.

"Oliver, if you weren't so goddamned dumb, I wouldn't have to pay for your car," he said. Ollie and I looked at each other totally confused. What did that have to do with anything? He just liked to be the big man on top. The kids were disposable. They were great as long as they just told him he was right, fabulous, the best dad ever, so smart, cool, thoughtful, all of it. If they had their own opinions, they were useless to him. He just needed them to stroke his ego.

I should have intervened. I always should have intervened in whatever he did to the kids. I talked myself into believing that I would make it worse if I did, then, I wouldn't be able to sleep because I'd have such terrible thoughts that this was all my fault. I felt like a loser because I didn't stop it. The truth was, I didn't know how to stop it. I had to at least say something, though. I was tired of being mad at myself. Eva and I had to go. Sophie and Oliver would still love me. I knew that. I couldn't stand the thought of them having to go to their dad's every other weekend without me there as a buffer. I hated that an evening or a day could turn on a dime, and I couldn't protect them. But they were getting older. They could both drive. They had a car. They could escape if they needed to. I'd talk to their mom before I left.

I had to be very careful. I could never tell anyone about the two hundred thousand dollars I saved. He'd sue me for that or half of that, and he'd win. No one could know. I'd use it to pay expenses, but I'd take out a loan for a house in a year or two. I couldn't do anything too quickly. I had to save enough of that cash for the down payment on a house, and to keep a decent savings. I had to figure out a way to get out without endangering our lives. I had no idea what that would look like.

11

Barb rode with the police to the hospital where they cleaned her up and gave her new ice for her lip. It was starting to throb. The detective asked her several times if there was someone she could call for her. Barb couldn't bring herself to tell anyone yet. She had to tell her husband and kids. There was no hiding her injuries. Her face was swollen and black and blue. Her lip was swollen and split, And she was terrified. Barb knew that when she told Marty, his world would change forever. Marty would blame himself. He protected his family. He took pride in his job. If she heard a noise downstairs at three a.m., she told Marty. He checked it out. If the kids got hurt by another kid at school, Marty had a little chat with the kid's parents. He even killed the spiders. This would devastate him. The kids would know first-hand now and forever that the world was scary. They'd know that people could and would hurt them if given the opportunity. It didn't hurt them to know that, she guessed. They'd find out anyway. Someone could hurt them, too. Neither of them had even had a big break up yet. They didn't know heartbreak yet... Barb needed to absorb it before she brought her family into it.

Detective Parker Engen understood. She survived an attack in college. She didn't like to think about it. Parker knew the boy and liked him. They were at a party, and she flirted with him. She'd had a couple beers from the keg, but she was completely wasted. That never happened to her. She didn't get drunk. Her friends Kelly and Teresa loved that she didn't drink much. Parker was always DD. She didn't mind. The girls could do their thing, and Parker loved to dance and socialize, she just didn't drink. The boy played football for the University of Minnesota, so he thought he was a big deal. He was really cute, and Parker wanted to get to know him better. She was flattered that he chose her to talk to at the party.

He tricked her up to a bedroom at the frat house where the party was. He kept telling her he had to show her something. In her drunken state, she followed. He shut the door behind them in the bedroom. He started kissing her right away. At first, Parker kissed him back. She soon put her hands on his chest and pushed him back a bit.

"Let's take this a little more slowly," she said. "I'm not comfortable with this."

"Oh baby," he said. "You're so sexy. I just can't control myself. I need you. Now."

"Please, I really don't want to. I like you, but I just met you. I don't want to have sex with you."

He pushed her on the bed, and started kissing her so hard that she couldn't tell him no any more. She couldn't breathe. He was too heavy to push off of her, and he made up his mind that he was having sex with her, and that was that. Parker had no say in the matter. But it was a party, so just as he was getting ready to rape her, someone knocked on the door. There was another couple who wanted the room, she thought. Thank God. But she heard Kelly and Teresa yelling, "Parker! Parker! Where are you?"

That asshole on top of her asked, "Is that you?" Parker started yelling back right away. "Kelly, Teresa, I'm in here. I'm in here." They banged on the door until the football player opened it. She'd never been so happy to see her friends in her life. The three of them ran out of the house and to the car. They hailed a cab. No one spoke the whole way home. Parker didn't go to the police because she thought it was her fault for getting drunk. But she did change her major a week later to Criminology. After graduation, she went to the police academy. She worked her way up the Minneapolis police department and became a detective.

On a trip up north, Parker met her husband, and she moved to Duluth. They hired her as a detective immediately. She'd been there ever since, and she loved it. Duluth was beautiful. Canal Park with the lift bridge and all the quaint restaurants, shops, and bars was still her favorite place in the world. She and her husband went there all the time on their date nights. Where Minneapolis was a boys' club and a totally racist institution,

Duluth was welcoming and forward thinking. Minneapolis could stand to learn from the Duluth police chief.

Detective Engen knew why Barb didn't want to tell her family yet. Parker still hadn't told her husband about the night that football player nearly raped her. She never talked about that night. She never uttered his name. She now knew it wasn't her fault, but she still felt ashamed. She understood female victims because of what happened that night, but no one knew that.

Engen and Townsend brought Barb to the police department to get her statement. Once they arrived at the police station, Barb was ready to call Marty.

Just as she knew he would, Marty raced to the station and hugged her and let her cry. He held her hand as she told her story. He only let go of her hand long enough for her to sign her statement. Marty was a good man. Once he grabbed her hand, she knew she could do anything. A sketch artist drew a picture of the man Barb described, but she only really saw him in profile. She couldn't remember him facing her. She'd blocked it out. The artist told her not to worry. And she drew his profile. It looked exactly like him, but she doubted anyone would ever recognize him from this.

"I'm so sorry," Barb said. "I tried so hard to remember everything about him."

"Don't worry, Mrs. Ellis. We'll get him. We've arrested offenders with less. A lot less." That made her feel a bit better. She and Marty went home to tell the kids.

12

Every summer, the entire Lewis family gathered at Michael's sister's family cabin. We brought our own tents and campers. I loved Michael's family, but I worried the entire weekend. I worried that he'd voice his opinions of everyone. I worried that his personality would alienate even his family. This year I told him that if he truly hated his dad, we shouldn't go. Michael hated his dad's attitude. His dad was pretty much deaf. He could hear almost nothing. His response to this was, "I don't need no hearing aids. I don't want to hear most of ya, anyways."

He was right. His dad was crabby, and he wasn't kidding. He didn't want to hear any of us. His dad, Ted, was a retired rancher. He had hundreds of acres and heads of cattle. It was a career that suited him. Solitude was what he craved. He didn't mind the work or the cattle like he minded people.

As his daughter-in-law, I saw the good and bad in him. He told me I wasn't his daughter-in-law in his heart. I was his daughter. Then, he'd turn around and insult me by reminding me that husbands liked obedient wives. Frankly, it didn't matter to me how sweet he could be. His meanness trumped any nice thing he ever said or did. He actually told Eva she was getting fat at her fourth birthday party. She was four. I could've killed him with my bare hands.

But, I hated a scene. I hated when Michael made snide comments and then told his dad or his sister or his mom off in front of everyone. It was rude and immature, and frankly, it just made him look bad. It didn't make me look fabulous either. He always dragged me into it by asking, "Don't you agree, Izzy?" I usually did, but I didn't want to offend the rest of the family. I didn't have to live with them, though, so I always agreed with him. It was uncomfortable.

Michael seemed to forget these problems every year. He got excited to go to the cabin. He could show off his skills on the grill to his family, fish all day long, and drink with his brothers-in-law.

He desperately wanted his father's approval. Every year, he showed his dad his huge fish, talked about his work successes, and prepared elaborate meals. His dad barely noticed. He couldn't hear him anyway. His dad would sit and chain smoke Marlboro lights on the deck and watch his family. That made him happy. He didn't care about anyone's individual successes. He just liked to watch them all together and think, "Look what we made." He loved his wife, Margaret, as did everyone. She was the glue. Without her, these weekends probably would have died out. Michael's sister, Jackie, who owned the cabin with her husband Nick, was not a big Michael fan. Neither of them thought he was particularly funny or kind. They didn't like his cooking or his stories. They saw through everything he did as a desperate ploy to get their dad to notice him.

"Don't you feel a little bit sorry for him, Jackie?" I once asked. "He tries so hard to get your dad to acknowledge that he's successful. He just wants to make him proud."

"That's all any of us want, and the rest of us have accepted that he will never acknowledge if he's proud or not. That's just who he is. He's an asshole. But I see him put down, Mom. He praises Dad, and he degrades Mom. Mom has always been there for him. She's always cheered him on and believed in him. Now, all of a sudden, Dad is a saint, and mom is worthless."

"I did notice how mean he is to your mom," I said. "There's no excuse for that. I can feel how uncomfortable he is around your dad, and everyone else gets Michael's wrath because he's so nervous and trying so hard to impress your dad."

"No, you're too nice, Izzy. I grew up with him. He's not mean because he's nervous. Michael is mean because he's mean. He doesn't need anything from the rest of us, so he ignores us or is rude to us. We only care about how he hurts mom. The rest of us can take care of ourselves."

This conversation with Jackie threw me a little. I didn't expect her to be so matter of fact in her feelings for Michael. She's a pretty good actress. She pretends that she's a little entertained by him, at least. And she pretends to like him very well. I never would have guessed that she didn't. In fact, because she believed in him, I cut him more slack. I thought there had to be more to him that I didn't see. I loved Jackie. She was so much fun. She had a ready smile for everyone. She made me feel comfortable the minute I arrived. She treated me like a sister. She and Nick were two of my favorite people in the world. She doted on her dad. She could pretend she didn't seek his approval all she wanted, but she wanted that as much as Michael did. The difference was, Jackie wouldn't do anything to get it. She stayed who she was.

Michael put on a show. It was more of a spectacle. His voice and laugh were the loudest. He planned and practiced the menu for weeks before. Eva and I ate the crab cakes and seafood boil many times before that weekend. It had to be perfect. Technically, we were in charge of one meal. I made fruit salad, cut up lemons, and made the crab cakes while he focused on the seafood boil. We put out newspaper on the tables and pitchers of lemonade.

Michael's big laugh radiated through the cabin. He made a

big show of being the chef, but he put on a cowboy hat instead of a chef's hat and bib overalls instead of an apron. He looked crazed. I'd never seen him try quite so hard. It was embarrassing. He had too much to drink, of course, in his nervous state. He put too many spices in. The boil was too spicy to eat, but we all pretended. My crab cakes and fruit were completely gone, and I replaced lemonade pitchers several times. I was jealous of the kids because they were eating hot dogs. That sounded better to me. I hated spicy food. I put out a couple of baguettes that I'd brought to help absorb the heat of the spices, and finally, a substantial amount of seafood boil was gone.

Dessert was a variety of sherbets. So we could all cool off our mouths. Michael was happy. He was too drunk to notice how everyone choked down the far-too-spicy seafood. I didn't even see him eat. He just drank.

His dad said, "Michael, put that Goddamned drink down, and come here."

"Did you like dinner, Dad?" he asked.

"No, I didn't. I was a cattle rancher. I like meat. A hamburger would've been better than whatever that cajun shit was you made. Everyone's breathing fire."

"Okay, I thought you'd enjoy a change from red meat, but whatever."

"We gotta talk about your drinking. You're embarrassing the entire family with this. I can't talk to you by noon most days. It's disgusting."

"Well, Dad, you piece of shit, maybe you're the reason I drink," he said. I could see Jackie, and his mom get very uncomfortable, but they didn't disagree with him. I hoped he didn't look for back up because I would have agreed with Michael on this one, and I knew the reason he drank, talked too loud, and showed off at family gatherings was because of his dad. What was the excuse the rest of the time? I wondered if his dad hurt him more when he was young than he let on. I wondered if his dad was responsible for Michael's complete lack of empathy. Who knew? Were you born with it, or did it develop as a coping mechanism? Who cared? The result was I married a psychopath. It didn't matter how he got that way, really. Did it? What mattered was protecting Eva from his psychopathy. Every time he lost it at a family gathering, Eva saw more of her father's true colors. She was a pretty patient, understanding kid who wanted to love her dad more than anything. But I know she saw. I know she heard. It broke my heart.

Every now and then, Michael would give me small snippets of his childhood. He didn't like to talk about it. I knew that he got up before dawn to do chores before school and had to go straight home to do chores until dark after school. But he always found time to ride his horse, shoot his bb-guns, hunt, fish, and hang out with friends. There were a million stories of his misbehavior in high school. Jackie said he was a really good kid and little brother until he hit about fourth grade. Then the lying started. She said Michael would lie about anything. He would lie about the stupidest things that were easily checked out. It didn't make any sense to her. He'd lie and say he didn't eat the last piece of chocolate cake with cake between his teeth. He'd say he was going into town because he had to work. He worked at the town restaurant. There was only one. I'd stop in with my friends, and he wasn't there. He'd say he had no homework, and his mom would get notes from the teacher saying he wasn't doing any homework. It was just stupid little things he chose to lie about, no one really saw the harm in it at the time. I wish they would have nipped that one in the bud because he still lies about everything. He lies about things big and small. I believe nothing he says without verification.

Michael's mom had a baby who died of crib death three days after he was born. Michael felt bad, but their mom was devastated. She couldn't get out of bed. She slept alone in a dark room day and night and wouldn't see anyone. Their dad was now in charge of the household. Luckily, they had neighbors who brought food over to help. This lasted about five weeks, Jackie said. Michael doesn't talk about it. I wouldn't even know if Jackie hadn't told me. Jackie said that during that time, Michael cried a lot, and their dad beat him for showing weakness. He hit him with a belt or a switch he'd find on the land. He blamed his mom for abandoning them with their father who obviously hated him and had no skills taking care of children. Jackie was in third grade, and Michael was in first when this happened. Jackie said he was the sweetest little boy until about fourth grade. I wondered if this was the trigger, and it just took a while before he let his new identity show or if something else terrible happened. I wasn't going to ask him, though. I felt terrible for him, but I didn't want him to know I knew. He, of course, saw it as weakness as his dad did.

Somehow, after his father's death, the stories about his dad changed. People only remembered the good. He was almost saint-like. Ted Lewis the cattle rancher and cold blooded man was elevated to sainthood in death. I found that absolutely ridiculous, but that wasn't for me to say. Michael wasn't the only family member to do this, either. Michael's mom and even Jackie and his other sisters told embellished stories about Ted the perfect man, husband, and father. It was bizarre. They totally rewrote history.

I wished Michael would have shared the truth with me. If I knew what happened to him, maybe I wouldn't be so angry with him all the time. I loved him, but I didn't understand him. His emotions were hollow. I could tell he tried to appear to feel what he was supposed to feel. He was always a beat behind. He looked around to see how he should react before smiling or looking sad. He truly did not know. It must be a terrible burden to not feel what others feel. I realized that if he couldn't feel sad or happy when people normally would, he couldn't feel love either. My life had been a complete lie. He didn't love me. He didn't love Eva. He didn't know how.

13

Sophie, Oliver, and Eva were best friends almost from the beginning. Poor Sophie had to deal with sleeping with a toddler in the room because we had limited space. As Sophie got older, she slept on the living room couch to have some space from her little sister. When they were little, there were issues about broken toys and who hit whom, or whose turn it was to push buttons in the lift. As they grew, however, they were as close as if they grew up in the same house and had the same mom. I loved to watch them play. Eva and Sophie were little athletes, and would have races in the back yard. Sophie was so sweet that she'd let Eva win every now and then. Her "win" would carry her through the week. She was so proud that she "beat" Sophie.

Ollie was more of a thinker. He liked to take things apart and put them back together. He was really good at it. Almost everything still worked when he was done. 'Almost' is the operative word in that sentence. I never did tell Michael why the lawn mower quit working. It remains a mystery to this day. Ollie also liked to hunt and fish. He liked things that brought him out into nature and let him be on his own. He was a great shot with a bow and had an abundance of patience in a boat. It was these passions that brought Ollie and his dad together. Michael loved the woods and the river. So, when Sophie and Oliver came for their weekends, Michael and Oliver hit the woods or the river, and Sophie, Eva, and I hit parks, playgrounds, Disney movies, Dairy queens, and Grandma's house. We'd come together for dinner, but during the day we were like two separate little families. Later, I felt guilty about this. I felt bad that I encouraged Ollie and Michael to go down the river so I could take Eva and Sophie to Monsters, Inc. and the playground. Ollie would have loved to have come with us, but he didn't have the option. He had to go with his dad. He didn't mind going with his dad, but he really wanted to go with us that day. Michael was furious. Ollie immediately back tracked and said he'd rather camp on the river, and Michael calmed down. He was like a kindergartener. He had to have his way. I didn't step in to help Ollie. I still feel guilty about that. I knew that if we did anything as a complete family, we'd all be going down the river and camping. Sophie hated camping. She hated bugs, tents, and she was no fan of fishing. Sophie liked to swim, run, and play. Eva was the same. Neither girl had patience enough for those outdoor, solitary sports. Neither girl would've enjoyed hunting either. Both were huge animal lovers. Ollie loved animals, too, but he did love the challenge of the hunt. He liked to know that the jerky we were eating came from his deer. He took pride in it. I still felt guilty. Eva and Sophie grew up knowing their dad favored Oliver. I didn't stop it. I loved my Saturdays with the girls, and I selfishly, didn't stop it. I couldn't have made Michael do anything the girls liked to do. I didn't even try to encourage it. I knew him well enough to know that he had zero desire to do what they wanted. The girls would have had to do whatever Michael wanted to do to spend time with him. They would have to hunt, fish, or camp to spend time with him. That is all. Looking back on their childhood, he never once went with us to the park or to a movie. Not once. Once the girls got older, he did go to their basketball and volleyball games when he was sober. The girls were so good at their sports that he loved to watch them. He glowed in the fact that he was the star athlete's dad.

I always had these talks with Michael in my head where I could convince him that the girls were worth spending time with because of who they were, or that maybe Oliver would rather do something else for once, or that he'd be happier if he could remember everything and wasn't hungover every day. He didn't drink too much in front of Ollie and Sophie. Eva saw everything. She would try to tell Sophie that dad was an alcoholic, and Sophie couldn't believe it. She never saw it.

I never could figure out how he could not drink in front of them when he was drunk every other day with us. I loved the reprieve, but Eva was furious. Sophie would say, "Eva, it can't be that bad," or, "Well, he never does that when I'm here." Eva thought that meant that her dad loved Sophie more. She was also angry that they could have been her support system, but they thought she exaggerated. Michael would drive that idea home with stories about how Eva was such a storyteller when she was little. Eva could leave the room when he'd start in, and he'd never let up. He didn't care that he hurt her. He just kept going. The kids laughed at the stories, too. They thought Eva over reacted to their dad's teasing, too. Given normal circumstances, I would have agreed with them.

I had a chat with them when Michael was on a work call once. I told them that Eva was not exaggerating. They did not know what happened when they weren't here. I didn't want to bad mouth their dad, but I wanted them to understand that Eva told them the truth. After that, the kids got pretty protective of Eva and wouldn't tolerate any teasing of her by their dad or anyone else.

14

Maria Morales was working at her family's Bodega near Dinkeytown. It was just on the other side of a bridge with foot access from the University area. The Greek houses were on the other side of that bridge, there were bars and restaurants that students loved, and it was a place students could bring their parents when they came to visit. It served many purposes. There was even a little mini-Target. Students who didn't have cars, walked to that Target and bought what they needed. You'd never have found power tools at this Target. At this Target, you'd find Gopher t-shirts and baseball hats, toilet paper, pizza rolls, Doritos, coffee, socks, underwear, fans, bean-bag chairs, etc... It was all student-oriented merchandise. Maria couldn't wait to start at the U. The first day of classes was only a week away.

    Maria's family owned the Bodega, and Maria had worked there in some capacity all her life. Finally, once she turned sixteen, her dad paid her for the time she worked the cash register or stocking the shelves. She loved the Bodega. She loved working with her family and the customers. Bodega customers mostly spoke Spanish. Her family only spoke Spanish. Maria was born in Mexico and lived there until she was five. Spanish was her native language. She thought in Spanish not in English. She could flip easily between languages, but given the choice, she'd choose Spanish every time.

    About two o'clock on Saturday, August 28th, a white man with longish hair came into the Bodega. He walked around and spent about an hour in the store. This was unusual unless someone knew her family. This guy didn't know anybody, he just stared at Maria when he thought no one was looking. Maria's grandmother, however, was always looking. She did not like this long-haired stranger. Maria thought he was handsome for an old guy. He had big brown eyes and his hair was like that of an artist. Maria imagined he was a painter or a poet.

Maria's abuelita, however, started mumbling under her breath. She took out her rosary and started to pray. She stared him down until he became uncomfortable and left.

- Abuelita, ¿Por qué no te gustó ese hombre?
- Él es el diablo. El diablo.

Her abuelita went to the back room to light a candle and pray to rid the Bodega of his spirit. She even took holy water and scattered it throughout the store and made Maria's mom call the priest to come bless it again. Maria laughed. She didn't believe like her abuelita did. Her grandma believed once that she had a curse put on her by her sister. She went to see a witch doctor who gave her a potion to rub on her skin and told her she had to swim in the ocean before the curse could officially be removed.

As carried away as Maria thought her grandma could get sometimes, she wasn't often wrong. She was a great judge of character. She told her sister that her husband would disappoint her if she let her guard down before she married him. She laughed and married him anyway. Two years into the marriage, her husband was arrested for embezzling thousands of dollars from his employer. The money he embezzled went right in his arm.

He became a terrible heroin addict. He's in prison now.

Maria's last boyfriend was not welcome around her grandma either. Maria caught him sleeping with someone else within weeks of dating. Maria ran all her dates past her grandma now. If her grandma liked him, she could consider dating him. If she didn't, there was no way. Maria realized that her abuelita didn't like many people. She was still single. As far as Maria was concerned, it was worth the wait to make sure she found the right man, and her abuelita could tell her if he had potential or not. She was only nineteen. It wasn't like she had to find a husband tomorrow, anyway.

As much as Maria put faith in her grandma's intuition about the boys she dated, she dismissed the idea that this guy who just shopped at the Bodega was the Devil. Maybe he wasn't a good guy, but the devil? She thought that was a little harsh even for her grandmother.

Maria got off work at four. She was anxious to get to Susana's house because they were going to the state fair that night. They were going to see Chicago and The Little River Band in the Grand Stand. Maria loved the love songs by Chicago. Maria was going to go home and change clothes, then go pick up Susana to go to the fair. Maria hummed "You're the Inspiration" by Chicago as she almost skipped to her car. The guy who sent her grandma to the back room to light a candle and pray the rosary stood in the parking lot leaning on her car.

What the hell? Who was this guy, and why was he leaning on her car? If she didn't have plans, she would've gone back to the Bodega to get her dad.

"Hey beautiful," he said. "I don't think I've ever seen a more beautiful woman."

"Good try," Maria said. "Could you please move? You're on my car."

"I know this is your car, Maria," he said.

How did he know her name? She stopped dead in her tracks. Maybe her grandma was right. Maybe he was the devil.

"My grandmother is praying for your destruction as we speak," Maria said. "She thinks you're the devil."

"The devil? Really? What do you think, Maria?"

"I don't think anything, Mister. I just want to get in my car and go home."

She didn't hear a response but she felt it. Before she knew it, she felt a huge pain in her head. She fell to the ground. She looked up and saw him standing over her holding a crow bar. She screamed, and he hit her again. Her world went black.

15

"You're wearing that?" Michael asked. Here we go thought Izzy.

"What's wrong with what I'm wearing? I've worn this before." I worked on my appearance for over an hour. It was as good as it gets at my age.

"Exactly. You only wear stuff like that. You look like a teacher," he said of my dress. It was navy blue and came just above my knee. It had a scoop neck and didn't show cleavage, but it wasn't an old lady dress either. What did he want me to wear to dinner with his potential client?

"Um... do I need to point out the obvious?" I asked.

"Yes, Isabelle, I get that you are a teacher. You just don't need to look like one when we go for dinner.

"Michael, when we go out in our town, I am still a teacher. I can't be dressed like you want me to here. I can't get a reputation, and the dress you want me to wear would give me one. I am not going to change into that dress. Not this time."

"You will wear the black dress. You are not an old lady, and you cannot dress like one. Go change," he ordered.

"Michael, I..."

He threw his beer bottle against the wall. It hit my favorite art print, and the frame shattered.

"I'm so sick of your shit, Isabelle. Get fucking dressed."

My instinct was to pick up the glass and vacuum so no one stepped on a shard of glass. I could see Eva or one of her friends stepping on a piece of glass and hurting herself. I was going to worry all night. But I went upstairs to change. While I was changing, I heard Michael fire up the vacuum cleaner.

I hated the dress that he wanted me to wear. I couldn't wear a bra with that dress. I was so uncomfortable. It was so short, that I insisted on wearing dark tights with it. Of course, Michael preferred I go natural, but it was about six inches above my knee. I hated it. I felt like my boobs would fall out, and it didn't cover enough because it was way too short. I didn't have a choice tonight. He scared me when he threw the bottle at my print. I would wear the damned dress.

I came downstairs in that ridiculous dress knowing that my night was ruined before I left the house. My print was gone. And everything was cleaned up. It was probably his way of apologizing. I noticed, however, that he didn't tell me that he wouldn't change a hair on my head, and that he loved me unconditionally. He still wanted me in this God-forsaken dress. He said nothing about the tights, and I had to count that as a win. I just had to worry about my boobs spilling out onto the dinner table. No big deal.

Eva bounced downstairs looking for her phone, and we passed each other on the stairs.

She had to have heard the fight. She slowed down when she saw me.

"Mom, you look beautiful," she said. I couldn't hide my shame at this dress in front of Eva.

I nearly started to cry, but that would have started another fight, so I bit the tears back.

My precious girl made sure to try to make me feel better. What a sweet and perfect soul she was.

This dress was great fifteen years ago when I'd go out dancing. But now, I felt absolutely foolish in it. I was that mom desperately clinging to her youth trying to wear an old dress that didn't fit great and exposed entirely too much skin. What did it say about my husband that he wanted me to expose this much skin in front of his potential clients? Whatever it said about him, it couldn't be good. He was supposed to be my protector. When he decided what I needed to wear, he felt more like my pimp.

I put a summer wrap around myself before we left, and Michael was satisfied. I wondered how long I could get away with wearing the wrap.

We arrived at the restaurant and luckily, the air conditioning kept it pretty chilly. I kept my wrap when we were seated.

"Who are we meeting, again?" I asked.

"For the hundredth time, we're meeting the owner of the resort up the North Shore, The Sandcastle."

"That's right. I knew that. I'm sorry." He rolled his eyes.

The hostess brought Andrew and Lydia Thomas to our table. Michael and I stood while they were seated. We all shook hands, and the drinks and conversation started to flow. Lydia was a lovely woman. She and her husband ran the resort together. She was the artist, he was the business. She made me feel comfortable despite my dress, and we fell into easy conversation. She wore a beautiful, conservative dress. It was expensive. I recognized it from Macy's. It was Calvin Klein, and was nearly four hundred dollars. It was as beautiful as she was.

We stayed at The Sandcastle once when Eva was a toddler. Lydia decorated with an up north feel. Everything was red and black plaid like a flannel shirt. She had chalk boards hung with quotes from Thoreau. "Go confidently in the direction of your dreams. Live the life you imagined," and, "All good things are wild and free." I loved the literary references, and I loved the motif. I loved the white lights, flannel, and pine cone themes. I loved the woodsy vibe the place gave off. I thought Lydia knew her clientele and played well to them. If she were designing an elegant hotel in a big city, I think she would have adapted and decorated that beautifully with clean lines and shapes. There would be modern prints on the walls and sculptures by local artists. Everything would be state of the art. But up the North Shore, the woodsy feel is exactly what her guests were looking for.

Michael was the odd man out at this dinner. I know we all noticed, I'm sure of it. He had one too many drinks before they brought out our main course, and his laugh was far too loud for the atmosphere. He acted as he would at a dive bar instead of an elegant restaurant. He also acted like Andrew and Lydia were old friends, when they were business prospects. Everything was off. I spent the evening trying to smooth out his rough edges.

"Lydia, your dress is hot," Michael said. "You look amazing."

"Your dress is amazing, Lydia. I love it. You look beautiful," I said. To her credit, Lydia ignored the hot comment and smiled and said thank you.

He did that several times during the evening. He referenced sex every chance he got and then laughed a little extra loud. He was the only one laughing. The second we all finished our coffee and dessert, Lydia yawned and told her husband that it was time to go.

"Lydia, you're a young gal, you should be able to stay up and party with us," Michael said.

"Well, Michael," Lydia said, "I haven't "partied," since I had kids. Somehow, parenting and running a business with a hangover is unappealing."

"That's why I don't drink much any more either," I said.

"Eva's not little any more, but she has a constant need for my taxi services."

"As soon as I put the ring on her finger, she stopped being fun," he said. Then he cackled like that was a hilarious observation. I was mortified.

"Isabelle, it was a pleasure to meet you," Andrew said, and he air kissed each cheek. When Lydia hugged me, she whispered "run" in my ear. I knew she wasn't impressed with Michael at all. I also knew that he would not be doing business with this lovely couple any time soon. They would buy their security system elsewhere. I didn't realize it was enough to make her tell me to run, however. Sure, Michael is a little too loud and has no filter, but for a stranger to tell me to run is on a whole different level. I would have loved to talk to her. I wanted to tell her that it's not that easy. If I could just leave him, I'd have been gone a long time ago. Part of me loved him and felt sorry for him, but mostly, I was embarrassed by him and scared of him. I wanted to get the hell away from him.

Michael went to shake Andrew's hand, but Andrew's back was already to him. Andrew would be dodging Michael's phone calls, I thought. He was as unimpressed as Lydia was. When we were in the car on the way home, Michael said, "I think that went quite well, don't you?"

I had a dilemma here. Did I tell him the truth or did I keep the peace? The loving thing to do would be to tell him. If I told him, maybe he could alter his behavior next time. Maybe people wouldn't dislike him upon meeting him. He'd be pissed at the time, though. I knew I would pay if I told the truth. He'd find ways to hurt me. I also had doubts he'd ever think I was right and change his behavior. He'd write it off to something I said to them when they rejected his services. It'd be my fault because it could not be his.

I opted for peace. The easiest thing to do was always to compliment him and agree with him. The path of least resistance, was the only way. It didn't matter if I disagreed with him, anyway. He wouldn't change his ways or change his mind. He wasn't capable. It was as though he had something missing. He couldn't read a room. How on earth he could have judged dinner a success? They were obviously embarrassed. He had absolutely no self-awareness. He was blissfully ignorant. I was relieved that he was, though. He could still be happy, forget that he broke her print with a beer bottle while raging at me to dress slutty, and not notice when potential clients can't get away from you fast enough. Part of me felt a little sorry for him. He missed out on some of life's greatest pleasures because he was so self-absorbed. He missed out on his daughter, his nieces and nephews, his mom, and he has no real friends. His life is surface level.

Where is that charismatic, sweet, funny, sexy man I met in the bar all those years ago? He disappeared. All I saw now was a shallow, self-obsessed, ignorant, narcissist. Sometimes, I think he could be evil. Where does he go when he disappears for days? He says he's gone on business, but I highly doubt that's true. The truth is, I have no idea where he goes, and I don't much care. Every time he goes anywhere, it's a reprieve for me. I get a couple of days to be Eva's mom without worrying about what he'll do or say to hurt either of us. The things he says cut like a knife and never go away. I live each day in fear of the other shoe dropping. I walk on eggshells or on a tight rope every day. One false move, and it's over. My little balancing act of keeping him calm while keeping my job, attempting to create a decent home for Eva, pretending to support his every move, following the rules he created but doing my own thing when he wasn't looking, will fall apart. It wouldn't take much for this house of cards to tumble.

I was desperate to get away from him, but I was too afraid he would hurt us. What would the easiest way to hurt me be? To hurt Eva, and he knew it. So, I hadn't left yet. Once he told me he could kill me without touching me. I took that as a threat to Eva. I'm still standing on the wire. I hadn't fallen off yet, and I know there'll be rock bottom. I probably will stay rooted in fear until I hit that bottom. Why am I so weak? I am such a loser. I can't bring myself to get us away from him. I wish I was stronger.

16

We had a couple years of relative peace. Michael travelled a lot for his job, and Eva grew into an absolute beauty. She was sweet, smart, and determined. Her kindness was unparalleled. It was her greatest asset and weakness. She was so kind that she couldn't imagine people didn't have her best interest at heart. It would come as a shock to her when someone treated her with disrespect. She wouldn't see it coming because she was so sweet that she always thought of others first. She figured that was standard for everyone. I wanted her to keep that quality as long as she could. Trust in human nature was hard to restore once it was gone. She had a great core group of friends, and they planned to move to New York City when they graduated next year.

    I hadn't left Michael yet because he was never around. What was the point? He'd come home for three or four days, and then, he'd leave again for three or four days. I never knew when he was coming or going. I didn't even keep track of where he went. I didn't care. He wasn't home. That was all that mattered to me. If he wasn't around, he couldn't hurt us.

    He still managed some incredibly insensitive comments and the occasional black eye. He seemed to be irritated by everything I did. Why didn't he just leave us? He told Eva she was fat, stupid, lazy, and boring. Eva listened to every word. Some days, it was all I could do to get her to eat anything. She was in no way fat. She had the body of an athlete. She was solid muscle. She worked out daily. When I asked her why she didn't go out for basketball or track, she said, "I'm not good enough to make the team." It broke my heart. She would have lead the team.

The coach tried to get her to go out for basketball every year. He was also her favorite teacher. While I had a mind for literature and writing, Eva had a math and science brain. Her favorite class was physics. The physics teacher was the basketball coach. Mr. Backe just got her, she said. He knew when she needed to be left alone, and he knew when she needed encouragement. He knew that it could only be good for her to go out for basketball. Eva would have been a great basketball player. She shot hoops in the driveway whenever possible after dinner. Michael loved to go outside and give her pointers. Soon, she stopped playing whenever he was home. When he was home, she spent most of her time with Tasha or Addie. They almost never came to our house, but Eva practically lived at theirs. I spent so much time thinking I was protecting Eva that I succeeded in driving her away. The girls came over once when Michael was gone. They brought their sleeping bags and were still awake watching scary movies when Michael surprised us by coming home.

"What the fuck are you still doing up, Eva?" he asked. Eva died a little inside.

"Dad, my friends are here," she pleaded.

"I can see, Eva. How are you ladies?" he asked.

"Fine, Mr. Lewis. How are you?" Addie asked. Tasha wouldn't look at him.

"I'm fine, but please, ladies, call me Michael. When you call me Mr. Lewis, I look for my father."

I heard this exchange, and I put on my robe and went to rescue the girls. Pretty soon, he'd be making them eggs and insisting they sit in the kitchen with him. Eva would be mortified. There was no way to tell him no once he got going.

"Hi, honey," I said. "You surprised us. We didn't expect you back until tomorrow. I'm so happy to see you."

He gave me a kiss and told the girls he was taking Eva's mother to bed. He cackled in a way that let the kids know what he meant by bed. He was always over the line.

Eva never invited her friends to our house after this. She was too afraid he'd come back when we didn't expect it.

I tried to protect her, but I just made her life full of fear and self-doubt. Physically, she was fine. I didn't take into account her mental health when she was little. I never wanted her to have to spend time with him without me there to buffer. I think maybe I inflated my value in this respect. She could hold her own. I didn't foresee it being this way. If I would have, maybe I'd have had what it took to leave sooner.

Part Two: Eva

Eva's mom was an English teacher at her high school. Sometimes, she loved having her there. She loved that if she had a really bad day, her mom was there to help her out. She didn't have to ride the bus, she could write permission slips, and she never had to worry about lunch money. But most of the time, it sucked. She heard about homework her mom gave or detention she assigned all the time. One time, she even kicked Eva and her friends out of her study hall because they talked too much. Eva was mortified. Everyone thought it was hilarious that her mom kicked me out. She only had to endure it for three more months. Her mom said that she would look back on it and laugh one day, Eva was just pissed all the time. She was mad that her mom was in her school, and in the next breath, she was mad that her mom wasn't around enough. She knew it made no sense, but she couldn't help it.

Her mom took a lot of shit from everybody especially her dad and sometimes even from her. Sometimes, Eva blamed her mom for all the shit her dad did. It was safer to yell at her mom. Eva knew her mom knew exactly what she was doing. She knew Eva was mad at her dad, and it was easier to act mad at her. Eva knew she needed to be nicer to her mom.

That day she told her mom that she hated her and she couldn't wait to go to New York so she wouldn't have to see her any more. It wasn't true, and she wasn't actually even mad at her mom, but her pride wouldn't let her admit her mistake. So, she let her poor mom be sad all day. She was still quiet when they got home. They had leftovers for dinner, and she offered no apology when her dad gave her a hard time about it. "You're home all day," she said. "If you hate what I make for dinner, you can cook," she said. If she wasn't still mad at me, I'd have found a way to high five her without him seeing.

He was a drunk asshole, and she was usually a jellyfish around him. She had absolutely zero spine. Eva wanted her to fight. She wanted her to stand up for herself. Keeping the peace was overrated. When he got mad, he could be really scary. Eva knew that her mom did the best she could with the hand she was dealt. But if she stuck with him because she thought Eva would be disappointed, she had it completely backwards. Eva would have been proud if she left him.

She was so happy it was almost the weekend. She could find things to do away from her family. Maybe, Gregg would text her. Eva wasn't positive she wanted him to. Of course, she liked him. He was a hockey player, so cute, smart, and funny. She had a crush on him for two years. She kept it to herself and only told her friends about it a couple of months ago. Eva could be secretive sometimes, but she didn't want to be secretive about Gregg any more. She needed advice, so she told her friends. Tasha blabbed as she always does, and Gregg found out. He told Tasha that he liked Eva too. Part of her wanted nothing more than for him to like her and want to go out with her. But she worried about him meeting her family.

Her dad was crazy. He could go off at any time. Eva never knew if he was going to even make sense. He was drunk all the time. He crossed the line all the time. There was a running joke in town. "There's the line, and there's Michael." They'd show the "line" and her dad jumping way over it with their hands as they said it. It wasn't just embarrassing. It was humiliating and degrading. When he'd cross that line and tell a dirty joke in front of Eva, she wanted to crawl under a rock. He didn't know his audience. He didn't have a filter. What kind of father told jokes like that or made comments like that in front of his daughter? He was sick. It only made matters worse when he got drunk which he did nearly every day. He talked about sex pretty much all the time. He didn't care if Eva heard. In fact, he wanted her to hear. He thought it made him seem cool to Eva. Eva just wanted a normal dad. She wanted a dad who was totally uncool who told bad jokes. She wanted a dad who went to her sporting events and cheered her on. She wanted a dad who liked to golf, watch football, and helped her mom. She wanted a sober, normal, complete nerd for a dad. Her dad was so embarrassing. He was old and tried to be cool. He told sick jokes, dressed like a teenager, wore his hat backwards, drank, and flirted with her friends. He didn't think she noticed, but she saw everything.

He also got mean sometimes when he got drunk. They thought they knew what he was capable of because they lived it and saw him in action. He threw beer bottles at art prints, he threw dinner plates against the wall, he called Eva fat, ugly, lazy, and stupid. He criticized everything about her mom, too. What was she thinking by staying with him?

She hoped it wasn't because her mom thought Eva wanted it that way. She didn't want him around. He was a pig. He devastated Eva's self-esteem, and she couldn't wait to get away from him.

He creeped people out. One of Eva's friends told her once that her dad had really blank eyes. She usually didn't see it, but when she looked at pictures of him, that was all Eva could see. It was like there was no soul behind them.

One night, he was out at the bar as usual. Eva and her mom both had gone to bed. She was sound asleep when she heard a loud crash followed by her mom's scream. Eva's dad was yelling that it was time to "end it." Eva's mom had the phone up to her ear and hung it up. She thought better of making whatever phone call she was making. Eva thought her mom should call the police. She stood in the hall staring at the madness in front of her. Her mom was sobbing, and her dad was outside the door with a gun. What the hell? Why did he have his gun? It was his hunting rifle. Eva was terrified and frozen in place. The phone rang, and her mom answered it. She said yes and turned her head. She saw me in the hallway. She grabbed me, and we went to the only room with a lock on the door, the bathroom. Eva jumped into the tub and stood all the way back against the wall. Her mom stood between Eva and the door.

She stayed on the phone with 911. They were sending the police. He yelled at her the whole time.

"Right. Go ahead. Call 911. Ruin my entire life, Isabelle." My mom didn't respond to anything he said.

The bathroom had a window, and to this day, they both wonder why they didn't go out the window. They were rooted in place.

"Seriously, Izzy. How could you act like this? How could you involve Eva? Good job, Izzy. Now my daughter hates me. You've always wanted that, haven't you? I hate you."

The gun went off. Then, there was nothing but silence on the other side of the door. The dispatcher warned us not to leave the bathroom until the police got there.

"Stay put," she said. "It could be a trick. Just stay where you are. Isabelle, Isabelle, are you still with me?"

"I'm here," her mom said. "We won't leave until they get

here."

"They're almost there," she said. "Hang on. You're about to hear them enter your house."

I heard, "Police. Police, On the ground. Put your hands on your head." As that was happening, a female officer knocked lightly on the bathroom door. "One more minute, ladies. We almost have him out."

They let us out of the bathroom in time to see him escorted out of the house. He shot off the gun and sat quietly after. He was quietly waiting. He faked that he shot himself or he at least wanted us to wonder. He was one sick bastard. She didn't know how her mom could stand it. At least Eva had her friends, and she was about to escape. Her mom didn't have that outlet. Yes, she should divorce him. Eva was afraid for her if she did, though. He thinks that if he can't have her no one can. He is so mean to her. He acts like she doesn't matter, but he will never leave her. He will never let someone else have her either. He's a fucking psychopath.

That night with the gun changed Eva. She didn't trust that things will work out like they're supposed to any more. She didn't believe people were basically good and have other people's interest in their minds or their hearts. Her childhood was over the minute she saw the gun and ran into the bathroom.

Once her own dad threatened her life, she became cynical. She looked for the worst in every situation. Tasha thought she had gotten bitchy, and Addie saw her side. She told Tash not to be so judgmental. Addie was an eternal optimist. Of course she was. She had the perfect family, the perfect house, the perfect dog, and even a great little brother. What the hell kind of lucky star was she born under? She was just little miss happy. It drove Eva crazy. Nothing bad had happened to her yet, so she didn't get it. But she always Eva's back. Tasha did, too. They both worried that Eva would become obsessed with the bad and miss the good in the world. They were already right. Eva had been crabby and hated people in general ever since the incident. Eva was so ready for her fresh start in New York. It was time. Maybe her mom could move with her so that she wouldn't have to worry about her all the time any more.

Eva didn't know what she'd do without her friends. Her friends were her family. She and Tasha had been friends since kindergarten and Addie moved here in first grade. The three of them were inseparable.

Tasha's home life was a little more like Eva's than Addie's was. Tasha's parents were divorced, and her mom was really cool. Tasha didn't think so, but Eva really liked her. She was the kind of mom you could have the birth control conversation with without feeling like a loser. She was the mom who would call you in sick because you were embarrassed that the boy you liked didn't like you back. She felt for us. She treated Eva like another daughter, and Eva could use all the love she could get. Tasha's mom was great. Tash wanted a more traditional mom like I wanted a more traditional dad. At least her mom wasn't mean, though.

When she really felt like she couldn't stand it in her house she knew she could go to Addie's or Tasha's and be normal for a little while. All Eva wanted was to be normal. Maybe in New York, she could be normal. She couldn't wait to go to New York. For now, she had to endure this last year of high school, and she wasn't sure she could do it. It all seemed incredibly pointless.

17

Oh my God. Could Señor White be any more boring? In her head, that was meant to sound like Chandler from Friends with the emphasis on be. Seriously though, could he? He was going on and on about his "perro loco" He was loco. It was like he tried to find the most boring things possible to talk about in class. She yawned and rolled her eyes.

"¿De qué color es mi perro loco?, Señorita Lewis?" That woke her up.

"No sé," she replied.

"Don't take the easy way out," he said.

"Blanco y negro," she said.

He said, "Muy bien," and that now she could go back to day dreaming. Sometimes, he was kind of funny. Eva gave him that. He was her favorite teacher by far, but not today. Today, he could cartwheel around the room, and he'd have bored Eva. She just want to start the weekend. She had things to do and having the ability to say what color his dog was in Spanish would not help Gregg like her or to find a job in New York City while she went to NYU. She already got accepted, and she couldn't wait to start. Eva wanted to be a counselor. She wanted to help kids who had shitty home lives. She wanted them to know that it gets better, and you can be whoever you want to be regardless of whether your dad's a drunk and beats you or your mom brings home men and makes you sit in the hall while she turns a trick. She didn't actually know any moms who did that, but she saw it on TV once. It was awful. At least she had a great mom who was willing to help her no matter what it cost her financially or emotionally.

It's always hard to pay attention seventh hour on a Friday. Seventh hour on a Friday is a waste of time. She supposed if the last class was sixth hour, then sixth hour would be a waste of time. All any of them wanted was for the bell to ring to spring them from this hell hole for a couple days. Thank God they were finally seniors. Tasha, Addie, and Eva were going to be roommates in New York City. Eva had huge ambition to be a graduate of NYU and get her Ph.D. in psych. Tash, was dying to be an actress, Addie would be a doctor. There was no doubt about that. She hadn't received less than an A in all of high school. She was always the nurturing one of the group. They all had their role in their little group of friends, and they are all important to the group. If one of them needed help, the rest of the crew would drop everything and be right there. Eva, however didn't talk much about her family shit because she was sure they'd come over and try to rescue her from it all. She didn't want them to see how her life actually was. She was pretty sure they wouldn't want her baggage. At least they wouldn't want that kind of baggage. She wasn't sure what her dad did on his little get aways, he was gross, mean, a drunk, and she didn't want her friends to look at her with pity. They had an idea, and she vented some things to them. But she didn't want them to see, and she didn't tell them everything.

Eva's mom still wasn't ready to face that asshole on her own. She could still see her vulnerability. When she looked alive in her eyes and started to speak her own mind, Eva could worry less. Next September, no matter what, she was going to NYU come hell or high water. She'd feel guilty leaving her mom to handle him herself, but maybe that would be enough to get her the hell out of there.

Today was particularly tough to endure Señor's incessant need to have the class repeat after him, for Tasha too. Tasha and

Eva had Spanish, Art, and Physics together. Tasha wondered if Señor could talk if his hands were tied behind his back. He was so animated. It helped us to understand, but today, it just bugged her to no end because she needed to go. She was jumping out of her skin. At six o'clock tonight, she was set to meet this guy who might want to be her agent. She figured if she did some modeling, she could afford to move to New York. She would model until she could get on stage. She was so beautiful and so talented that Eva had no doubt she'd be a Broadway star someday. An agent was the necessary start. She needed an agent, and then a manager.

Tasha starred in every school play we had since we were freshmen, and it lit a fire in her that no one could extinguish. It was a given she would make it big as long as she got rid of that idiot she was dating. Why would someone as beautiful and talented as Tasha want to date a dick like him? She thought it was cool that he was older, but that was part of why I couldn't stand him. Addie, had no opinion. "It wasn't for her to judge," she'd say. I wish I had it in me to be so easy going. I didn't though. I was a hundred miles per hour or sleeping. I really didn't have a happy medium. My dad hated laziness. He interpreted rest as laziness, and that had been beaten into me.

We all wanted to get the hell out of this God-forsaken town, and I think Tasha saw Owen, the gross boyfriend, as a ticket out. He was twenty-two, and he went to New York City all the time. I thought it was weird that a twenty-two-year-old even wanted to date a seventeen year old. It wasn't even legal, was it? She thought it was cool because he had his own place. It was his place in life she liked, not him in particular. Owen set up the meeting with the agent, so the girls and I decided not to give her shit about Owen until she met with her agent. That sounded so cool and grown up. "Her agent." It made them all giggle with happiness.

Tasha's mom didn't have the money to help her get started in New York. Neither did Eva's. Eva worked a part time job at a movie theatre in Duluth. The job sucked, but the people were the best. Her favorite people who worked there were all guys. She didn't really get along with the girls. She knew she was jaded and a bit introverted, but it hurt that they made plans and never invited Eva. The guys just laughed and joked and had an easy-going attitude. They were so much easier to be around than the girls. The girls all talked behind each other's backs and were in constant competition for the attention of a couple of the guys who worked there. Maybe they didn't like Eva because she was friends with them all. Maybe they wished they could easily hang around them. She didn't know. It probably had a bit to do with jealousy, but she wouldn't have gone out with them if they asked anyway. They used to ask, and she always had an excuse not to go. She only had eyes for Gregg. She didn't want to risk the friendship of these guys either. They were her protectors, and they made work so much more fun. Eva wished the girls would just talk to her and get to know her, but until then, she was happy hanging out with the guys.

Most of the time, she was so happy when everyone left the house, and she was on her own. Addie, or Tasha could call, and she'd still come up with an excuse if she had the house to herself. She felt crazy. What teenager chooses books over friends? Why would anyone her age crave alone time? She just needed peace. When her parents were gone, she loved the quiet. Sometimes, she even turned off her phone so it'd be perfectly quiet. She wouldn't even turn the TV on. She really should be more social. But she couldn't pass up her alone time.

18

Eva had lots of flashbacks to her younger years. Her mom made her go to a therapist, and she says this is normal. Eva didn't really mind going to the counselor. She felt better whenever she went. Sometimes, she thought her friends got tired of hearing her trash talk her dad, so she didn't really talk about any of it any more. When she went to therapy, she could talk without worrying about that. If she needed to talk about her dad, she talked about her dad. If she wanted to talk about corndogs at the state fair, her therapist let her babble all she wanted about corn dogs. She would steer her back to the important trauma stuff, but Eva never felt guilty in her therapists office. She was safe there. Her therapist was the reason Eva decided to be a therapist. She wasn't sure how she'd function every day without being able to hash it all out with her counsellor. She always had her back. She was always on her side. Once a week, Eva felt normal and not like such a freak.

One of the flashbacks that keeps popping up is the time he took Eva camping by herself. She was in about seventh grade. Her mom was working on her Master's Degree and had to go somewhere for that. He decided they should go fishing. Eva was not a fan. She did like swimming, though, and they camped on the river, so she could swim across from where he fished.

She was in the river in her own little world when she heard a four-wheeler. There was a blonde woman on it. Her dad was happy to see this woman. Eva had seen her around town before. She was the bar owner's daughter. It looked like she came here just to see him. No one accidentally takes their four-wheeler to this remote spot.

Her dad reeled in his line and went to her. They hugged for longer than was appropriate. Eva just had a gross feeling about this. He made her a drink and they sat at the fire. Eva swam until she was frozen. She couldn't stay in the water any more. Her fingers were shriveled, and her teeth chattered. They sat by the fire, and she went into the tent to change. She decided to stay in the tent and read her book.

She could hear the two of them getting drunk. They were way too loud, and her dad never even came to see why Eva didn't come out of the tent. He didn't care. It was supposed to be father daughter time, and he invited a date. Crazy bastard.

All of a sudden, the two of them got very quiet. Eva heard nothing and wondered if she left. She opened the tent about an inch and peeked out. He and this gross drunk girl were doing it by the fire. Soon, she heard grunting and moaning. They didn't even attempt to hide what they were doing. Eva thought that he forgot she was even there. Eva pretended to be asleep just in case he decided to peek into her tent. He never did, and she never slept. First thing the next morning, he was making coffee and smoking by the fire like he always did. She rolled up her sleeping bag and took down her tent.

"Already had enough," he asked. "I thought we'd hang out here today. You can swim, and I'll fish."

"That was the plan yesterday, but you brought a date," Eva said. She did not disguise the disgust or the sarcasm in her voice. In a heartbeat, he was directly in front of her. He pushed her with both hands on her shoulders. He took Eva so off guard that she stumbled backward. She fell into the fire pit. There were still enough hot coals to warm his coffee and to burn the hell out of her back. Both Eva and her dad smelled the sizzle of Eva's long hair on the hot coals. She rolled off the coals and ran to the river. She jumped in and couldn't get out. Anytime she did, the pain was intense. He thought that might be bad because she could get an infection. He decided to get them out of there. He quickly took down his tent and poured water on the coals.

Her dad started to worry about what her mom would say or do, and he started to act like a concerned father. They rode a side by side to their camp spot on the river. She laid on her stomach in the back. Sometimes she bit back tears when they hit the bumps and sometimes she let out blood curdling screams. She never experienced pain like that before in her life. When they got home, her dad could tell that she needed a doctor, so he took her to the Emergency Room. They sent her to the burn unit at the hospital in Duluth, Miller Dwan. Eva's mom got there minutes after they admitted her. They had Eva on pain killers and had to do a skin graft.

She was in the hospital for almost two weeks. Her dad never came to see her, and her mom never left. They gave Izzy a cot to sleep on in Eva's room. It made her feel better to have her mom there. This was the first time her mom didn't try to make excuses for her dad. Eva was terrified of him and absolutely disgusted by him. Her disgust trumped her fear, and she never forgave him. When she got a smell of a campfire, Eva was back to that camping trip in her mind. She relived it often and hated him for it.

Her mother, who Eva would never understand kicked him out for a while, but little by little he weaseled his way back in. Eva was so disappointed in her mom when she took him back. She knew her mom was disappointed in herself as well. She could barely look at Eva. She was so ashamed. Once, she told her that she didn't know all that went on behind the scenes. Eva told her that it didn't matter. If her child had been pushed into a fire pit, she'd never accept that guy back into her bed. She just nodded and walked away. Nothing seemed to work. They stayed in that house. She would not leave him. She did not understand his hold on her. Izzy wouldn't tell Eva about all the threats on their lives, the lives of their family members, or the threat of what Michael would do to Eva. He told Izzy often that he knew the best way to get back at her was to hurt Eva. He'd leave little notes with threats in Izzy's car, on the bathroom mirror in her mailbox at school, everywhere. She didn't want to tell Izzy because that was too much for anyone to bear.

Another incident that Eva would flashback to often, was when she was five or six, but she remembered it like it was yesterday. He was drunk. Shockingly. He was always drunk for these little horror stories. Eva played soccer. She loved to run with her friends and kick the ball. That was all she really understood. She especially liked to play with the other kids.

The particular game that gave her flashbacks, Eva's mom stood with her parents, and Michael stood alone. Even at her young age, she knew that meant he would yell when they got home. But the yelling started early. He started yelling at Eva from the side-lines.

"Move it, lard ass. Come on, Lewis, move those tree trunks. Pretend there are treats on the other side. Run like someone broke a piñata. Go, bubble butt." Eva saw her grandpa start to lose his mind. Her mom pushed him aside though and handled it herself. Eva never found out what her mom said to him, but he shut up and sat in the car. Eva's mom grabbed her at half time, and they dropped her dad off at home, her mom packed some clothes, and they went to grandma and grandpa's for a long time. We stayed there that whole summer. Eva loved it. She was the princess there, and plus, they lived on a lake. Grandpa took them on boat rides, grandma and mom swam with her and taught her how to paddle board. She paddled to the dock, and their dog, Max, would get on her board. They paddled endlessly around the dock. She never had to worry about yelling. At that age, yelling was the worst thing she could imagine.

Eva never forgot his words. "Lard ass, bubble butt, tree trunk legs, etc..." He was so mean. Eva's mom, grandma, and grandpa said that it was because he was drinking. He didn't know what he was saying. Sometimes, when people drink, they don't know what they're saying or doing. Of course, Eva didn't have a fat butt, and her legs were strong enough for her to run, paddle board, and swim. A lot of kids aren't lucky enough to have strong legs. So, her mom told her it was actually a compliment.

She got over it at the time. She was proud of her athletic body as she got older, and she forgot all about that incident until she heard a boy in class call a girl "bubble butt" Eva started to cry. She couldn't breathe. She fell out of her desk onto the floor. The whole time, she was gasping for air. Her whole body shook. She passed out. The next thing I knew, paramedics were loading her into an ambulance. A sixth grader, at the time, all she could think about was how embarrassed she was. She was pretty sure she'd get teased the next time she went to school. The boys were relentless at that age.

It turned out the kids just thought it was super cool that she got to ride in an ambulance. She didn't even have to give them the story she made up about her panic attack. She was going to say they thought maybe she had cancer and they were doing tests. Then she wouldn't look like an idiot, they'd feel sorry.

Eva perpetually worried about her butt getting too big.

Sometimes, she'd starve herself after she ate too much so that it could even out. She got carried away with both eating too much and starving herself sometimes. She never got fat, but that wasn't healthy.

Everyone worried about her. She passed out several times while fasting. If she wasn't careful, her mom would take her to the hospital where they'd force feed her. She couldn't get so bad she passed out any more.

Eva didn't think she would ever have kids. It was too risky. She could screw them up with all her issues. She just wanted to live in NYC in a great apartment overlooking central park. She'd have an office where she treated her famous clients, and she and her friends would still hang out like the Sex in the City ladies. They'd probably go to watch Tasha in the Broadway shows. Eva kept her eye on the prize and saw the big picture. Good grades would get her into a good grad school. Good grades in grad school would make it so she could charge people a lot of money per session. She would, of course, marry Gregg and live happily ever after, but no kids. They were not part of the plan.

19

Tasha had their apartment all planned for the fall. She planned little dividers so they could each have their own space. It was a tiny space but that didn't mean they had to live like savages, she said. They'd have black and white prints on the walls, black furniture, and red accents with throw pillows and candles. Addie and Eva said she was in control of the decorating.

"Of course I am," Tasha said. "You two would have no taste if not for me!" She was teasing them and they laughed, but Addie and Eva knew she was not wrong. Addie's claim to fame was her kindness and intelligence, Eva's was her brain and grit, and Tasha was the artist. Tasha and Eva were intense. Addie was too in her own way. Addie just worried about everyone so much it was like having another mother. She reminded them to be careful. She was their protector. She would be the one to lock the doors and turn out the lights. She'd be the one who knew where everyone was all the time. Eva felt safe with Addie there.

Tasha didn't have Eva's vigilance to safety. She was intense, but her intensity was all focused on her career as an actress. She worried constantly about her figure, her skin, her teeth, and her age.

"Oh my God, Tasha, you are seventeen," Addie said. "Get over it! You are going to be a star."

"Some people my age have already starred in movies," Tasha said.

"They will probably burn out by the time they're twenty.

You'll have a long career like, like, um..."

"Like who, Addie?" Tasha retorted. "You can't even think of anyone."

"I can," said Addie "I can see who I'm thinking about but can't think of her name."

"So, she's super famous," Tasha said sarcastically.

"Yes, actually, she's the most famous."

"Jane Fonda," Eva offered.

"Yes, Thank you!" she said. "Liza Manelli, Julia Roberts, Kyra Sedgewick, and so many more. Now I can think of tons of them! Betty White, Cloris Leachman, Sophia Lauren, Audrey Hepburn, Glenn Close, Angelina Jolie..."

"Okay, okay, I get it," Tasha replied. She went back to worrying about her appearance.

Addie threw up her hands and said she tried.

The girls told Tasha to call them when she got home from meeting the agent. Tasha told them all to quit worrying. She was fine. Owen wouldn't set her up with a loser, and they all needed to get over it. But yes, she'd call.

Tasha left to meet this agent Owen told her about. Even Tasha had to admit it was shady to meet a guy at Kwik Trip. Really? Kwik Trip? Who had a meeting in the Kwik Trip parking lot? Hookers were the only people Tasha could come up with, but she never voiced her concerns to the girls.

Tasha was early, so she went into Kwik Trip to get a Diet Coke. Trent Osborne was working behind the counter. He stared at Tasha when he saw her. Tasha had always thought Trent was cute, but she always had a boyfriend, so they never talked.

"Hi, Trent," Tasha said.

"I wasn't sure if you knew me or not," he said.

"Of course I know you," she said. "Our school isn't that big."

"We don't exactly travel in the same circles was what I meant," Trent said.

"What do you mean?" Tasha was confused. She didn't see that their circles were so different.

"You don't have to know because you're popular," he said.

"Am I?" she asked. "I don't feel popular. I have two best friends and one sort of boyfriend."

"When did he become a sort of boyfriend?"

"Since he hasn't called me to hang out in weeks. I'd have broken up with him, but he set this meeting up with an agent so I can make some money to move to New York with. I didn't want to look ungrateful."

Just goes to show you that you don't have any idea what's going on in someone else's world. He figured Tasha was a little rich bitch who would never have noticed him and probably would think he was a loser if he did notice. Tasha brought her pop up to the counter to pay.

"Let me know if he becomes an ex-boyfriend if you want," Trent said. "I'd really like to take you out sometime."

Tasha beamed at him. Take her out sometime? That was so old fashioned and sweet. She liked his crooked smile and dimple on his left cheek. He had dark hair that fell in his eyes and a quiet demeanor. She would love for him to take her out sometime.

"I'd like that," she said. "I have a feeling he'll be an ex-boyfriend by next week." Tasha walked back out to the parking lot just as Owen was walking up.

"Hey, babe," Owen said.

"Hey," Tasha said.

"What, no kiss?" he asked.

"No kiss. You've ignored me for three weeks, Owen. You do not, in fact, get a kiss."

"Wow, babe. I set this all up for you, and this is the thanks I get?"

"You wouldn't even pick me up. I had to walk here. It's freezing."

"I know. Sorry about that. I was coming from somewhere."

"What's her name?"

"We don't have time for this now," he said. "He's here. He's in the black SUV over there."

They walked to it together, and Owen knocked on the window. Larry rolled down the window and told Tasha to get in.

"Hi," Tasha said. "I'm Tasha Lind."

"Tasha Lind, call me Larry."

"Nice to meet you, Larry," Tasha said. He kind of gave her the creeps. He was all sweaty like he just came from the gym, but he wasn't exactly the gym type. He was a big guy and didn't look like he got a lot of exercise.

"Where do you see yourself in five years, dear?"

"I see myself working my way up on Broadway in five years. Modeling is to pay the bills until I can land a Broadway job," Tasha said. She hoped she didn't sound crass.

"Okay, I can get you a few modeling jobs, I think," he said. "Let me look at you." Tasha just sat quietly.

"I'm gonna need to see you without the shirt so I can see your dimensions."

"Larry," she said. "That is not going to happen. I am not that kind of girl."

"What kind of girl? The kind who gets modeling jobs? You're not that kind of girl?"

"I just meant that I don't flash people in the hopes of getting a job. It's not my style."

"You may need to rethink your style, dear," Larry said. "If

you want jobs, we have to know your body. You will not model clothes if you are too big or too small. We need to see."

"I'll be happy to show someone in the proper setting, but your car in a Kwik Trip parking lot is not a proper setting."

"You're a real bitch, aren't ya?" he asked.

"Yes, sir," Tasha said. "I can be."

"That's a turn on," he said.

"What?" she asked. Tasha realized she might be in trouble here. She looked out the window. Where the hell was Owen? She looked all over and didn't see him.

"You heard me," Larry said, and he grabbed her arm with one hand and yanked her close to him. He tackled her onto the back seat. What happened to the driver? He's gone, too? They planned this, she thought. Owen had to have known because he got the hell out.

What did he get out of this? Money? Drugs? He was a son of a bitch. She should have listened to Addie.

"Please, Larry, please let me up and I'll take my shirt off. If you just let me up, I'll be nice, I promise.

He slapped her across the face. "Shut the fuck up, bitch," he said. "You had your chance to do this civilly."

Tasha started to kick and scream, twist and turn. The door opened.

Larry sat up and looked toward the door. Something was sprayed in his face. It was Trent.

He maced Larry! "Run, Tasha!" he said. Tasha went out the other door and ran behind him.

"I called 911, asshole," Trent said. "If you think it's our word against yours, look up. That's a camera, you idiot. You planned a rape in front of a camera. That takes a special kind of stupid."

Larry was screaming about his eyes. He told the 911 operator the guy might need an ambulance because he didn't have mace. He grabbed bug spray and sprayed that into Larry's eyes. He didn't want to blind the guy, but he did want him to get off Tasha. Trent stood his ground with the bug spray pointed at Larry like a gun. He dared him to move. Apparently, the bug dope was not pleasant because Larry just sat there trying to wash out his eyes with a water bottle. He didn't risk getting sprayed again.

When the cops arrived, they arrested Larry. There went her big modeling and Broadway dreams.

"Thank you," Tasha said to Trent. "You saved me."

"It wasn't that big of a deal," he said. "Anyone would have done it."

"Maybe," Tasha said. "But that doesn't change the fact that you did it, and I appreciate you."

"Well, you're welcome," he said. "Guys like that are scum. They give us all a bad rep."

"Men do kind of suck," he said. When he looked at her, she was smiling, and she elbowed him to encourage him to laugh too.

"Still want to take me out?" she asked.

"Very much," he said.

"Good," Tasha said. She fished a marker out of her purse and wrote her phone number on his arm.

Tasha was happy about the prospect of going out with Trent, but she couldn't believe this nearly happened to her again. Was she a magnet for these assholes? At least this time it wasn't her fault, she thought. She felt so guilty about the first one that she never told anyone what happened. She knew that someday, she would have to tell someone about it. If she was smart, she'd come clean with her mom first, then with Eva. But, she wasn't going to think about that today. She'd think about that later. She was good at that.

20

Detectives Engen and Townsend knocked on Barb's door at eight a.m. She was still in her bathrobe drinking coffee. Townsend was Detective Engen's partner. He was the trench-coat wearing type. She liked him, but he liked to dress the part of detective, and she was embarrassed for him. He was a good guy, though. He was a fierce protector of anyone he felt was wronged. She knew he'd do whatever it took to help Barb and her husband find the creep who abducted and tried to rape her. They were both beginning to think there was a serial killer in the area because several young women had gone missing lately. Barb didn't really fit the guy's type, but who knew. Sometimes, they couldn't hunt the type of victim they usually hunted. If they were desperate for a victim, they'd take who they could get. Admittedly, they usually went younger if they couldn't find their type. They were easier to manipulate. But their minds were open.

"Marty, can you let them in? I'm still in my robe. I didn't know they were coming today," Barb said.

"Of course," he said. He opened the door and greeted the detectives.

"Did you guys find anything?" Marty asked.

"We are sorry to bother you, Marty," Detective Townsend said. "We just have a couple questions for Barb."

"Would you like some coffee?" he asked. They said they would and he poured them each a cup and heated up his own. Jordyn and Brock were still asleep. There was no school that day, so the kids would sleep until ten or eleven. He woke up to use the bathroom at two a.m. and heard them in the family room watching a movie. He was glad they were sleeping. They'd been through so much. They all had. Marty never really fell back to sleep after two, and Barb was prescribed Ambien to sleep. Sometimes, that didn't even work. She'd take her sleeping pill, and still be up watching television or reading for hours. She tried meditating, hot baths, spa music, and journaling her feelings. While all these activities helped, they didn't always work. Each time he felt her toss and turn, he felt guilty. He wished he could have protected her. He should have protected her. But that was selfish. He didn't want to make any of this about him. He knew it was about Barb, and he thanked God every day that she survived that horrific attack.

Barb walked into the room and greeted everyone. She got herself another cup of coffee and joined everyone at the table. Marty got up to leave her alone with the detectives. She grabbed his arm and asked him to please stay. She knew he would want to be a part of the process, and everything was better if he was near her. She trusted no one any more, but she always trusted Marty.

"What brings you two over today?" Barb asked.

"Well, we've connected your case to several others in the area. Many women are missing, or their bodies have been found," Townsend said. As he said it, Parker glared at him. Was he too blunt? He never really knew.

"We want to go over your statement again because we've had some cases of missing women in the area. We are wondering if they are connected in some way. They have definitely not been connected to your case yet."

"There is one thing that sent me into a near panic attack," Barb said. "I don't know how this could possibly help, but Marty and I took the kids out for dinner a couple weeks ago. Marty almost never drinks, and if he does, he has a beer. That night, for whatever reason, he ordered a Captain Coke. I thought it was weird because I didn't know he even liked Captain Morgan. He said he just wasn't in the mood for beer, and his boss liked it. So he thought he'd try it. When the waiter brought his drink, he asked if I wanted to taste it. When I did, the smell really freaked me out. All of a sudden, I was back in that car. I realized his car reeked of Captain Morgan. There's no doubt."

"Actually, Barb, that could be really helpful. Can you think of anything he said or have you remembered any tattoos or scars?"

"I don't remember any. I do remember patterned socks. His socks showed below his blue jeans, and I could see his socks. They had those little dogs that look like they could be big dogs but have itty bitty legs. The Queen of England has them. I can't remember what they're called."

"Corgis?"

"Yes! That's it! Corgis were on his socks. They were black with those little dogs pictured on them."

"Thanks, Barb! That's amazing. Thank you! If you think of anything else, please call us."

"I will."

Engen and Townsend were elated. One of the bodies had a Corgi hair on it. They knew now for sure, at least those two cases were linked. The other two bodies had identical black fibers on them. So, they were fairly certain they were all linked. They could only prove that two were linked, and the other two were linked. It was just so coincidental that they had four bodies with the similar wounds to their heads, and Barb had been threatened with a tire iron. There was a hair consistent with a Corgi on the second body found, and Barb's attacker had Corgi socks. Barb said his car was black, and Victims one and four had matching black fibers on their shirts and were both found without pants or underclothes. All four had a shirt, but no pants or underpants. Just the two had the fibers. It was safe to link the cases now, they decided. They'd keep these details close to the vest if they could. The press could help, but really only if they had the description. The press already published the sketch Barb helped create. Too bad her recollection of him was only in profile. He was so nondescript that he could have been anyone. The boogieman doesn't necessarily look like the boogieman.

21

Sometimes Eva wondered, "What if he's right?" Maybe he's right and she was too lazy. What kind of dad says that to his daughter, though? Last week, he said she was lazy and ungrateful. This week, he called her a fat pig. She put on her work out clothes and found an old Billy Blanks Tae Bo on YouTube. Her mom used to love these. She said they made her feel tough. Eva needed to feel tough. She couldn't let him be right about her. If he was right, she should just quit everything. Just walk away from everyone and everything. She could just be a sad, pathetic lonely person with no friends and work in a library so she could read and not talk to people. She'd have peace. Right now, that sounded better than anything. She would rather live with peace and boredom than this. She fought off all of his comments and criticisms by trying to fix whatever he thought was wrong with her. If he said she was lazy, she never sat down while he was around. If he said she was stupid, she would study until she got straight A's. This time, he called her fat. He pushed the teenage girl's worst button. The fear that their bodies were imperfect. They all worried intensely about that. She had already lost twenty pounds that she couldn't afford to lose.

    Billy Blanks was next to impossible. She couldn't believe her mom used to do this all the time. It was super hard! But she was right, Eva felt kind of bad ass. Her dad could suck it. She was a size three now, and she didn't want to be smaller than that. She felt faint most of the time because she was dehydrated and starving.

In Oak Creek, you didn't have to post anything. Someone would make you their business and it'd be all over town that you had a doctor appointment for a rash or whatever the case may be. Eva didn't pay attention to the gossip, but she knew it was out there.

Sometimes, she would hear it when she was pumping gas or at the grocery store. The gossipy ladies loved to talk about her dad. He was at the bar several nights a week, and Eva's mom never went with him any more. The gossipers loved to talk about her parents' marriage, and Eva would hear he had an affair with the lady who runs the Community Education program or with Tammy who worked at the bar. She heard once, he was sleeping with Lily Olson who ran the post office, and another time, Eva heard he was having a full-blown affair with a local mom named Cyndi. He denied the rumors, of course. People just liked to talk. Her mom at least pretended to believe him all the time. She needed a bit of confidence and to get the hell away from him. If someone just threw her a bone, she'd be all set. Her mom needed someone to tell her she was beautiful or to get compliments about her teaching from her students, something. She would. It wasn't a stretch. She was really pretty still, and everyone loved her as a teacher.

22

Eva always walked this one loop around the school because she knew Gregg's locker was there. He had to wonder just how many classes she had that direction because she was always there.

Last Friday, Eva went to the movies with Addie and Tasha, and Gregg and his friends were there, too. They sat with them, and he held her hand. He still hadn't texted her or anything, but he held her hand for the whole movie.

When they parted ways, Gregg said he'd call or text. He didn't. Not one text or phone call all weekend. Eva took her phone everywhere with her. She checked it incessantly. Luckily, her dad had disappeared for a couple days. He did that sometimes. He just left for a few days, and we didn't know where he was. He said he needed space. Neither Eva nor her mom really cared. They were just happy he wasn't around. Life was so much more peaceful when he wasn't around. But for her mom to just blow it off like that was weird. She always told Eva that things were much more complicated than she knew, but she knew this, no husband of hers would take off for days and be accepted back in the house whenever he felt like it. No way. He had to be absolutely committed to her or he could get the fuck out. How much more complicated could it be? What could he be doing other than having sex with someone else during these little disappearances, anyway? Nothing. There was nothing else he could be doing. He was such a lying cheater. Eva heard that he once hit on a bridesmaid or something at a wedding he and my mom were at together. What kind of guts does it take for someone to do that? What kind of stupidity? It's like he has a death wish. If he had a divorce wish, he should just get divorced. Bye. See ya. Don't let the door hit ya in the ass on the way out!

With her dad gone, she could have talked to Gregg freely on the phone. But by Monday after school, still nothing. She avoided Gregg in school. She didn't walk the loop by his locker once. At about eight that night, Eva finally got a text from him asking if he could call. Her dad was still AWOL, so he could. Eva was so happy!

They talked for an hour. There were some silences at first that were awkward, but once they got talking for real, they couldn't stop. He was so much fun. We were well into hockey season, and he asked if Eva would go to his game on Thursday. It was a home game, and we were playing our rivals, Duluth East. Eva wouldn't have missed the game anyway. She loved to go to East games because Oak Creek needed to beat them. They were the rich kids. They acted like the Oak Creek kids didn't exist, so they had to pound them on the court, the ice or the field. That was where Oak Creek had the advantages. They knew how to work hard. East didn't. Everything was handed to them.

Eva was so happy to go to the game as someone Gregg liked. She wasn't officially his girlfriend yet, and that was important in her world of high school. But they were close.

They spent some time together, they held hands, and kissed. Gregg was sweet and he seemed to really like her. She had liked him for so long. Now that he liked her back, she was afraid her dad would scare him off. After the game, she would stop talking to him, she decided. She'd spare him the stress of meeting her dad and interacting with her messed up family. She had to.

If She let him, Gregg would be her first real boyfriend. All her friends had had several boyfriends by now. Eva liked Gregg since junior year. It was easy. She didn't talk to him. She didn't tell him she liked him. She didn't tell her friends she liked him. She just liked him from afar. If anyone knew, it would be real, and he could reject her. That was better than him actually liking her and finding out how sick her dad was. She was in no position to like anyone until she left the hell of her house. Her mom tried really hard, but their house was torture. Eva and her mom were told they were useless so many times that they believed it. They trusted no one with the truth about their home. It was embarrassing. Eva's mom thought everyone would blame her for not getting Eva out. But they didn't understand. He threatened to kill Eva if her mom didn't remain compliant. For some reason, looking like a normal family was really important to him. He couldn't consider being divorced. That was normal too. Half of America was divorced. He'd never let them go that easily though. So, they stayed to protect each other from the monster. He couldn't live a long time. His liver would give out, he'd drive drunk and run into a tree, an angry husband or father would shoot him, something had to give. He burned every bridge he walked over. He was quickly becoming the most hated guy in town no matter how many drinks he bought people. He was so stupid that he didn't realize a drunk guy wouldn't remember who bought him the drinks. It seemed pretty obvious. And there was this saying her mom always said that she thought applied to anyone who associated with her dad, "There's no loyalty amongst thieves." On Law and Order or in her books the smart guy took the deal first and ratted out the other bad guys. The rat got six months, the other guys got life. It seemed pretty obvious to her, but her dad was sure these village idiots were his buddies. All Eva could do was pray that one of his "buddies" ratted him out or got rid of him so she didn't have to walk on eggshells any more. And her mom deserved someone sweet who would adore her. If they left him soon, they could both be happy very soon. Or at least, they could have some peace.

Tasha came over about six. The game was at seven-thirty. They had to get there by seven or there'd be nowhere to sit. Everyone in town went to this hockey game. Oak Creek hated East. They decided to head to the hockey shelter as soon as she was done with Eva's makeup and picked out her clothes. Eva laid a couple pair of jeans and two sweaters on her bed to choose from. She picked some Calvin Klein jeans and a red sweater. She thought the sweater would look good under Eva's black jacket. She did her make-up and used shades of brown on her eyelids. She said brown made blue eyes pop. She was the expert. But Eva felt good.

"Wait!" Eva said. "I can't wear red. That's an East color."

"You're right," Tasha said. "Let's go with purple. That way, we look like we didn't try too hard, and we show school spirit."

"We don't have school spirit, Tash."

"I know, but we can pretend," she said. "And if you start dating a hockey player, you need to have school spirit."

"This is too much work," Eva said.

"It'll be worth it," Tasha said.

"He's adorable," she said. Eva beamed.

"I think I might have met someone," she said.

"I thought you were dating Owen," Eva said. She could not help saying his name sarcastically. None of the girls could. They really did not like that guy. Addie tried not to judge, but even she couldn't say his name normally.

"Shut up, Eva!" She said and punched my arm. She was blushing.

"Oh my God, Tash," I said. "You like him, like him. Who is he?"

"His name is Trent. He's in our physics class, he's so cute, and he's really nice to me. I talked to him at his job at Kwik Trip the other day."

"Speaking of Kwik Trip, you haven't mentioned your meeting with that agent guy in a while. When is that?"

"That didn't work out," she said. She wouldn't look at me when she said it. Eva could tell she didn't want to talk about it.

"I'm sorry, Tash. I really thought that would be it, and you'd be all set," Eva said.

"So did I," she said.

"Well, the Trent thing sounds promising. I know who you're talking about. He sits in the row by the windows in the back. He's not with Gregg and his crew, but he sits by them."

"Yeah. That's him," she said. "He is one of the nicest guys I've ever met."

"He's the anti-Owen?" Eva asked.

"Totally. We better go. Addie texted that she was already there, and she saved us a seat."

"I'm nervous," Eva said.

"Don't be. You look perfect," Tasha said and she uncharacteristically gave Eva a hug. Tasha was not a hugger. That was Addie's job to dole out the hugs. Eva and Tasha didn't go there.

When they got there, the pep band was playing, and the guys were warming up. Gregg gave Eva a head tilt when he saw her. She couldn't see a smile, but his eyes were happy to see her. Addie waved Tasha and Eva over. They found a spot near the East goalie. They knew they wouldn't be able to see the action as well on the other side, but for two periods, the offence would be right in front of them. Besides, all the best seats in the middle were taken already.

"Oh, shit," I said. "Shit, shit, shit."

"What?" Jenna asked.

"My dad is here," Eva said. He was such an asshole, and he always seemed to show up at the worst possible times. He was gone for four days, and he showed up here? Why? After spotting him, Eva knew she wouldn't be able to pay attention to the game. She would have to have one eye on him at all times to be sure he didn't humiliate her. She didn't know what she thought she could stop by looking at him, but it helped her feel some sense of control, anyway.

It was a fairly even game throughout the first two periods, then Gregg exploded on the ice! He scored twice in three minutes. He was awesome. Eva cheered so loud that she thought she would lose her voice. She was so proud to be the girl he asked to come to the game. She couldn't date him, but she would have the memory of tonight, she decided. It was almost worth all the pain of loving him from afar for the last year and a couple months. She was sure that she would love him from afar for the last few months of school and beyond, too.

Tasha went to the ladies' room between the second and third period, and she didn't even see Gregg score his goals. That was pretty common with the lines on the girls' side. She came back to her seat looking like she was going to be sick.

"What happened?" Jenna asked.

"Nothing," she said.

"No way, it's not nothing. Your face is pale, and your eyes look kinda wild," Eva said.

"It's nothing, Eva," Tasha said. "Could you please just drop it?"

She stared off into space, and the girls wondered what they did to make her mad. Addie didn't mince words, ever, especially not with us.

"Spill, Tash," Addie said. "There's something going on. I see it, too."

"I broke up with Owen, okay?" she said. So, we all hugged her and told her we loved her. We all, against the advice of our mothers, told her what a loser Owen was anyway. What was a twenty-two-year-old doing with a teenager, anyway?

Addie, who really hated Owen although she professed to be neutral, actually held back here. She didn't tell Tasha she thought Owen was a dick here. Eva thought it was her big opportunity, and even Tasha looked surprised that Addie told her she loved her and left it there.

The next day in study hall, Addie said she didn't buy Tasha's story about Owen. "Why not?" Eva asked. Eva didn't mention Trent. If she wanted Addie to know about it, she'd have told her.

"Because it was too convenient of a reason, and she looked too horrified for it to be that. She doesn't really like Owen. She thinks it's cool that a guy with his own apartment likes her. Haven't you noticed that she doesn't gush about him, like, ever?"

"Now that you mention it, you're right," Eva said. "She doesn't even really talk about him let alone gush. But what the hell else could it be? She went to the bathroom, and she was fine when she left. When she came back, she looked mortified."

"Something had to have happened with someone in the hockey shelter," she said.

"Oh my God," Eva said. "My dad was there. I saw him in the stands, and his nose was red. His nose being red tells me right away that he's drunk."

"It was cold out, though, and that can make your nose red,"

Addie said.

"I know, but I know him. I feel it when he's drunk. I can't explain it, but I always know immediately when I see him. So does my mom. You live with a drunk long enough, you figure it out fast. It's survival."

"I didn't think of that."

"My dad did something to Tasha, I know it. I can feel it in my bones. That is what was bothering her, and because it was my dad, she didn't want to tell me."

"Want me to find out what he did?" Addie asked.

"Only if talking is the right thing for Tasha. I don't want to hurt her more to satisfy my curiosity. I know he hurt her, though. Her face was so haunted," Eva said. "He's such a dick."

"Maybe someone or something else is bothering her. You never know. It might not have been your dad."

"Addie."

"Maybe…We'll know soon enough. In the meantime, enjoy your new relationship. You're entitled to enjoy life, Eva," Addie said.

"Not at the expense of someone else, and I will hurt Gregg. I'm too fucked up to have a normal relationship and to trust someone," Eva said.

"The only way I see you fucked up is assuming Gregg is better off without you. You have no idea how great you are. Please at least think about it."

"All right. And Thanks Addie," Eva said. But she knew she was in no shape to date anyone right now.

When they were at the game last night, she could hear her dad do his loud, cackle laugh from the other side of the arena. It made her want to throw up. She wondered what he did to Tasha, because she knew it was something. She was happy, saw him, and shut down completely. Come to think of it, Tasha never came to her house without asking if her dad was home. If he wasn't, she came over. If he was, she didn't.

Gregg called the night of the game. He said he liked having Eva there to watch him. He said he felt good that the prettiest girl in the school was there to see him. God help her, but she couldn't stop herself from dating him right away. It was the only thing in her life that felt right. Gregg and Eva started holding hands in the hallway, and we were officially boyfriend and girlfriend now, not just hanging out.

"Hi," Eva said.

"Hi," Gregg said. "What are you up to?" Eva liked that he called. He mostly texted, but he called her at night when her dad wasn't home.

"I was just talking to Addie," she said. He asked if Eva wanted him to let me go so she could go back to talking to her. Eva said no, that they were done.

"What are you doing?" she asked. "What were you up to before you called me?"

"I was helping my dad build a bed in the shop. It's really cool. You should see it! We used diamond willow. It's so pretty. The dark colors of the wood contrast so well with the light-colored wood."

"I can't wait to see it. You and your dad get along really well, don't you?"

"We do," he said. "What about you and your dad?"

"With my dad? No. I don't know if you've heard, but my dad is the town drunk," she said. She was pretty sure he'd say he had to go. Now that he knew what a loser her dad was, they shouldn't talk any more.

"I know he drinks, but a lot of people in town do. The bar wouldn't stay open if it was just your dad," he said. God bless him! That was exactly what she wanted to hear. It was good to know she wasn't alone. It was a relief to know. Her therapist had been all over her to hit up an Alanon meeting so she could see how many people there were who lived exactly like her. She hadn't had the nerve to go yet, but maybe she could go. She wouldn't tell her dad. He thought shrinks were there to make you feel okay within yourself in order to get permission from a professional to bail on your family.

"Gregg," Eva said. "Are you sure you want to go out with me? My dad is a crazy lush, and my mom and I spend most of our time figuring out how to avoid him. She won't leave him because he threatened to kill me if she did."

"I'm positive, Eva. I like you. I don't care about your dad except I care if he hurts you. I'm not embarrassed by him, and you shouldn't be either. His actions aren't your fault. You're not him," he said.

Eva was crying and said, "I'll understand if you change your mind at any time. He can be completely repulsive."

"It's okay, honey. Stop worrying about me, anyway. I am in this because I like you. That's it, I accept whatever comes with you because I like you."

Eva had never thought of this. Her self-esteem was still so low. When you're told you're a loser enough, you start to believe it.

23

They left him once. Eva's mom went to therapy before she left him, so he's pretty sure the therapist talked her into leaving him. It couldn't have been the affairs, the booze, the threats, pulling a gun on us, the name calling or any of the million offences he committed against both Eva and her mom. In the psychopath's mind, it was advice from the therapist.

About a year later, they ended up back with him. Eva's mother missed her family time with Sophia and Oliver. Sophie called crying almost every time she was at dad's because she missed her stepmom. Eva's mom missed them just as much and started spending Friday evenings at his house with them. That turned into spending the night on Friday, and then, she just stayed the weekend. She started sleeping where she used to, and before Eva knew it, they were back there. She insisted on couple's therapy, and he did whatever she said. He knew how to play her. Eva's mom was so happy. He acted like he really wanted help and to change. They went for about six months when their therapist told them she was sure they would make it. She was graduating them from therapy. She said she knew they were honest, and earnest in their desire to be their best selves with each other. The very night they graduated therapy, her mom helped her dad pack a bag for the next day. He had to go to International Falls for business. Eva remembers that clearly because it was spring break. He was staying at the Holiday Inn.

Eva asked her mom why they couldn't stay at the hotel with

him. He could work, and we could swim and go out for lunch or something. Eva was about eight years old. Her dad left already. She called him to say they were coming. They'd just meet him up there.

"Izzy, no, you can't come up here," he said.

"Why can't I?" She asked.

"Um, cuz it's snowing," he said.

"It's Minnesota. It's always snowing," she said. She was immediately suspicious because he always wanted Eva and Izzy with him. He was obsessive about it. When he'd take a load of recycling to the dump, he made her ride with. He had never warned her off because of snow. That just didn't happen.

"Okay," she said. "I'll tell Eva. She'll be disappointed."

"Okay. Bye. Talk to ya later," he said and hung up. It didn't seem to bother him at all. She knew without doubt that something was wrong.

My mom went to his work room in the basement and just started digging through things. She didn't know what she was looking for, but she dug through receipts, drawers, cabinets, everything. Finally, she decided to look on his computer. She shook the mouse, and he didn't exit his email before his computer went to sleep.

She underestimated him. He was so brazen. He asked her to pick out a shirt for him to wear to dinner. He told her he was having dinner with clients but didn't want to wear his work shirt. So, her mom packed a nice green button down shirt that she bought him at the Mall of America.

My mom couldn't believe she was so stupid and gullible I heard her tell Beth. But it didn't occur to her since they graduated from therapy the night before. She just could not believe the balls he had to do what she saw on his email.

"Hey, just checking in making sure we are still on for tonight," he wrote.

"I'll be there about six," she said. "I can't wait to see if actual sex with you is as good as our phone sex." I heard my mom scream downstairs. I ran to the top of the stairs to the basement and asked my mom if she was okay.

"I'm fine, honey," she said. "I thought I saw a mouse, but I was wrong."

"Okay," I said and went back to watching iCarly.

She read on. She found that the woman, Elaine, sent my dad inappropriate pictures. She had a tramp stamp; I heard my mom tell Beth this whole story. Even at eight, I knew what he was doing was sick.

He chose the tramp stamp lady over them. Eva felt bad for her mom. She didn't want to go there anyway, but she was mad that he picked sex with a new lady over being with his family. What was wrong with him? Eva would never forget this rejection. She knew her mom wouldn't either. She wished she never went back to him. Sophie and Oliver didn't get why they left him in the first place. Their parents worked it out so Eva's weekends with her dad were the same weekends Ollie and Sophie had with him. That way Eva didn't miss any of my time with her brother and sister. Her dad was always good in front of them. He never drank too much when they were there. Or he hid it better, is probably more like it. He can't drink that much and then just stop two of every fourteen days. That's not what Eva read about alcoholism, anyway. That fact made her wonder if he really was an alcoholic. God, he made her question everything.

Over the years, Eva came to terms with the fact that he was an evil person and an alcoholic, but she didn't think Sophie and Oliver had yet. He never took his normal dad mask off in front of them. His mask made him funny, smart, clever, and kind. When he took that off, all pretense of humanity vanished. He didn't even try to be nice or pretend to have a conscience sometimes.

His nastiness escalated over the years. At first, he was passive aggressive and would just sort of hint at the fact that he found Eva and her mom repulsive. He'd say things like, "All the women I talk to say carbs are the root of all evil." As we are eating chicken noodle soup with home-made bread. Or he'd see a gorgeous girl on tv and say, "I wonder what it's like to be absolutely surrounded by beautiful people. What do you even do with that?"

Most of the time, things like that made my mom cry, and made me hate him. He got worse; he'd just flat out say he ruined his life when he married my mom. He could've done a lot better. Women approached him all the time asking him why he married her, he'd say. He was just so much better looking. He'd hit Eva in her most vulnerable places as well. He'd tell Eva to cut out the carbs or she'd look like Mrs. Larson down the street who weighed about three hundred pounds. "They could do a show about you. You could star on 'My 600-Pound Life'," he'd say. When she tried out for the play, he'd say, "Don't you have to be attractive and popular to get parts in plays?" Sometimes, he'd park the car far from whatever business they were going into and tell her to run to the doors.

Junior year, he teased Eva about not having a boyfriend. That was the year that she loved Gregg from afar. One night, they put together an air hockey table together. It was their Christmas present. Ollie, Sophie, and Eva would have a blast with it. She was so excited. Ollie would just have fun, and Soph would get all competitive like always. Tasha and Addie, she thought, would love it too. The three of them were so competitive. They loved to play horse or race each other even now that they were seventeen. Eva was happy, and her guard was down. She should never, ever let her guard down around her dad. She learned that that night what happened if she did. He was downright evil.

He said, "I'm going to bed with my wife. I know you don't even have a boyfriend yet. Are you the only girl without a boyfriend? I notice Tasha has had lots of boyfriends." Eva sat there with her mouth open. She couldn't believe her own father gave me shit about not having a boyfriend. "Maybe someday you can have a boyfriend, too." Who does that? Eva never touched that air hockey table. None of them did. Ollie and Sophie were already in college by the time he bought that thing. They came for visits now. They didn't come for weekends. They would actually sit and chat. Sometimes Sophie came without Oliver, and sometimes Oliver came without Sophie. He was always on perfect behavior with Sophie. He talked down to Oliver sometimes, but never Sophie.

One night Sophie actually spent the night, and they stayed up late talking.

"Why are you going so far away to college, Eva? I'll miss you!" she said.

"I have to get out of here, Soph. I'll lose my mind if I don't."

"Quit being so dramatic," she said. "Why would you even say that?"

"You don't see it, Sophia, but I live it every day. He's such a manipulator. He's scary and a drunk. I hate him."

"People drink, Eva. Wait until you get to college. Everybody drinks. You just have to ignore it and find people who don't."

"Oh Soph, I'm happy for you that you still think it's just me being dramatic. I'm happy for you that you didn't live here. Dad is cruel and a drunk. You just don't see it. He's always on his best behavior when you guys are here. Look at me! I'm a great dad. I'm such a good guy. He's all about appearances."

"Did you ever stop to think that maybe he does the best that he knows how? It's not great, he doesn't know a lot, but it's the best he knows how."

"Again, lovely thought. But he's mean, Sophie. He doesn't care who he hurts. I think he enjoys watching us hurt. If I cry, he smiles and cackles. You know that laugh." We imitated it, and we laughed together.

"My mom used to say that he'd cackle after he said something hurtful and think that because he laughed, that made it a funny joke," Sophie said. It was the first time Sophie ever sided with me. I told her that.

"I'm always on your side, Eva. I see what he does. Remember that night he made no sense during the political debate?"

"Yeah, Ollie called him a Republican, and he freaked out."

"I never forgot that. He was vile to Ollie and to you, and I've heard him say bad things to your mom. I always understand exactly what you guys are saying, and I'm happy not to live with him. I say what I do to hopefully make it seem better to you."

"It won't be better until he's out of our lives for good," Eva said.

"I love you, Eva."

"Love you, too, Soph."

24

That conversation with Sophie sustained Eva for a long time. It helped to know she wasn't in this alone. They had to know the truth about him. She thought they thought she was crazy, and that her dad hung the moon. She didn't know they didn't totally buy his holier than thou act.

They didn't want to make it worse for anyone. Knowing Sophie, she thought all that through. She probably didn't want to believe Eva 100%, but she also knew she wouldn't out and out lie. Eva guessed she thought the truth was somewhere between what they saw, and what Eva said. She hated that someday, reality would crush them. She knew he was evil and came to terms with it a long time ago. She didn't really know the term for it except for psychopath. She read everything she could get her hands on about psychopathy. She knew that didn't make her an expert, but from what she read, he checked most of the boxes. He had a flat affect, he got bored easily, he never felt guilty about anything, his thoughts always went to himself, one time, she saw him kick their dog, Bailey, and laugh, he used people for his amusement, he could be incredibly charming, and he thought he was the best everything. He was the best father, husband, business man and even fisherman. Those who didn't appreciate his perfection were missing out, he thought. He lied all the time. Sometimes the lies were huge, and sometimes they were small, irrelevant and stupid. He couldn't help himself but to lie. He coerced people to do what he wanted all the time. The "vacations" he convinced them to go on were like torture for them. They were always in the middle of nowhere in a tent and fishing. He conned Eva's mom into buying a boat when they didn't have money for heat. The list went on and on. Eva hoped, for Sophie and Oliver's sake, that they didn't find all of this out at once. Their whole belief system in who they were could change. Eva's did, but hers was gradual. She knew her mom talked to their mom all the time, and so she just couldn't take responsibility for that too. It was too much.

Eva and her mom tried their best to make everything perfect for him when he was around. They even tried to keep Bailey from barking, and Eva walked her so her dad didn't notice her as much. She was so afraid he'd hurt her again. They made sure there were no loud noises. Bailey was so little and cute. If she had normal sized legs she'd be a medium sized dog. But those little Corgi legs were adorable. Even the dog walked on eggshells for her dad. Eva was disgusted by him.

25

Tasha hated this piss-ant town in the middle of nowhere as much as Eva did. Although Eva didn't know it, Tasha wanted to get away from Michael almost as much as she did. That man had the ability to crumble Tasha's world down around her. He was the big humiliation of her life. The shit that went down freshman year with him would bring his world down even more than hers, but it didn't stop her from worrying.

If what happened that night ever got out, she'd leave town immediately and never talk to Eva again. Her best friend could not know what her father did to her or her own role in that night from hell. Eva hated her dad enough without Tasha's story adding to it, she thought.

She figured her ticket out of town would be modeling. Everyone told her she was photogenic, and that she should model. However, the "everyone" she thought about were people from the wrong side of the tracks in this redneck village. Oak Creek wasn't far from Duluth which was its only saving grace. It was only a twenty minute drive to Duluth. She liked Canal Park with its cool coffee shops, tourists, fun restaurants, and the lift bridge. She, Eva, and Addie went to Canal Park almost on a weekly basis. There was no better place to have girl time than with a Caribou Coffee than on the ledge by the lighthouse. Tasha could close her eyes, feel the breeze off Lake Superior and think about life. She thought about Trent and how he saved her from Larry the Pig. She could forget about the terrible secret she'd been hiding from Eva and the girls for the past four years and just be a girl with the world at her feet.

Sometimes, people said they were jealous of her good looks or her youth or whatever else of hers that they wanted for themselves. Tasha always thought they should be careful what they wish for. She may have had pretty eyes and a trim figure, but she was full of anxiety and depression. Her dad died when she was little, and her mom had lots of boyfriends through the years. Tasha didn't like most of them. If she liked them, her mom didn't, it seemed. In her spot by the light house with her tall sugar free green tea, she tried not to worry about her anyone learning about freshman year and Eva's dad, Larry, being able to afford NYC, any of it. She was just Tasha Lind from a small town in Minnesota with the best friends anyone could ask for and a passion for musical theatre. She was normal, she told herself. She was just a normal girl who had a secret that would destroy her life, and her best friend's life if anyone found out.

26

A young woman went missing or was found murdered every two months like clockwork for the last three years. They were all either in the Twin Cities area or the Duluth area. A couple went missing from the Casino in Hinckley.

Eva became suspicious of her dad's disappearances about a year after they started. The first year, she just reveled in him being away from the house. She could be herself when he was gone. She didn't care where he was as long as he wasn't home. When he started to leave for three or four days at a time every month or two, she started to wonder if he had another family somewhere. Did she have a sister or brother she didn't know about?

"Mom, do you ever wonder where dad goes all the time?" Eva asked.

"He's just working, honey. His sales territory takes him all over Northern Minnesota."

"Yeah, but it's like getting to be more of a regular thing. And, where does he go? Can't he do everything online now?"

"Well, he has to actually meet with customers to install their computers," her mom said.

"Oh, so when he's gone, he brings computer equipment with him, then. I get it." Eva said and was fairly satisfied with the response. It made sense that he had to go to the customer site to install equipment. That couldn't exactly be done online. But her mom got a far away look on her face like she hadn't really thought about it. Like maybe he didn't always have computers with him when he went out of town. Maybe he was meeting other women like when he went to International Falls when she was little. Her mom was devastated that day. She tried so hard to hide it. She took me to Barnes and Noble and let me pick out two books. Then she took me out for pizza. Eva felt her mom's tension and asked her several times what was wrong. She finally figured it out when she heard her mom on the phone with Beth.

But when Eva heard about the missing and murdered women in Minnesota, she wondered if her dad had something to do with it. First, he was gone often and she didn't know where he was. Her mom didn't even really know where he was. Second, he was just evil and gross enough to do something that vile. Psychopaths weren't necessarily serial killers, but serial killers were always psychopaths.

Eva wrote all the dates out for her mom to check against her journals. Since she started having insomnia years ago, the doctor told her to create a bed time routine. So every night, she took a bath with lavender oil and wrote in her journal. Then she meditated until her Ambien kicked in. Eva did the same, but She just used melatonin for now. It worked for her. Sometimes, the Ambien didn't even work for her mom. She's experienced more anxiety causing moments with her dad than Eva did. She knew that her mom had a lot of secrets. She didn't want anyone to actually know her or her story.

Luckily, for their investigative purposes, she never missed a day with her journal. Some entries were a lot longer than others. Some didn't make a lot of sense if she wrote after ambien, but it was a place to start. They could at least check to see if he was around or if he was on one of his "business meetings." Eva was putting the final touches on her list of dates girls went missing when Addie texted. "Jenna Olson wants us to meet her at Daily Grind."

"Jenna Olson from Spanish class? Why?"

"Yep. Didn't ask, just said I'd be there. Want me to pick you up?"

"Sure. Tasha coming?"

"Yep. She's driving herself, though."

"See you in ten."

"Sounds good."

Half an hour later, they were all at the Daily Grind. They had the best blended coffee drinks! It was totally geared toward our age group. They played popular music, had comfy chairs, great Wi-Fi, they sold ice cream and healthy food, and they let you buy one coffee and hang out for hours doing homework if you wanted to. It was half an hour from our house in Duluth, but it was totally worth it.

Jenna looked a little like she wanted to throw up, and her little hands just shook.

"Hi Jenna! I'm so glad you came up with this! I don't think I've ever even seen you outside of class!" Tasha said.

"I know," Jenna said. "You all seem to have so much going on all the time that I didn't want to intrude. You guys have all been friends forever, and I didn't want to just invite myself. "We have a blast in Spanish. I just wish I'd have thought of us hanging out earlier."

"Um. That's really sweet, but when I tell you this, you will all hate me." Tears were about to spill out of her eyes.

"What are you talking about, Jen?" I asked. "We couldn't hate you," Addie reached over and patted her hand to show her how much we meant it.

"I didn't mean to," she said. "He just looked so evil the last time I saw him at the movie theatre with your mom, Eva. His eyes were blank and soulless." She took a drink of her blended White Chocolate Raspberry Mocha, and swallowed and looked pitifully at Eva. She wanted to hug her. She knew that soulless look. Jenna was really perceptive. It didn't surprise Eva that she caught it.

"I decided to follow your dad, Eva," she said, but she couldn't look at me. "I wanted to know if I was imagining that I felt that day I saw him. I was totally OCD about it. I couldn't sleep. All I could see were those eyes. He was staring at this girl in a short skirt. But it wasn't like a "Hey baby" stare. It was more of a "I pick you to be a victim look. He never took his eyes off this girl, and his eyes were like black. I was so creeped out, and I thought maybe I was the only one who saw. So, I followed him after the movie, and a few more times." She looked at Eva to judge her reaction. Then she looked at Addie and Tasha to see if they were mad at her for saying this to Eva.

"Eva, please don't hate me."

"That doesn't make me hate you," she said. "I hate him, but I could never hate you."

"Yeah, you will when I tell you the rest," she said. "He went to Tasha's house, a lot. He watched her and followed her. He never went into her house, but he looked in the windows and took pictures."

"Like a Peeping Tom?" Addie asked.

"Yes, exactly. Well, I thought it was really weird, but I didn't want to tell you guys, so I told all of this to Detective Engen. I went to the cops and told them I saw your dad peeping in Tasha's windows. You have to hate me now. I called the cops!"

"Good," Eva said. "That's exactly what you should have done. But I'm pretty sure following him is dangerous, so I wouldn't do that any more. The cops know. Let them do their job."

"What I don't understand, "Jenna said, "Is why he fixated on Tasha. He's a grown man. He could have gone anywhere to peak into an adult's window. It really freaked me out, you guys."

"I know," Eva said. "I've been realizing just how scary he is more and more every day. I didn't worry before too much because he was just mean to me and my mom when he was drinking. Otherwise, he was weird, but tolerable. Lately, though, I'm scared, I'm scared of what he could do."

"Eva, you and your mom need to get out of that house. Now! I think he's really dangerous. He climbed really high in a tree just to look in Tasha's window." Jenna said.

Tasha shuddered. She knew she should probably tell Eva what happened now. Then, maybe Eva and Izzy would leave him and be safe. Was she being selfish telling them? Or was she being selfish keeping it to herself. She couldn't decide but thought it was better to be honest. If Michael hurt Eva and Izzy, and she could've done something to make them leave him, she'd never forgive herself. It was time.

Eva had knots in her stomach. She almost couldn't breathe. Tasha looked gray. Eva had never seen her so nervous.

"Eva, Addie, Jenna, I have to tell you something. It might make you hate me, but if it keeps you and your mom safe, Eva, I'm okay with that. I never wanted you to find out. I was so ashamed, but I have to tell you."

Eva said. "What did he do, Tash?" It was her turn to take a few deep breaths. She just knew it was something her dad did. That was why Tasha looked so upset at the hockey game. She knew he did something creepy to her. She hated him with everything she had in her. What kind of psychopath spied on his daughter's friends. Gross. He's a pedophile and a psychopath. Did it get worse than that?

"The summer before freshman year, I was thirteen. I was starting to be curious about boys. I had a couple want to date me, but they were boring. I was dressed in a halter and shorts, and my mom would have killed me if she saw me in that outfit. So, this was my fault."

No one was going to buy that, but they listened. They could contradict when she was done.

"I was walking to your house, Eva, it took forever to get from down town Brookston to Oak creek. So, when your dad pulled over and offered me I ride, I said yes. I might as well have been wearing a neon sign that said take me, I'm yours. I was dressed so slutty, and I acted so stupid." Her face turned red. She tried to decide whether to tell the girls the whole truth, but she saw where I got you to keep something big to yourself.

"Eva, your dad raped me. He leaned over and kissed me. I almost wanted him to at first, but when it was happening, I was screaming no… no… no! So he knew I didn't want it. He had to use vaseline. I'm so sorry I didn't tell you before. Please don't be mad at me. I didn't want it to happen. At first, I thought it would be kinda cool to have an older guy think I was hot. So I played right into it. But I was only thirteen. I didn't know how it hurt, and I didn't know he'd take it so far. I was so embarrassed. It was totally my fault. I mean, he did it, but I totally asked for it. I was such an idiot. I'm so, so sorry."

Tasha started to sob. She ugly cried. The kind where sobs wrack your body, and you can't catch your breath. Eva just hugged and hugged her. She clung to her.

"You're not mad?" she asked. "Even though at first I thought maybe it was cool to kiss an old guy? I'm pathetic."

"Is that why you didn't go to the police?" Eva asked.

"That's why."

"Oh honey. Did you wonder what it would be like to have him rape you? Did you tell him you wanted him to do what he did?"

"No."

"I didn't think so. Tasha, you did nothing wrong. You were thirteen for Christ's sake. He was a forty year old man by that time. Did the #metoo movement teach you nothing? This is a hundred percent on him and zero percent on you."

Tasha started to cry again. "I will get help," she promised. "Obviously, I've still got issues."

"Don't we all," added Jenna. "Except for Addie. Add, you're perfect."

"Shut up," Addie said as they laughed through their tears.

"Don't forget, though," Eva said. "Don't forget you're not to blame."

Tasha just nodded her head. She was obviously relieved to have this off her chest, but it was a big secret that she carried for a long time. The confession took a lot out of her.

They all went for a walk in Hartley Nature Centre before they went back so they could get back to a better frame of mind before they went home.

When Eva got home from the coffee shop and the hike, her mom was in the kitchen. She was making a venison pot pie and listening to her audiobook. Eva heard the name Bundy mentioned, so it was one of her murderer books.

"How many times have you listened to a Bundy book?" I asked.

"Too many to count, baby. How was The Grind?"

"Dad raped Tasha," Eva said matter of fact.

"What? Are you sure it was rape?"

"Mom! Tasha was thirteen so yes, it was rape."

"I didn't mean it like that I just meant…"

"Mom, how else could you mean it. I know this little bit of information uproots our entire lives, but dad is a sick, fuck."

"Eva, your language," her mom said.

"Seriously mom, you're worried about my language? Listen to me. Dad raped Tasha when she was thirteen years old. He's a pedophile."

"Oh my God," Izzy said. "Oh my God."

"Yes, mom, oh my God." We have to do something about this right now. We can't pretend it's all right any more. He'll hurt someone else."

"I didn't know." She whispered. "I had no idea."

Eva's poor mom looked white as a sheet. Her hands trembled. She blinked about hundred times a minute. Was she blinking back tears? What was up with the blinking? She had to snap out of it because they had to get away from him. Now.

"It smells great in here," Eva's dad said as he walked in the kitchen. God he had bad timing.

Eva and her mom both stiffened and stood a little straighter. Eva's guard instantly went up.

"What are you girls talking about?" He asked.

"Nothing," Eva said.

"Can't be nothing," he said.

"We were talking about her classes, honey. Physics is about to do her in. Eva, I'll call you when dinner is done so you can go study." Sometimes, Eva's mother was a genius. She knew exactly how to handle that idiot. Eva didn't get a chance to tell her what Jenna said about him looking in Tasha's windows all these years later.

Poor Tasha. Eva would never be able to look that psycho in the face again. What a disgusting excuse for a human being! He was such a loser. She couldn't believe he did that. I guess she could actually believe it. She believed he was evil more and more every day.

27

"Are you okay, Tash?" Eva texted later that night.

"Sort of. I'm sorry I had to tell you. I never wanted you to know."

"It makes me sick that he'd do that, but I'm not even a little surprised. He's so disgusting. I'm so sorry he did it to you." Eva said.

"Well, at least I came clean about it, and now I can start to heal. I told my mom, too. I felt so guilty because I dressed slutty on purpose. I wanted to show off. And then I was curious about kissing a man, and I, honestly, was kind of proud an older guy thought I was hot, at first. It was so stupid. I was so stupid."

"It wasn't your fault at all. Will you go to a therapist?" Eva asked.

"Probably."

"Let me know what it's like, okay? I could really use some help, but I don't want a loser shrink. I've had a couple of those."

"I will. Do you have any guns in the house?" Tasha asked.

"Yeah. The dick is a hunter. He won't kill us. He needs us so he can look normal."

"You should be afraid still, Eva. Stay vigilant around him. Don't let your guard down. If he gets desperate, I believe he'd do whatever it takes to save face."

"You're freaking me out."

"Good. Just stay on your toes. This is not the time to let your guard down. We can do that when we go to school."

"I have to go to bed. It has been one of the longest nights of my life," Eva said.

"Mine too," Tasha said.
"We'll get through this," Tasha assured Eva.
"Good night, Tash! Love you!"
"Good night," Tasha said. "Love you too, Eva. Be safe."

28

Against Eva's better judgement, she invited Addie over to study Physics a few days later. It was so hard that she needed Eva's help. People came to Eva for English, Social Studies, Art, and Spanish classes. Everyone went to Addie for Science or Math help. She was crazy good at those. She was going to be a doctor, so she always focused on Science and Math. She knew she wanted to be a doctor when Eva finally figured out how to crawl. Addie was so smart that it just wasn't fair. None of the girls had never seen her get a test back that wasn't an A. She'd still get mad at herself for the one or two things she'd get wrong.

Eva worried about her family whenever anyone was over. Addie's house was so peaceful. Her dad was quiet, smart, and kind. Her mom was funny, and took pride in her home and kids. They weren't rich, but they weren't poor. Eva loved it there. Nobody was drunk there. She looked at her watch. It was seven-thirty p.m. on a weeknight. They probably had a couple hours before her dad would be home. On weeknights, he usually came rolling in about ten. Sometimes, he ignored Eva which was her preference. Other times, he needed an audience, so she was summoned to wherever he was so she could watch him perform whatever rant he chose that night. He usually ranted about how her mom had changed, and she disrespected him now. Or he'd complain about the democrats in the Senate. It depended on his mood. Eva could deal with the Senate complaints, but the mom complaints got scary and embarrassing. He made too many sexual references.

Addie and Eva went up to her room and closed the door. Immediately, her mom poked her head in and said, "Hi, Addie!" Eva thought her mom was thrilled she had a friend over. She loved her friends like they were her other kids, but Eva always went to their houses. No one ever came to their house for obvious reasons. They finished their physics right away. Addie explained it in a way that Eva finally understood, and it was actually easy. Then they had to gossip.

Addie loved a boy named Nick from school. He supposedly didn't know she loved him, but he was all she talked about, and Eva caught him staring at Addie more than once.

He had a girlfriend, but we didn't like her. She was popular and bitchy. She reminded the girls of the main character of mean girls, Regina George. Her passion was finding fault in everyone else. Why Nick went out with her was beyond Eva. She was good looking and she put out. Boys liked that, Eva guessed. But Eva thought Nick was deeper than that.

Apparently, he wasn't immune to her feminine allure, but he'd be much better off with Addie, and everyone knew it.

"Do you think they'll ever break up?" Addie asked.

"Of course," Eva said. "He likes you. I see him looking at you all the time in Econ."

"But Ashlee is so pretty and perfect."

"So are you, Addie. And there's no such thing as perfect," Eva said.

"Well, she looks perfect. I wonder what zero percent body fat feels like," Addie said.

"Malnutrition," Eva said. They laughed until they cried.

"How's Gregg?" Addie asked.

"Actually, he's really good. He's so sweet."

"You got a good one, Eva," she said.

"I know. I got really lucky," she said.

"He's the lucky one."

"He likes me just like I am. I don't have to drink or be more social. I don't have to wear certain clothes or put out. I don't have to be an athlete or not smart or whatever it is they say boys want. He just likes me, and I just like him. It's kinda perfect. I don't want to jinx it, but he gets me."

"The 'Cool Girl' speech in Gone Girl is the greatest. She says that men want the cool girl. She has to be a size two but eat shitty food, smart but not too smart, she has to like sports but not know more than he does. She has to be a lady but not care about men being pigs... or whatever she says. I never want to be that "cool girl" it'd be too hard to keep up the show," Addie said.

"I know. I promised myself a long time ago that I'd never pretend to be something I'm not," Eva said. She'd seen her mom do it to keep her dad happy all the time.

"Me too," Addie said. "Or is it me either?"

We laughed because we played that speech over and over. It was our mantra. She promised herself to learn from her mom's mistakes. She watched her mom attempt to be everything my dad wanted. She did it for survival. If she didn't do it, he'd be so cruel that it'd be impossible to be near him. When he left the house, sometimes she'd collapse on the couch. She was exhausted from all the pretending. Eva was too. She decided early on boys could either like her or not. She didn't care, but she wasn't putting on a show. Addie knew this about Eva and felt the same. She learned that the opposite way. Addie's mom didn't fake a thing. If she wanted to go shopping or get a massage, that's what she did. If she wanted to have left overs or take out for dinner, they did. She didn't do things just to please her dad. If they had pot roast, mashed potatoes, and homemade bread with an apple pie for dessert, it was because that was what her mom was feeling like cooking that day. No one expected anything different. Addie wanted to be treated exactly like that. Eva hoped they never changed their minds.

They went downstairs and raided the cookie jar. Eva's mom had just bought Oreos. They were Addie's fave, and Eva knew it. They grabbed the Oreos and a glass of milk each and went up to Eva's room. They were having so much fun that Eva forgot to keep track of the time. It felt good.

"Remember when we were little, and we used to get grounded from each other all the time?" Addie asked.

"Totally," Eva said. "It was a good punishment because we hated it. When your mom and dad busted us riding our bikes on the street instead of the sidewalk, we didn't see each other for two weeks!"

"Yeah," said Addie. "I never rode my bike in the street again!"

"Me either," Eva said. "What made you think of that?

"I have no idea," she said, we laughed again. It felt so good to be "normal" for a while. It didn't last.

Her dad came in the door to her room. He did the usual pushing of the door rather than turning the handle so it banged open. Eva jumped every time he did this. It pissed him off that she jumped. He saw a movie on Scientology where they did drills to try to make people not jump at loud noises. They called them drills. They'd make a loud noise or yell in someone's face, and they couldn't reveal any surprise or fear. He thought it was cool and showed discipline. He kept trying the drills out with Eva and her mom, but it never worked with them. Their anxieties were stronger than Scientology drills.

His entrance stopped all their fun. Addie who was bubbly and giggly, and in love with Nick one-second turned into a quiet little church mouse at the sight of him. Eva never talked about what it was like at home for her. She didn't talk about what a dick he was or how he abused and manipulated them, but Addie had a strong reaction to him. She made herself as small as possible with her knees up to her chest and she would not look at him.

She didn't want to be seen or heard by him. He would see this as weakness, for sure.

"Hi, girls," he said. Eva could smell the booze from ten feet away.

"Hi, Dad," she said.

"Hi, Mr. Lewis," Addie said.

"Hey, don't call me Mr. Lewis any more. Call me Michael. Mr. Lewis makes me feel like an old guy."

"Okay, Michael," she said. She was itching to leave, Eva could tell. They still had our books open near them just in case this happened. They wanted a ready-made excuse for hanging out on a school night.

"You ladies talking about your boyfriends?" he asked. That was none of his business, and Eva would never tell him.

"No, Dad," Eva said. "We are studying for our physics test tomorrow."

"Well, you should be dating boys," he said. "You won't have those tight little bodies forever." Addie and Eva cringed. Eva glared at him. If looks could kill, he'd be lying on the floor.

"What?" he asked. "Over the line?"

"Ya think?" she asked.

"I was just kidding, ladies. It was a joke. I'm sorry that you took it seriously." Was that an apology? It sounded like he blamed us for him making a disgusting comment about his daughter and her friend's bodies. He was always over the line. Eva hated him so much. Poor Addie. She'd never come over after this. Son of a bitch. Eva would get back at him if it was the last thing she did.

Not shockingly, Addie said she had better head home. She asked if Eva wanted to come with her and spend the night. Eva's dad heard this and put a stop to the conversation.

"I don't care how old ya are. It's a school night. Eva, you sleep at home on school nights."

Eva looked at Addie and mouthed "I'm sorry!" She smiled at Eva with knowing eyes. She gave Eva a quick hug and said good bye to her dad. Eva walked her down and watched her get into her car. Eva wasn't afraid that some stranger would get Addie. She was afraid her dad would.

29

Izzy

As I pulled into the church parking lot for my Alanon meeting, I realized I hadn't been here in weeks. No wonder I was starting to lose it. Alanon kept me grounded. Alanon reminded me that I'm not alone.

I made friends with Kurt. He can relate to almost everything I say. His wife is the same type of alcoholic as Michael. Neither of them admit a problem, and both of them are champion gas lighters. They make us feel crazy if we ever point out their alcoholism. No one else thinks they have a problem, they say. They have jobs they are good at, and they have friends. Kurt says his wife's "friends" are just people at the bar just looking for a free drink or an excuse to drink. Michael regularly told me how drunk his buddy, Pete, was down at the bar.

"He passed out with his head on the bar," he'd say. "He was drooling and talking to himself. He puked everywhere." He loved to tell me how drunk other people were so he didn't look so bad. Kurt's wife was more of a home drinker, but she talked about what a drunk her dad was growing up to make herself look better.

Kurt and I decided to go out for coffee after the meeting. The meeting was long and pretty boring. The woman we call "the rambler" talked for about twenty-five minutes, and I don't think she ever really did make her point. So, coffee with Kurt was just what I needed. "Did you tell him, yet?" Kurt asked.

"That I go to Alanon?"

He nodded.

"No, have you told Carrie?"

"Oh for sure. I tell her everything even if she doesn't like it. Carrie is aware of everything I think. But, she drinks anyway. Shows ya how much I matter," he said taking a sip of his coffee.

"I'm such a loser," I said. "I can't make myself stand up to him. I thought I could, for Eva, at least. But I stammer and stutter, and I can't say anything. I get so mad at myself.

"What did he do lately? You didn't share at the meeting, so I figured it was Eva related. You look like shit, by the way."

I laughed, "Thank you very little."

"I don't mean it like that. I mean you look like you haven't slept and you could cry any minute. But I know you. God forbid little miss perfect cries."

"What's that supposed to mean?" I asked him.

"Izzy," he said. "You are the most tightly wound person I know. You haven't taken the first step of Alanon yet. If you don't take it soon, I'm afraid we'll lose you forever."

The first step is to admit that I am powerless over alcohol and my life has become unmanageable. It sounds like a no brainer. If I'm going to Alanon, alcohol is a pretty huge problem or I'd never waste my summer mornings in a church basement with terrible coffee.

Admitting to that, was like accepting defeat. Am I ready to accept defeat yet? Can I admit that? I have spent my entire adult life trying to control the environment around me so Michael won't be such an ass. I still cater to him, compliment him, sleep with him, and act like I'm his number one fan. I did that in the hopes of having a good day the next day. I always looked to the next day. I wished that was the real Michael. The "good day

Michael" was the real version of him, and "Pretend-sober Michael, and 'Drunk Michael' were exceptions. He doesn't apologize, but I want those good days. I want to see the Michael I fell in love with, and I can deal with the stress I know. I know this fear. I know this life. I'm more afraid of what could happen than what has happened before. I know I am wrong and weak. I am used to the torrent of criticisms that come out of his mouth when he's drunk. I'm used to the mocking and the threats. I'm not afraid of that any more. It's a given that I will regularly experience that, then, he goes to sleep, and it's over. That's the usual routine. I know, however, that he is capable of much worse. I've seen his temper, and I've felt his desire to hurt or kill me. His face gets red, and he balls his hands into fists. It's all he can do to keep from punching me.

He's also a gun enthusiast, so there's just no telling what a completely enraged drunk, like Michael, will do when tested. That fear kept me in line in his eyes, and kept me a weak loser in my own.

"Izzy, what is it?" Kurt asked.

"Nothing," I replied. "You just hit a nerve."

"Because..."

"Because I can't admit that I have lost control of my life to alcohol. It's like saying everything I've done for the last seventeen years is for nothing."

"It isn't for nothing," he said. "You love him, and you love Eva. But has hurrying home after work, quitting drinking anything yourself, and never sleeping or relaxing in your own home changed him? Does he admit he's a dick because you're home in time for Jeopardy?"

"Of course not, but if I get home in time for Jeopardy, he's less likely to be at the bar when I get home from school."

"How much less likely?"

"Okay, he is at the bar when I get home from school two to three nights per week. So, I guess it doesn't really help," I admitted.

"Does he drink less because you gave up alcohol?"

"No."

"Does he straighten up because you work full time, handle all of the parenting, and work yourself sick trying to maintain his standards?"

"God, no."

"See," he said. "Unmanageable."

This is why I loved Kurt. He should be a lawyer. He lets me get away with nothing. But he does it in such a good way. He's right. It's time to stop rushing home to "save the evening." It never works, anyway. The good evenings happen on the good days. On the other days, he drinks. That's all there is to it.

"You're right," I said. "It's time to stop. Maybe I'll try the 'Just for today' exercises. That seems a little more doable than pledging to never try to manipulate my surroundings again."

"Good girl," Kurt said. "Now, let's talk about something else."

"Is there anything else," I asked. Sometimes it felt like there wasn't.

"There is so much we are missing right now while we are so wrapped up in all of this. We both should leave them," he said.

"I know," I said. "I know."

30

Makayla Madison went to a baseball game in Moose Lake with her friends Gretchen and Taylor. The three of them had boyfriends on the opposing team, the Esko, Eskomos. Young people thought they should change their name because Eskomos was racist. Esko maintained that it was a play on the word Esko, and their mascot is an igloo not the Inuit Eskimo any more. Makayla thought that if it offended anyone, they should change it, but that was not up to her. Moose Lake is about forty-five minutes south of Duluth on I35, and Gretchen's parents let her take the car. They felt so free! They loved listening to their music as loud as they wanted cruising down the interstate just the three of them. Makayla's boyfriend, Grant, was the starting pitcher for Esko. All three girls loved baseball, especially Makayla. Her dad coached one town over in Carlton. Carlton and Esko hated each other. They were rivals because they were both really good at football. Football and hockey were the source of most rivalries in Northern Minnesota. Carlton and Esko partnered with a bigger town, Cloquet, about five miles down the road for hockey. Esko was a basketball town. They didn't have enough kids to make a hockey team, but they had plenty to have a baseball team of their own despite the school's small size. Makayla's dad thought Grant was a great pitcher and actually had a shot at a scholarship. That'd be so exciting for him. He mowed down Moose Lake. They couldn't catch up to his fast ball or figure out his curve. The game was going really fast! Makayla thought Grant looked adorable on the mound. He had a little ritual before every pitch. He took his hat off and put it back on, tapped his toe on the rubber as he leaned forward for the sign, and as long as he wasn't pitching from the stretch, he had a really high kick before he threw the ball. His coaches were trying to get him to stop that because it was taking too much energy. At sixteen, that wasn't a big deal. But, Makayla's dad thought it was a good idea to work on his form immediately. Then, as he got older, he wouldn't be so invested in a style that would take extra energy. Grant hated that he had to change his delivery. He said it was really hard to train himself to change. But, he wasn't using a high kick today, and he was killing it.

Makayla thought she should use the restroom before they headed home. She told the girls where she was going. The bathrooms were on the playground on the other side of the field. It was a hike, but they'd been sitting forever. Her Apple Watch kept yelling at her to get moving, so, she'd walk over to the bathrooms. The walk wouldn't hurt her. Gretchen was busy texting her boyfriend who was sitting on the bench. Coach would not approve of him texting, Taylor reminded Gretchen. She said she knew, and she just said she'd talk to him after the game. Taylor's boyfriend was third base and batted sixth. He was pretty good, but wasn't going to get any kind of scholarship. He was high school good not college good. He just played for fun, anyway. Grant was the only one of the three who could have a baseball future.

Coach pulled him in the fifth. In high school, they only played seven innings, so he had a good game. His arm felt a little rubbery. He looked around for Makayla and didn't see her anywhere. He was sure she wasn't far away. He saw Gretchen and Taylor, so Mak couldn't have gone too far.

Esko won 15-5. It was a blow out. Grant was happy. They were actually worried about Moose Lake. They were always good for a small school. Before heading to the bus, Grant ran over to Gretchen and Taylor.

"Where's Mak?" he asked.

"She went to the bathroom, but that was a long time ago. You just got pulled when she went. It's a pretty long walk over there, but she really should be back by now," Gretchen said.

"I'm worried," Taylor said. "She doesn't answer texts or calls."

"I'll tell coach, and we'll all go look. I'm sure she just got side tracked walking around. She does that sometimes."

"Yeah, but not without us," Taylor said.

Taylor was a little melodramatic, Grant thought. But he was a little worried, too. He was pretty sure it was all good, but he wanted to see her, now.

The whole team spread out. When the Moose Lake team and their parents heard what was going on, they all spread out to look for her. She had a yellow sweatshirt on, so she should be easy to spot. A few parents got in their cars to look around the neighborhoods for her in case she went for a walk.

Grant's coach called the police. Grant was shocked at how many squad cars showed up.

Until he saw all the cops, he was sure she was just walking around looking at the Lake.

The Lake wasn't far from the ball field. That's where he'd be if he wasn't playing, he thought. He was sure they'd find her and she'd be embarrassed that they all made such a big deal about it.

Her parents showed up. Then, really he got worried. Mak's dad had his uniform on. He had to have come straight from the baseball field. This is really serious, he thought. Everyone called Mak's Dad, Coach Madison or just coach. He ran over to Grant. "Grant, have you seen her?"

"Not since the fifth inning, Coach. That had to have been an hour and a half ago."

"I'm so sorry she got lost while coming to watch me, Coach."

"It's not your fault, Grant. I'm sure she just got turned around and couldn't find her way back to the field. We'll find her."

Grant hoped he was right, but wow. Coach looked so freaked out. It freaked Grant out. Before he knew it, it was dark. Makayla still wasn't back. Grant's bus had to go back to Esko. Grant didn't want to leave, but Mak's mom and dad told him they'd text him when they found her.

The cops put up the tent and fired up spot lights. She just disappeared.

31

Eva and I ate dinner in front of the evening news. I made Tater-Tot hot dish, a Minnesota classic. Eva loved it. I baked up some Grands Biscuits to go with it. Michael loved those with butter and Jam.

Michael knew we would eat without him if he wasn't home by six. We gave up any pretence of eating dinner as a family a long time ago. Eva and I would just eat, and I'd put a plate for him in the fridge. He was a big boy. He could heat up his own dinner if he was late. It seemed he was late at least three times a week.

The Duluth news was usually fairly entertaining. The big investigative piece was about pot holes in the road. Duluth was pretty peaceful. They had what appeared to be nine year old reporters. It was hilarious.

Eva and I cringed watching poor little Emily or Ken stumbling through their stories about a new CVS coming to town or a blueberry festival in Northern, MN. Big news in Duluth wasn't usually life threatening. We were ready for a story like that when they cut to Moose Lake baseball field and talked about Makayla's disappearance. Eva gasped.

"Do you know her?" I asked.

"Yes. Oh my God. She's Addie's friend since childhood. We've hung out with her a million times. When she's at Addie's, we always see her. She goes to Esko."

"Oh no. Eva. That's awful. Maybe she just went for a walk

and got turned around. That kind of thing happens all the time."

Eva frantically looked for her phone to call Addie, and I kept watching the report. "Both the Esko and Moose Lake baseball teams searched until dark. The Sheriff's department states that they have no information to give at this time. I talked to Coach Swanson from Esko, and he said they are all together to help Grant get through this crazy time. They are all still assuming that she went to walk around the lake and got lost somehow, but so far, there have been no sightings. She no one has seen her since about five-thirty this evening."

"Last night, we reported a rash of women who have disappeared or whose bodies have been found along I35. The Sheriff said they have no reason to believe that Makayla Madison has met with foul play as of right now. Wondering if this could be related to this disappearance is premature. Ken Isaakson, Channel Six News."

Eva was panicked when she heard about the other missing women and the bodies they found. What if Makayla was one of them? What if she met with a serial killer. What if someone took her? Oh poor Addie.

"Eva, if you go to Addie's I need you to text me when you get there, do you understand?" I asked.

"Uh-huh," she said while looking at her phone and texting Addie.

"No, Eva, listen to me. Look at me! I need you to text me to tell me you made it safely."

"Yeah, Mom, okay, God," Eva said.

"Maybe I should drive you."

"What? Why?" she asked.

"Because you're upset. Because there's a psychopath out there taking young girls. I'm not saying that happened to

Makayla. It's too soon to say that, but you have to be careful now, Eva. Very careful," I said.

She finally looked like she understood me, and she asked if I would drive her over there and pick her up when she texted. I told her I would. I didn't think any of the kids should be alone right now.

I knew that Makayla wasn't missing. She was dead or kidnapped. She was not lost. There's no way to get lost in Moose Lake. I've been to that baseball field. It's just off the main drag about a quarter of a mile, and there's a park and the lake. It's wide open. She was wearing yellow. She would be seen by the helicopter or the teams of people searching for her. Moose Lake is not a big place. It would be a miracle if Makayla was seen alive ever again. Those poor parents. They showed her dad on the news arriving at the field in his own baseball uniform. He was a coach in Carlton. His eyes were wild, and he knew his life would never be the same again. Her mom arrived a few minutes after her dad, and they showed her crying in her husband's arms. Why did they think they had to show that kind of sorrow on the evening news? Their worlds were crumbling, and the cameras captured it for the whole northland to see. It wasn't entertainment. This was their daughter.

This one hit awfully close to home, I thought. Eva even knew her. Yesterday, when I first heard about all this on the news, it freaked me out. Most of the women were young girls like Eva. Some were a bit older, but most were close to Eva's age. My heart broke for those parents. I'd die if something happened to Eva. I don't mean that to be callous or as an exaggeration. Physically, I would stop living. I could not go on. I wasn't strong enough to handle it. Those poor girls, and their parents nearly broke me.

It was one thing to listen to a Ted Bundy documentary on

audible while I made dinner or as background while I did something else. It was nearly fifty years ago, and it was in Washington, Oregon, Utah, Idaho, and Colorado. Oh, yeah, and the worst ones were in Florida. He's been dead since 1989. Florida executed him for killing so a twelve-year-old. I didn't fear him because I knew his story, and I didn't live through the fear people lived through while trying to find him. I was about five when they got him for good. I didn't worry about serial killers. I was fascinated by them. I was curious as to what made them tick. I read and listened to whatever I could find on psychopathy trying to figure out what made those guys go over the edge. I wondered if Michael was a psychopath. He checked so many boxes. But I didn't know how someone became that way. Was he a psychopath? A narcissist? A malignant narcissist? There was some kind of a personality disorder there. I'd love to have someone diagnose him or at least interview him to see what a professional thought. As an amateur, I thought he was at the very least a narcissist. But I wouldn't rule psychopathy out. It really didn't matter what I thought.

 Where in the hell was he? I never knew if he was coming home or not. I never even knew where he was. Every now and then, he'd text me that he was going out with friends and would stay at one of their houses so he didn't drink and drive. I called bullshit on that excuse. I never really asked him because I liked when he was gone, and I knew he would lie anyway. I needed to leave him. My dad told me that it wasn't a good sign that I was happier when he was gone.

32

The girls wanted to go join the search the next morning. I excused Eva from school, and Addie's parents brought the girls down. They knew Makayla's parents well because the girls knew each other from church. I managed to teach that day, but I don't know how. All I could do was worry about the kids. What if they found her body? How would they handle that emotionally? Maybe I'm wrong. Maybe she's alive? I tried to hope, but I really didn't. I knew she was dead. How could this happen here?

I was also livid because when Michael finally strolled in at four am, he was pissed that I was upset.

"I have to go out without you or I'd be stuck in the house every day of my life, Izzy. You know how to fix this? GOYA."

He loved that term GOYA. Once he figured out what it stood for, he used it all the time. Get off your ass, it meant. So he could say that without actually saying it. He thought that gave him a free pass. Leave it to him to twist reality and gaslight me. He thought he still fooled me with that. He did not. He gets home at four in the morning, and he makes it out to be my fault.

After I got a grip on my anger with him, I told him about Eva's friend being missing in Moose Lake.

"It was bound to happen," he said.

"What? Why?" I asked. I could not fathom this reaction.

"Have you noticed how those kids dress now days? Eva is fine, but the rest of them are falling out of their tops and their shorts are so short that their asses hang out the bottom."

"What does that have to do with anything?" I asked. "Are you saying they ask for it because of the way they dress?"

"You know that's not what I meant."

"What did you mean, then?" I asked.

"Well, I'm just saying that a guy can only hold back so much. When they see a woman dressed like that."

"First, they are girls, not women. Second, they always get to say no. No matter how they're dressed. No one asks to get raped or murdered or kidnapped or whatever has happened to this child." I was mortified by his reaction to this. I could not comprehend how he could say something like that. He was obviously a misogynist given how he treated me, he was a pig with how he always crossed the line when he was "joking" he cheated on me, and I knew it. But this, I could not rationalize away. This reaction was inexcusable.

"I get it, Izzy. I'm not blaming the women here. I'm just saying most guys have no control. I'm not saying it's okay."

"Again, she's a girl. She's sixteen. She's a student at Esko High School."

"Whatever," he said.

Oh my I couldn't talk to him about this. I just wanted to punch him when he spoke about this. I was so mad that I could barely breathe. I pictured her parents trekking through the woods around Moose Lake praying they find their daughter and not her body. I pictured our girl and her best friends desperately trying to help their friend find her friend and support her through something terrible like this. I pictured her boyfriend feeling bad that she was at his ballgame when she disappeared and the two girls she went to the game with who didn't walk with her to the bathroom. It wasn't their fault by any stretch, but I knew kids. They would blame themselves. Everything was about them. They saw the universe from their perspective only, so they'd blame themselves. Poor kids. I hoped they were getting some counseling. I wondered about my own students. Did they know her, too. Oh I should think of her in the present tense. No one knows what happened yet.

I texted Eva to see how things were going. She didn't answer for over an hour. "Not good, mama."

"We haven't found anything."

"Addie is completely freaked out."

When I texted her back, I told her I loved her and to hug Addie for me. I was heartbroken for them, and I was disgusted by Michael's reaction. I shouldn't have been surprised by it. I was happy that Eva didn't hear him.

I sat at my computer and looked up Makayla Madison. There was a site about all the missing and murdered women along Interstate 35. There were several missing from near the University of Minnesota, and their bodies were found on North Interstate 35 near Hinckley. They listed the dates the women were last seen. They started disappearing about two years ago. Makayla was the youngest, and most were under twenty-five. They were all smart and beautiful. They all had the world at their feet and their absence was felt by their friends, family, and community. They were smart, ambitious, and sweet according to interviews with their families. Their Grade Point Average was a combined 3.8. The police didn't know if that meant anything or not. I didn't really see how that was relevant. It just made me sad. They had so much to look forward to. Any one of them could have changed the world. Some kind of psychopath took these young women away from their loved ones. Who would do something like that?

Part 3
Izzy

My plans to leave Michael were all in place. I found the cutest apartment that had a swimming pool and took dogs. There were woods around the place, so I could take Bailey all over back in the woods. Bailey was coming with me. She was my baby. Michael never paid any attention to her. He was all about hunting dogs. He had a lab, Max, who I adored, but that was Michael's dog. Bailey the Corgi rescue was mine. There were trails, so I could let her off leash. Hardly anyone went back there. I loved the place. It was a cute little two bedroom with a balcony that looked out over the trees. If I squinted and hung off the balcony, I could almost see Lake Superior. I definitely could hear the honk of the horn on the bridge. It was morse code for the ships. The bridge operator and ship captains talked to each other this way. They signaled before the bridge went up so the cars would clear and people would get off so it could be raised for the ships to come into the bay or leave the bay. I never got tired of watching those ships. If I spent the rest of my life alone, I was okay with that. I'd go to Canal Park, walk Bailey on the lake walk and in the woods by the apartment, cook what I wanted or just have cereal. I might never have the same relationship with Ollie, but he knew I loved him always. He was settled and living in Minneapolis with his wife. He was a grown man, and I was so proud of him. He knew that, but it wouldn't be the same after I left his dad. I didn't think an ex-stepmom would rank high enough to try to squeeze me into his already full and happy life. I'd see him sometimes, but I would have to push myself onto him.

Sophie would live and work in Duluth when she finished college. She was close. She had a year of classes and another six months of internships left before she had her degree wrapped up. I knew she'd stay because her boyfriend was the love of her life. She sparkled when she was with him. The two of them would get married, I knew that. Also, Sophie and I spent so much time together when they were little. Ollie always went with his dad, and Sophie and Eva came with me. At the time, it felt right, but now, I felt guilty. I loved my days with the girls, but Sophie and her dad's relationship would never be close, and my relationship with Oliver was affected as well. I probably shouldn't feel guilty. It's not like I had a choice. I didn't speak up, but even if I had, it would have changed nothing.

Michael did what Michael wanted. Nothing would ever change that.

Ollie was the biggest drawback of the whole scenario. I vowed to drive to see him when I could and when it worked for him. But I had to get out. I was dying here. He started trying to be a better person right before Eva's graduation. I was not impressed, nor was I convinced that he was actually making changes. I found bottles of captain Morgan and Windsor tucked away in dark corners of the garage and the house. He was sneaking the alcohol, but I knew that. I could smell it, and his cheeks got red. His nose had a nice Gin Blossom that fired up as the alcohol hit his system, but he didn't realize it. This was something only I knew, so I was never fooled by his act. I also caught him stalking me that June. It was weird, but everywhere I went, he knew about it. He always knew who called me and for how long we talked. He'd mention it in passing, but the creepiest thing he did was to hack into my email.

I realized it one day when I was I was painting some trim on the side of the house. I heard the truck pull up. I was pissed because I should have had another two hours of blessed freedom before he came home from work. It was June, so I was off for the summer. I hated when he came home early. I felt robbed of time to feel free, and nervous about him approving of how I spent my time. I was "on" like I was when I was at work when he was home. I let loose a string of profanity. "Goddamned it. I have two more hours before I have to deal with this," I said out loud to no one. I had to pull myself together before he saw me. I shook my whole body to get rid of the nerves and irritation I felt and went back to painting. This was an activity he would approve of.

"Hey, babe," Michael said. "I thought maybe I should take you and Eva out for dinner and to a movie. You've been talking about craving seafood."

Oh my God, I thought. He's reading my emails. The only person I told it would be nice if Michael wanted to go to dinner and a movie tonight was my friend Beth over email. She didn't have cell service at work, so we emailed each other here and there throughout the day. He thought movies were a waste of time and going out for dinner was a waste of money because he could make it better than they could anyway. He never thought about what Eva or I wanted. Never.

I panicked. What else did I say in that email. What else have I said to her? I couldn't check now. The trim was less than half painted, and he'd see that I just walked away from it. So, I kept painting. My mind was racing, though.

I sucked in a big gulp of air. Oh shit! Two weeks ago, Beth and I were emailing about her boyfriend. I know I told her to leave him. He never put her first, and she should leave him.

Michael would not like that. His mind would automatically go to me wanting to leave him. He saw everything through his own lens.

Eva bounded outside. "Why is dad home?" she asked while crunching an apple?

"He must've finished up early," I said.

"Well, he wants to go out for dinner and a movie, but I told Addie and Jenna, I'd go to a movie with them."

"How about, you go to dinner with us, you guys go to your movie, and we'll go to our own movie. Does that sound good?"

"Yep. Good plan," Eva said. "I'll text them now."

Oh thank God. I could not imagine going for dinner without Eva there as my buffer. He'd have his perfect little family together, and he could bask in that pride. If he saw anyone he knew, he'd look like the perfect husband and father. I would pay for this night out in private, and I knew that. It was almost worth it. I decided to enjoy it, and pay later. "Please don't wear the jeans with the holes in them," I begged Eva.

"Mom, everyone wears those."

"I know, I'm a teacher. I see it every day. Whatever, I'm just glad you're coming with us," I said and kissed the top of her head.

I needed her, and I knew it. I wasn't proud of myself for thinking I needed Eva for protection and for things to talk about. I was the worst mother ever. I couldn't imagine sitting with Michael for hours without Eva there. He saw everything I've said to Beth at work. I felt sick. He is running scared at the moment, but now he knows I want to leave him. I know I talked about that. It was all I thought about. I hated my life. I was scared all the time. I hated him. Beth encouraged me to leave him. I was terrified. But this was my usual. He did terrible things, and I worried. It happened all the time.

Michael gets all his self-esteem by looking like the world's greatest dad and husband. And suddenly, I knew what to do to save my ass. I sent a quick email to Beth and said, "Wow! It's almost like Michael can read my mind. He's taking Eva and me out for seafood, then we're all going to a movie. She's meeting friends, and maybe he and I can see that one with Denzel that's up for an Oscar. I seriously have the sweetest husband. He does so much for this family and to make me happy. I'm so lucky."

Then, I went into the bathroom and shut the door so I could quickly text Beth to say NEVER say anything bad about Michael over email. He's reading them. I caught him today.

She texted back, "Omg. What an ass!"

"I know," I said.

"Maybe we can play with him with it for a while. I'll email you tomorrow. Don't worry, I won't say anything bad."

I didn't have time to even wonder what she meant because he barged in the door.

I couldn't even have five minutes of privacy in the bathroom. Sometimes he'd just barge in and not say a word. He'd just turn around and leave. He'd leave the door open so I was exposed in there. Not all the time, but enough to make me nervous to even enter the bathroom.

Sarcasm dripped from him all night. I didn't want to know what would happen when he got drunk. I was so screwed. My ass was not saved by the complimentary email. Eva was immune to my nervousness. She was used to it by now. I was nervous all the time.

"My bride needs a night out, we go out," he said. "I take care of her. It's what I do."

I would have to thank him profusely and stroke his ego to

avoid a fight. Eva rolled her eyes a couple of times. That was how I knew I was over doing it. I was laying it on a bit too thick.

Beth thought it would be fun to play with him a little with this, but I wanted everything in my inbox and sent file deleted. I texted her my password, and she was breaking in to delete everything. If he asked why, I'd say I just cleaned out my email. Then, I'd ask him how he knew. He'd have to admit what he did It wasn't worth it to play with him. I had to set up a new account so I could talk to Beth without him knowing what I said. A lot of things he'd been saying to me lately made much more sense. He never had a problem with Beth because he knew she was strong. He knew he couldn't break her. She held nothing for him. He couldn't win with her, so he usually left her alone. All of a sudden, he hated her. He thought she was a "bad influence" on me. I couldn't figure out why he did such an about face with her. He absolutely despised her. It made sense now.

I could hardly breathe. I was absolutely terrified. I had no idea what all he read. I vented to Beth alone, and he found that password.

He sat proud as a peacock at dinner watching Eva and me as we pretended to be having fun. We each ate lobster. Eva actually ate which made me happy. She hasn't been eating lately, and it was freaking me out. I watched her like a hawk, and Sophie and I decided to talk to her about all of this soon. She was spiraling out of control, but she could control her food intake, and she was getting obsessive. Sophie and I were worried.

"Mom, if you think I'm throwing up my dinner, you can go back to the table," Eva said. "I haven't felt the need to control my food for two weeks almost. I'm up two pounds already. I liked myself at a four. My bones are jutting out all over, now, and I have this extra hair all over me. I don't like it. I started eating again and decided to control it at a four or six."

"Okay, honey," I said. "But you don't just will yourself out of an eating disorder. You need help, so I'm watching."

"Well, watch me put the weight back on then, because I'm fine. I would go to a shrink for lots of reasons, though. We both need to go," Eva said.

"You always refused to go. I've brought it up to you a thousand times. This makes me so happy. I've been secretly going to Alanon for a while, now. Would you go to that with me?"

"I think so," she said.

"Mom, don't believe that dad is fine now, okay?"

"Don't worry, I am not fooled by him," I said. "But why do you say that?"

"Because he's creepy. I am happy he's good now, and I'll take it. But I don't trust it. We've had too many years of shit with him to believe he's all of a sudden better. Besides, I found a stash of liquor in the garage. So, I know."

"I saw the stash, too," I said. "Not a super creative hiding space."

"He didn't think we'd look," she said. "He underestimates us all the time. That'll be his downfall."

"When did you get so grown up," I asked.

"I leave for college in less than two months, mom. Do you have a plan yet?"

"Actually, I do. I have an apartment rented already. I paid cash. You'll love it," I said.

"I'm so proud of you, mom. We'll get out safely. He'll never hurt us again. I believe that."

"I know," I said. What I meant was "I hope so." I wasn't so sure, and I didn't believe Eva's story about all of a sudden deciding not to be anorexic. Maybe she wasn't exactly anorexic.

195

Maybe she just decided to control food when she couldn't control anything else. I knew I did that. Maybe she did too. But I couldn't take chances with her health. I found a counselor in Duluth who worked with anorexic patients. I decided to make an appointment with her for Eva, and I made an appointment with another counselor for me so I could help her. The problem was that Michael thought therapists were Satan. He thought their mission was to break up families and to encourage women to walk out on their husbands. He said that every woman he talked to, who went to a therapist, left her husband, so no, he wanted nothing to do with marriage counseling when I brought it up. So, we had to sneak. I decided to put my work address on our insurance papers, and to give my work address and phone numbers to the therapist. She wouldn't be able to call us, but I'd figure out an explanation for that. If I tell the truth, they have to report it, and Social Services would get involved. I couldn't risk that right now. We were so close to getting out. What was the point of getting out if Eva died from an eating disorder that I ignored, though? So, I made up my mind that it was worth the risk.

We got back to the table, and Michael had already paid the bill.

"What'd ya fall in?" he asked.

"Clever," I said with a little more bite than I intended. "We're fine, just woman stuff," I said to kind of smooth over my first response. I also knew that "woman stuff" was enough to stop any man from asking more questions. Michael included. He wanted no part of that conversation.

We went to the theatre, and Eva met up with Addie and Tasha. The three of them went to see some summer Blockbuster Marvel film that was in no way something I wanted to see. But the military action film we were going to see looked even worse.

Oh well. I said dinner and a movie. I didn't specify the movie in my email to Beth. At least he was at the theatre with me, and we had a nice dinner. We were safe here. He couldn't get drunk here. And he couldn't hurt us here.

Eva went home with Addie and Tasha and the girls had a sleep over at Addie's house. Addie was still completely devastated about her missing friend, Makayla. The girls spent as much time with Addie as possible to help her through.

Michael and I went home, and as I knew he would, he started to push going to the bar. It was only eleven o'clock, so there was almost no way out of it. I hated that bar. Michael loved it. He was king of the castle there. People from town loved him. He bought drinks and held court. He flirted with other women, and left me to sit alone. Still, he always begged me to go with him. I almost never went. It was humiliating and boring. I decided to reward him for taking us to the movie and dinner by going to the bar. I made him promise that he wouldn't get drunk, and we'd be home before one.

"God, you act like going to the bar with me is absolute torture," he said.

"No, no, I'm sorry. I just don't like to stay a long time, and you know how I feel about you drinking," I said.

"Always the booze, right, honey?" Honey was said with such sarcasm. He said it like he hated me.

"You never look in the mirror and ask if you're the reason I drink sometimes, do you? Do you ever think it could be you? Maybe you're the problem?" he asked.

"What? Sometimes? Michael, you're drunk several times a week. And you know what? When you're "not drunk" it's just a day you decide to pretend you're not drinking. You drink daily, and you know it. I found a few stashes of Windsor and Captain. Do you think someone who isn't an alcoholic has a stash? Have you found my stash?" I asked. I knew I was over the line, and I didn't care. I was so mad that he tried to blame his drinking on me. Look in the mirror? He needs to look in the mirror.

"You bitch," he said. "You are so high and mighty. You're such a martyr staying married to a loser like me. Oh, poor Izzy. She's so abused by the big bad alcoholic," he said. I hated when he mocked me like that. It made me wonder if it was true. Was I acting like a martyr? Maybe this was me. How could it not be partially me? It had to be. He wasn't like this when I met him. Maybe I was the reason he drank.

"What, Izzy? No snappy response?" he asked.

"No, Michael. I'm sorry. I know you like to go there, and I don't. I'm not trying to make you feel less than me because you drink. I'm not better than you, I have different issues. I'm so sorry I make you feel that way," I said.

"Yeah, Izzy, you've got issues. You and your friend Beth, you two are planning your "escape" from me. I know you two gossip about me behind my back. I think you do it with Eva, too. If you turn my daughter against me, I'll kill you."

"I'd never do that. Eva makes up her own mind about everything," I said.

"What are you saying? Are you saying Eva hates me all on her own? It's her decision to not like me? Like if you acted like you liked me ever, maybe she wouldn't think I was such a dick."

"Michael, Eva doesn't hate you. She loves you. I love you," I said trying my best to calm him down.

"I'll drop you off at home, and I'm going to the bar. Isabelle, a social life is a good thing. If you weren't so fucking awkward around people, maybe they'd like you more. No one in town likes you. They think I can do better."

Wow. That was an attack I wasn't expecting, and I had no ready answers. I had no way to retaliate. I wanted to tell him he had it backwards. I hear from people who hang out down there and accept his free drinks but hate his guts. They tell me about the women he leaves with, and he gets into a fight every couple of weeks. I was so angry that I don't know what to do. I just sat there, shaking. We rode the rest of the way home in silence.

He dropped me off in front of our house and headed to the bar. I wish I would've known how awful it would be to live so close to a bar when we bought this house, but he didn't drink then. He wasn't an alcoholic at least. He always had an addictive personality, but I didn't predict his alcoholism. I hated how he made me doubt myself. I doubted my sanity, my personality, my parenting, my perceptions, everything.

"Well," I said. "I'm sure you could." He dropped me off at home and sped off to the bar. It was so terrible to fight because we lived together. I hated having him around me when he was so pissed. He didn't hold a gun to my head to terrify me. I was terrified nonetheless. I never really knew why I was so scared of him. A lot of people threatened violence, and not many followed through.

Why didn't I listen to my mother all those years ago in the restaurant? She told me he would ruin my life. I was so in love with the charming Michael, that I thought she was being dramatic. He was so charming when we first met. When anyone asks me how I ended up with this guy, I remember how he looked at me that night he bought us all a beer and looked so intensely into my eyes. I remember our first date when he made me dinner, and we laughed and had so much fun. I conned me into believing that was who he was. This personality and his alcoholism didn't show its face until I was pregnant with Eva, married to him, and we owned a house.

33

I woke up and looked at my phone. It was seven past four in the morning. Michael wasn't home yet. He's such a dick.

I just got up and made coffee. It was going to be a long day. Eva was at Addie's, and I had a counseling appointment at ten. I decided not to talk to him when he got home. I was really scared though. I was afraid of what he'd be like when he did get home. I took a shower and got ready. I waited for him to come home. Every noise made me jump. I made the bed, got dressed, and left. I texted Eva to stay at Addie's as long as possible today because I wouldn't be home for a while. I told her dad and I got into it a bit of a fight last night, and it would just be better to stay clear until I got home.

"Just be home in time for me to get ready for my date, k?" She texted back.

"I'll be home by 3:00," I said.

"Perfect, Addie said that was okay. So did her mom. Love you."

"Love you more."

"Not possible."

I put my phone to my heart. Oh how I loved that girl. If he wanted to get back at me, The worst thing he could do to me was hurt her. That was why I was so scared. I was scared he would hurt her in order to hurt me.

My therapist told me that this was the most dangerous time for an abused person. When he or she leaves, that's when the shit hits the fan. Even if the abuser feels the victim will leave shortly, he or she can lose control. He told me to try to always stay between him and the door and to leave sooner rather than later. He also thought I should send Eva somewhere safe immediately.

    I left his office determined. I would be out within the week. I wanted to tell my therapist that I was out on my next appointment two weeks from now. I had no choice.

    After therapy, I went to the grocery store and bought some pantry items, soups, pancake mix, spices, things like that. Then, I went to target and bought bathmats and towels. I made sure to pick up a couple things for the house so he didn't notice a target charge and no target bags.

    I went to my new apartment and put things away. I had the cable and Wi-Fi hooked up right away and brought the tv from the guest bedroom. He never went in there, so I didn't think even knew there was one in there. It was small, and I'd need a bigger one. Next time I went to town, I'd bring the rest of the cash and stop and get a TV. I wanted a smart TV set up with Netflix and Hulu. I needed regular channels so I could watch football, and I was set. So, I signed up with Sling TV for good measure. I had a lot of blue and yellow in this apartment. The couch that was delivered was almost a denim, and I bought happy feeling yellow throw pillows. Yellow made me happy. So I got a blue and yellow comforter for my new bed, too. My new bed had an adjustable frame. I couldn't wait to write in my journal with my dog and the head of my bed up to make it easier and more comfortable. I stepped out onto my balcony and let the wind whip through my hair. I felt nothing but peace here. I was afraid I would feel like I was crammed into this condo with not enough room, but I had exactly enough room. There was a room for Eva and one for me. Two full bathrooms, a decent sized kitchen and a pantry that opened up into the living room. The dining room was small, but I wasn't a big entertainer, so it didn't matter. What I was going to love was the pool. I couldn't wait. It was time.

34
Detective Engen

Detective Parker Engen was looking at Barb Ellis's file for the millionth time. She knew she was missing something. She felt it in her bones.

He had her strip naked and crouch on the floor of the car when they hit the intersection, she saw the tire iron tucked between the seats. That's when she knew he was going to kill her. She quit believing she'd get out of this alive if she played her cards right and decided she needed to run. This assault happened in the middle of the day. She was missing something, she knew it.

She checked for similar cases in the state of Minnesota, and she found that there were seven women, who went missing in the last three years, who were seen in the morning, and not after dinner. Aside from Barb, and the girl walking home from the theatre, no one was seen after the dinner hour. They went missing from parks, parking lots, and again, walking home from the theatre.

They were young, beautiful, and had so much potential. She paced the tent they had set up in Moose Lake by the playground. There still was no sign of Makayla, and Parker knew it was time to look on the Interstate. If she were alive, they'd have found her by now. It had been two days since she went missing. A beautiful, intelligent, kind girl was snatched from her parents and friends. It wasn't fair. Parker was pissed.

Barb was older than the average victim, but she looked young. Her hair was long, and she was short and thin. From a distance, she could pass for twenty-five or thirty. Could her case be related to this? She decided to send the composite drawing of Barb's attacker out to the public. She called the local news stations and told them she'd give a press conference that evening at six. No, they didn't have anything new, it was just to update the public as to where they stood in the search for Makayla.

The usual crowd showed up at the press conference from the local channels, but Parker was shocked when she saw the big networks there ABC, NBC, CNN MSNBC, everyone. Apparently, others have put these cases together with one person as well. Otherwise, they wouldn't be here. Of course, Makayla was young, beautiful, and white. So, her story would sell. Parker cursed herself for thinking that. Whatever the reason they were here, she was thankful for the publicity. It was the best way to end this.

Parker walked up to the podium more nervous than she'd ever been while doing a press conference.

She stayed out of the shot of the cameras for a moment while Makayla's photo was displayed on the projector. She wanted everyone to see it.

"Makayla Anne Madison went missing from the baseball field and park in Moose Lake, MN around five-thirty p.m., Tuesday night. She is five-foot-seven-inches tall, approximately one hundred and forty pounds, blonde hair to the middle of her back, blue eyes. She was wearing blue jeans, an Esko Baseball sweatshirt and navy tennis shoes from Nike. If anyone has any information as to her whereabouts, please call the number on the screen. Five bodies of young women have been found along I35 and two more are missing. We have no confirmation as to whether or not the disappearance of Makayla is related, but we do have a composite drawing of a person of interest in the other murders and disappearances. He is a white male, age thirty-five to forty, brown hair to his shoulders that he often pulls into a ponytail. He has an average build and a tattoo on his wrist that says YOLO. It was a saying popular in the nineties meaning "You Only Live Once." He speaks as though he is educated. If you have any information on this man, we'd just like to speak to him about the homicides and disappearances. We think he can help us find the killer. Thank you," Detective Engen said. "I'll take a few questions."

"Where did you get that composite?" he asked.

"I can't answer that, but from a reliable source," she said.

"Is he a suspect?" a reporter shouted without being called on.

"No, we just want to talk to him," lied Parker.

Parker gestured toward the MSNBC reporter to say she was next to ask a question.

"Do you have a conclusive link to all the bodies? Is this person a serial killer?"

"Given my gut, I'd say yes, but no one has yet to go to prison based on my gut instinct.

"We do not have a conclusive link, and we just want to talk to the man in the composite drawing. If you would all put it up on your websites, we'd appreciate it. Thank you."

At that, Parker hustled out off camera. She'd never done that before. It was a rush. Reporters could be rude and pushy, but they definitely served a purpose here, so she had to give them a little. Parker knew the tattoo would get him just like Richard Speck who was "Born to Raise Hell." That's what his tattoo said, and a nurse who lived through the attack on her roommates reported the tattoo. When Speck tried to kill himself and ended up in the hospital, the doctor recognized the tattoo, and called police. He was arrested and died in prison. Parker hoped this asshole would die in prison as well. He had definitely earned it.

35
Izzy

I put the dry cleaning in the back of the car, and jumped in. I had a love-hate relationship with running errands. I loved being out of the house, I loved listening to my audio book as I drove, I loved the freedom of being out and about without worrying about Michael getting pissed. Most of my errands were for him, so he didn't get mad when I ran them. I hated spending my Saturday afternoon in Menards, Fleet Farm, and the grocery store. He never went into town. Today, he was off on some four-wheeling adventure with his buddies from town. I'd known about these plans for a long time. These idiots would get hammered drunk while driving four wheelers for hours, then, they'd come back to Weasel's cabin and shoot Clay Pigeons. The guy's nickname was Weasel because he could weasel out of anything. I didn't even know his real name. If any of the guys had little boys, they came with. The young boys thought it was awesome running around on four wheelers and shooting guns. It had disaster written all over it. Eva had no interest, but they didn't want girls there anyway. Ollie never went on this traditional weekend. Thank God. I told his mom about the drinking and the guys, so she just made plans that weekend every year. I'd give her the heads up, and she'd handle it from there. We saw no need to confront Michael about it. If he hurt himself, fine. I wrestled with telling the cops about this weekend all the time. Instead, I reported it to social services. I'm a mandatory reporter, and I saw this as abuse. This absolute disregard to the safety of others absolutely should be illegal on some level. Not that anyone who fills out paperwork for social services ever hears back from them, but I wanted to know. I always wished they would call and tell me what happened. They never did.

With Michael occupied, this was the perfect day to meet with my therapist. She had weekend office hours and was closed on Mondays. I really liked my therapist. She was starting to grow on me. She had her Ph.D., so she was a doctor, but not a medical doctor. She knew what she was doing. Dr. Sánchez was the only one who ever asked me questions or played devil's advocate with me. She didn't just nod and ask me how that made me feel. Isn't it obvious how it makes me feel, when my husband calls me stupid, uncoordinated or selfish? She thinks he's projecting his own fears onto me. She made me think deeper, and I was starting to believe that I mattered a little at least to the people who loved me. Michael picked at my self-esteem for so long that I didn't care if I lived or died, and I didn't think anyone else cared either. I didn't want Michael to know I was seeing a therapist. He would flip out. In his mind, a therapist is just someone who makes you feel okay about dumping your family and thinking only about yourself. There were days when I thought maybe he was right. I did pledge to love him in sickness and in health. I'd have to say, this is sickness. But I think there are deal breakers to that vow, too. He shouldn't be able to call me stupid, lazy, ugly, or whatever adjective was his favorite for that day and think that I have to take that because I took vows eighteen years ago. I took those vows before his alcoholism ever started. I didn't know. He was on his best behavior. He was in his charming phase until we bought the house. Now, he was an asshole more than he wasn't. I wouldn't even recognize that sweet man who cried when our first dog died and when he found out his dad had cancer. I loved him then.

One night, at his parents' farm, he and I took a drive into town. We never made it to town because the Northern Lights were out. Out where his parents' farm was, there were no town lights to obscure our view. We got out of the car and laid on the hood. We just stared up at the sky and watched the green and yellow lights dance across the sky. Michael sat up on one elbow and said, "How'd I ever get so lucky?"

"I love you so much."

His eyes were brimming with tears. I hugged him tight and told him how much I loved him too. I'd never felt so close to anyone. I loved being his wife. I loved him so much. This Michael was the good Michael.

I didn't even notice that my parents and friends were getting pushed out of the picture little by little.

"Honey, I'd like to have my mom and dad over for dinner," I'd say.

His usual reply was something to the effect of, "That's fine, but you know your mom will find fault in something. She'll think you cut the celery too big or the yard is too messy, or that dessert is delicious, but a little too sugary for her taste. But go ahead and invite them." I'd never invite them. When I wanted to go out with my friends, sometimes, I'd lie about which friends. He didn't like Beth, (I didn't need that negativity). He didn't like Sue (she left her husband, and he didn't want me getting ideas). He didn't like Sarah, (too bossy) or Jennifer (just crazy). That didn't leave many Michael approved people to make plans with. He liked when I hung out with Hannah Keppler or Rebecca DuPuis because he liked to drink with their husbands. They were sisters, and they were married to big drinkers, and so they were on my Michael approved list of friends I could see. I didn't notice this happen all at once. It happened little by little, until I felt totally alone. I couldn't talk to Hannah or Rebecca. I didn't want them to tell their husbands. So as far as they were concerned, my marriage was always bliss. I didn't like going out with them. They were so kind and fun. But they made me feel like such a bitch because I hated Michael's drinking. I know it was different for their husbands. They never seemed drunk even after ten beers. But Michael drank the hard stuff, so I could tell on him immediately. I really fit nowhere. One day, I picked up the phone to call a friend. I wanted to talk. But I realized, there was no one to call. Not one of my friends would want to hear from me after I consistently cancelled plans and never asked them to do anything. For a month, I got voicemails from Sarah, and I never called her back, not once. She told me that friendships were like house plants. Without attention and love, they wither and die. That friendship was over. I felt so alone.

If Michael decided I "wasn't going anywhere," I wasn't going anywhere. I didn't mean to ignore people. Jennifer, last time I talked to her, I picked a fight with her. Michael thought she was tacky. He didn't think I needed friends like that. I figured she didn't want to talk to me either. I'd burned my bridge with David ages ago. Shortly after I met Michael, I knew I didn't want Michael anywhere near David. He'd hurt David's feelings without a doubt. So, I made a choice. I chose Michael. I couldn't be with Michael and still be friends with David. Michael could not have handled that as he proved many times over. I couldn't call my parents until I was ready to leave him. I didn't want to put them through more. They hated Michael almost more than I do. There's no one left except Beth. He hates her most of all, so it's not like I can have her over for dinner or go out with her.

Especially since the whole email reading episode, he made it impossible for me to see her. He said I don't need her influence. I was in this all alone, and it was no one's fault but my own. I bought all his lies. I made my own choices. I can't put it all on him. I used to have so many friends, and now, I am alone. How could I have let this happen?

The more isolated I felt, the bolder Michael became.

How did I not see this coming, I wondered? He moved me to the sticks, hated all my friends, couldn't tolerate my family, and now, I have no one. I had to get out of there. Eva left in a couple months for New York City, Then, I could leave. If he hurt or killed me, so be it. Eva would be too far away to hurt. So, that was my plan to get out. When Eva was at college, I could leave. I already had that apartment that I loved. I brought stuff over there little by little. I didn't take things from the house, I bought new things from Target or wherever. All I wanted from the house were my clothes, my art prints, my Great Grandmother's dining room table, and my life. I had a therapist to talk to, to help me get by until I could call my friends and beg their forgiveness for how terribly I've treated them. I didn't think I had any choice in the matter, though. He made the rules. I didn't even want to know what would happen when defied him.

It's about more than physical fear, though. I know he could and would kill me just to prove his fucked-up point. But I am humiliated by so many things that I have done in the name of keeping the peace. What do people say first when they hear a story about an abused woman? The very first thing out of most people's mouth is, "Why doesn't she just leave?" I would have said the exact same thing. Before it happened to me, I thought women who let men abuse them repeatedly were weak or stupid or both.

Abusers have a lot of work to do when they meet someone in order to get what they want out of them. First, they have to pick out someone with a vulnerability. Jeffrey Epstein picked girls with no money, whose fathers had just died, women who were highly ambitious, or even women with good family ties. The girls who came from good families, would be highly embarrassed if their actions came to light. They were as young as fourteen years old, and didn't know what to do when this old man hit on them or raped them. If at first they went along with it because they didn't know what else to do, he had them. What if their mom or dad or pastor etc… found out what they did with this dirty old man? How embarrassing, they'd think. So, they stay because their secret is threatened to be exposed. If their father just died, at first, Epstein was portrayed as a father figure, giving money to the needy young girl whose dreams of Broadway he "nurtured" until one day he told her to take her clothes off. By this time, she thought she owed him because he'd been so nice. Abusers don't bother with people who don't have an Achilles heel they can easily pick out.

Then, they turn on the charm. I had low self-esteem. That was my Achilles heel. He picked up on that immediately and started charming the pants of me. He was such a gentleman. He told me I was beautiful. I was his sunshine. I made his life worth living, I was what he'd been looking for his entire life, and life was good now that we found each other. He was romantic, he brought me flowers and delivered them to work for me, He was funny, witty, loved the theatre and baseball. Come to think of it, I asked him how he felt about those things, and he answered with a question. "Well, how do you feel about the theatre?"

I, of course, went on and on about my love for the music of Phantom of the Opera, the voice of Idina Menzell, the showmanship of The Lion King, the story of the optimist Don Quijote de la Mancha, etc... I couldn't get my stories out fast enough. He said he loved Les Miserables. My first clue to his lying here should have been his absolute murder of the pronunciation. I didn't want to be a snob, though, so I ignored it and was so happy he loved musicals. With baseball, I could tell he was lying when he said he liked it because he knew nothing about it. He didn't even know how many innings constituted a game. He could not name one member of the Minnesota Twins. I thought it was kind of cute that he'd pretend to like it because he liked me so much. Who was I to judge? I said I wouldn't mind learning how to hunt. I'd never considered learning how to hunt before. I said that to please him. I'd do it, but I wasn't exactly interested in it.

Once he had me charmed, he started to point out the flaws in my friends. Often. He'd say things like, "I can't believe you're friends with her, she's so fake. She's so full of herself, or she's such a liar." He knew my priorities and morality by this point and would find any flaw in my friends and exploit them. He belittled David's sexuality, Teresa's love of Tyler who cheated on her regularly. "There was something wrong with her if she let Tyler cheat on her all the time." Alicia was crazy, Carmen bragged too much, how could I stand it? He had something for everyone. He let it be known that he would not be spending time with my friends. I thought there had to be something wrong with me. Who was the common denominator there? It was me. I picked all those "flawed" people to be my friends. What was wrong with me? So, I backed away from everyone.

Then, he started in on my family. He wouldn't bad mouth my dad. I think he respected or feared him. I think he knew the threat to our relationship was my mom. He knew my dad stayed out of my personal life and didn't give advice unless I asked for it. He really hated my mom, though. It got to the point that I didn't want her to have to be around him. I called her when he wasn't around. I stopped inviting him to go to dinner at their house with me. They never asked where he was. I knew that the feeling was mutual between Michael and my mother. After their first meeting, my mom knew he was not going to make me happy. She knew he was a misogynist, and that he'd belittle me every chance he got. She hated him with the most dramatic, over the top, feelings I could imagine.

"He will destroy your life. Can you imagine having kids with that man? He'd assume it was your job to take care of them. He'd show up on picture day. He's narcissistic." And on and on she went. After looking up the word 'narcissist' and doing some research on the term, I thought there was no way my mom came up with that one on her own. That was pretty extensive. It wasn't terribly common, and you'd have to have some psychology training to spot someone who was a narcissist. They hid it well, usually, and he or she could just be confident. Like I said, she poured on the drama. Michael wasn't a narcissist, I thought. He was kind, thoughtful, and loved me. I decided that she never liked any of my boyfriends, why would Michael be any different? If I liked someone, she hated them. If I wasn't that into a boy, she thought he was perfect for me. I was sick and tired of her trying to manipulate my choices like that. I pulled away from my parents, too. But not before I gave my mom a big piece of my mind about how she treated me and how she tried to be my puppet master. She was mortified, but I didn't care. I was such a brat. I wanted Michael. I did not care what anyone who loved me thought. I pushed them all away. This is part of an abuser's plan as well. I made it too easy for him.

I went so far in the things I said and did that I didn't think I'd ever be able to talk to most of the people I disrespected ever again. I assumed they would hate me forever. They should have. I could never crawl back to them. It'd be like admitting defeat, and if I did, I'd have to be prepared to give Michael up. That just wasn't going to happen.

So, when we got married, there were plenty of dry eyes. No one was overwhelmed by the romance of it all. My mom smiled through clenched teeth, and David looked like he could not wait to get out of the reception. When I went to talk to him, he informed me that this would be the last time he endured that asshole, as he put it. He said to let him know as soon as I ditched him. He'd always be here for me as long as I dumped the husband. I pointed out how little sense that made.

He said, "It makes perfect sense. If it takes twenty years for you to figure out what an enormous mistake you made here today, call me first. No questions asked. I will have room, and I will be happy to take you and whatever kids you have by then in. But I will not subject myself to his hatred for me for another minute. He's cruel," he said.

I started to apologize for Michel and explain how he just doesn't get it or know anyone, etc… David was having none of it. "Let me know when you leave him. I'm sorry Izzy, but I will not subject myself to that treatment, and I don't want to watch it happen to you either."

"If I wasn't gay, he'd find something else to pick on." David said. "That guy is a psychopath."

I told him I was sorry he felt that way, but I understood.

Beth told me to fuck off. She wasn't going anywhere and Michael could kiss her ass if he wanted to, but she was my friend and that was that. Michael eventually gave up but not until he'd given it the old college try. He set her up to look like she was cheating on her boyfriend, like she lied to Isabelle, like she was a thief, etc. I told Michael to stop. We both knew what he was doing, and I'd leave him if he didn't quit trying to get Beth out of my life. He, of course, denied all of it. I knew he was guilty, though. I, for once, didn't let him get his way on this and neither did Beth. He dealt with it. But I had no one else. I'd pushed everyone else away. Beth couldn't be there for me one hundred percent of the time. I couldn't put that on anyone. I couldn't lose her, so I didn't want to sufficate her. Michael hated the fact that he couldn't get rid of her. It drove him crazy. But I was careful to only talk to her when he wasn't around. We didn't email each other any more, obviously. I'd call her from the grocery store parking lot where I'd sit and chat with her for an hour before finally returning home sometimes. I couldn't do it often, but I did it enough.

The nail in my coffin was Oak Creek. We were by the railroad tracks, in the sticks, where no one would just stop by. In the summer, I still got up and got ready every day in case someone did stop by, but no one ever did. My parents called every now and again, but they did not interact with him on the phone if he answered. They simply asked for me. Sometimes, I could hear him tell my mom that I wasn't home. I was, of course, I was in the other room. But the less I talked to her the better, according to Michael.

I hated Oak Creek. In Oak Creek, our house was a block from the neighborhood bar. The bar was a hole in the wall where the local alcoholics and single girls hung out. There were a few men who came in who had hunting land up there, but that was it. Michael was very popular there. He bought rounds for everyone at least twice a night. That kept him in everyone's good graces no matter what he said that rubbed them wrong. A lot of people got angry about him hitting on their wives or girlfriends. Buy an alcoholic a beer, however, and a lot can be forgotten or forgiven.

I was so alone. When I found out I was pregnant, after I told Beth, I didn't know who would take my call. I called my grandparents. I knew they'd be happy for me. When I finally got a hold of my mom, she said, "Oh no." I was so offended.

"Mom, how could you react like that to your grandchild, who will be in your life in a few months?" I asked.

"I'm thrilled for that," she said. "It just makes getting out of this marriage a hell of a lot harder for you. That's all I meant by oh no."

"Mother, I am having his baby. He is my husband. I have no intention of getting out of this marriage, I need you, mom!" I said.

"I love you, Izzy," she said. "Don't you ever forget that." And she hung up. I didn't know if that meant not to call her any more or what. So, I didn't. She and I didn't speak until after Eva was born. It was a very lonely existence for me. Once Eva was born, I was too busy to be lonely for the first four years. Once she went to school, things started to slow down a little bit. I got a full night's sleep again for the first time in years. When I rested up and came out of my raising a baby and toddler fog, I started to notice that Michael was hardly ever around.

He loved to play the martyr. If I was tired, "Sure wish you had time for me, too." If I was happy, "Sure wish you got this excited to do something with me."

If I talked about Eva, "Sure wish you talked about me like you talk about her."

It was ridiculous. It grated on my every nerve. This is your daughter, asshole. You aren't supposed to be jealous of your daughter. I thought that was really weird. But who could I talk to about it? Beth was sick of it, I'm sure. So, while I filled her in on things, I tried not to complain too much. I didn't want to burn my bridge with my dearest and only friend.

He picked at my self-esteem until I had nothing left, he had a wicked temper that scared the hell out of me, and he reminded me often about sinners leaving their husbands and how they went to hell and their husbands would have reason to send them there. I was terrified, alone, ashamed, and friendless. Once the weird, gross sex stuff started to happen with him, I was totally alone; I would never talk about it. I didn't know that a husband would rape a wife. Why would he do such a thing? By the time he started doing that, we'd been married about fifteen years. If I said no, he'd pin me down and take it anyway. I'd come out of those nights with fat lips and black eyes. I ran into a lot of doors in those days. I don't think anyone believed me.

So, why doesn't an abuse survivor just leave her abuser or his abuser? It's complicated, but for me it was utter embarrassment, the fear of having to start over in my forties, where would I go? I had no family to speak of. We were cordial to each other, but they hated Michael so much that they could hardly look at me. I couldn't turn to them, I thought I'd be humiliated. So, I started to squirrel money away. I actually started this process years ago. I knew there'd come a time that I couldn't stand another second with him. That's how I finally got my new apartment and furnishings. I even had enough to furnish Eva's room for when she'd visit. After doing all this, I still had well over a hundred thousand dollars left in cash. I didn't put this money in bank accounts. I didn't want there to be a record of it. I squirreled it before we had direct deposit. He thought I made a hundred dollars a pay check less than I did. Then, once we got direct deposit, I used my debit card at Target and Walmart. I always got an extra forty dollars and hid it. The amount was so little, and since it came from checking out at Target or Walmart, he didn't suspect a thing.

    I told no one for the longest time, I didn't even tell Beth. When Eva asked me, I told her. I even took her to our awesome new place. It'd only be home to her on visits, but still, I thought of it as our new place. I couldn't wait to live there. It was in Duluth for one, had a pool, great views, and everything was brand new. My bed, my dressers, patio furniture, dishes, silverware, towels, rugs, everything. I even had the pantry pretty well stocked. When the time was right. When I knew I could safely get out and Eva was safely in NYC, I would leave. Then, I didn't care who said, "I told you so." They did tell me so, and I didn't listen. But I was listening now, and I had my Eva. So, I had a comeback to anyone who said it was too bad I didn't listen sooner. If I would have, I wouldn't have Eva. Exactly Eva. I wouldn't change anything about her. This child needed to be born and exactly how she was meant to be. Without her, the world wouldn't be as bright or as beautiful. They would agree with me and leave me alone about it, because on this, I was right.

36
Michael

For as long as Michael could remember, he was unusual. He was different from his siblings, his parents, his teachers, his friends, everyone. He didn't know what made him unique, but he could not help it if he was special. He knew that sometimes, he had to hide his differences because people were just too stupid to understand him. Sometimes, he needed things from people, and he had to play his cards right to get them to go along with him. For some reason, some people didn't see his difference as a good thing. They judged him as a troublemaker, mean, selfish, and uncaring when he'd forget to pretend to be like everyone else.

Before he realized that some people didn't like his specialness or didn't understand it, he didn't know to hide it. Michael sometimes saw his brother or sister cry while they watched a movie, and he thought they were the crazy ones. Why did they care what happened to a fake person? He'd see his brother walk into the kitchen and help his mom put groceries away. Michael had just been thinking to go in the kitchen and get the cookies and bring them to his room before his stupid brother saw them. He'd remember the helping tactic next time.

One time, in school, Laurie Simms caught his eye. She was really cute. She had pretty blonde curls, and she always wore a dress. Sometimes, when she played on the jungle gym, he could see up her dress. Michael always found a spot under the monkey bars where he knew she'd be. As always, she had a dress on, and she loved to climb to the top. Michael pretended to play in the sand. When she climbed over head, he stared up at her. He laughed to himself because he thought he was so clever. None of the other boys thought of this, and he knew they wanted to see up her dress, too. Laurie heard him laugh and she realized what he was doing. She screamed, Michael ran and pretended to have been playing soccer the whole time. He hoped Laurie didn't know who he was. She was in Mrs. Harmon's class, and Michael had Mr. Lindquist. So, she probably couldn't tell on him. She didn't know who he was.

But the playground lady told him the principal wanted to see him right now. Michael thought about running away, hitting the playground attendant in her tummy, she obviously had a baby in there. That'd hurt her enough to stop bothering him. But then he thought, why should I risk getting in trouble? I didn't do anything wrong. If she didn't want boys to look up her dress, she shouldn't climb onto the monkey bars. He knew better than to say that though. He'd tell the principal Laurie was lying. "Okay," he said. "Right now?"

"Right now. Do you need me to take you there or can you get there yourself?" The playground lady asked.

"I can do it myself," he said. He didn't want that lady telling him what to do any more. He still wanted to punch her baby.

Michael walked into the school building and easily found the principal's office. He told the secretary who he was when she asked. He almost said Spiderman, but he didn't think she'd find it funny. He thought he was funny, though.

He sat in a chair that was really big. His feet didn't touch the floor. It was fun to swing his feet back and forth. If he swung harder, and someone walked by, he'd kick them and could tell the secretary it was an accident.

Mrs. Carlyle walked by, but she wasn't close enough to kick. A few minutes later a kid in sixth grade walked by and he kind of smiled at Michael. Michael thought he was making fun of him, and he kicked him. The sixth grader went straight down. He wanted to gloat and tell the boy he did it on purpose, and not to mess with him again. But he knew he'd get in trouble. So, he said he was sorry, and that it was an accident. The sixth grader would have been embarrassed to have been dropped by a third grader, so he just said that was okay, and he walked away giving Michael a lot of room. He never got in trouble with that. He wondered who else he could get with that trick. If someone was embarrassed to be taken by such a young kid, they'd keep their trap shut. They wouldn't tattle on him.

The principal called him in. She told Michael that he was suspended for the next two days for looking up Laurie's dress. She told him it was really naughty, and if he did stuff like that when he got older, he'd go to jail. Jail scared him. When his dad went to jail, he didn't come home the whole time Michael was in first and second grade. He got home right before he started third grade. So, you go to jail a really long time.

"But Mrs. Adams," Michael cried. "I didn't do anything. I never looked up her dress. That's wrong to do. Why would I want to look up a girls dress anyway? Girls are yucky." Principal Adams almost let out a laugh at this proclamation. She'd have to say, he probably didn't do it. She looked at his little watery eyes, and his very serious face when he denied looking up her dress.

"Okay, Michael. I wasn't there, so today, just this one time, I will believe you. If it becomes a habit that I see you in here. I'll wholeheartedly believe your accuser. Today, it's possible she pointed out the wrong boy. But Mr. Lewis," she said.

"Yes, ma'am?" he asked.

"I'm watching you."

"Yes, ma'am," he said.

She bought it. He learned to throw in some tears when he denied an action today. The tears sealed the deal. "I looked pathetic," he thought. "But I didn't get in trouble. When school warned me about something, they usually didn't call my dad. My dad used to go places all the time in his great big truck. He was gone on Wednesdays, Thursdays, Fridays, and he came home late on Saturday. We always cleaned and made dad's favorite food when he came home from a "trip" Now he doesn't go anywhere. He didn't work at all. He was always home.

"He yelled at me all the time. I wanted to run away. Maybe I could be friends with a kid at school who had nice parents. I could stay there when I wanted to. That was a good idea. His mom just sat on the porch smoking lots of cigarettes and ignoring us. She was clumsy, too. She always had a black eye or a bloody nose. She should be more careful," Michael thought.

This is what made him special. This is what made him better than everybody else, he thought. He was smart and could con a principal, and a playground lady. He could kick a sixth grader and look up a girl's dress and not get in trouble. Michael knew he thought of bad things long before the other kids. He also didn't feel bad when he got caught like they did. When the teacher said things like, "You should be ashamed of yourself," Michael never felt ashamed of himself. On the contrary, he was proud of himself. He figured out when people could tolerate or buy the lies, and when he had to "apologize" and "cry". He could read people and know what they needed. He was eight years old.

He knew he was special too because he didn't feel bad about. He lies he told or things he stole or people he hurt. Some people might think that was a bad thing. But he thought it was stupid to feel bad about things that didn't hurt him. Why should he care? He could tell his dad that no, he didn't climb the tree. He swore to God. Even with birch bark in his hair and

scratches on his face and arms, he denied what he obviously did. But he cried and was so adamant that he made people question the obvious. That questioning, is called gaslighting, and Michael would become a professional gas lighter. He was already good at it by the time he was eight. At twenty-eight, he could make you believe you were crazy because you saw something happen, did not really happen. Others would stop and wonder if it was possible they didn't actually see him take that pair of pants. He'd go into the dressing room and come out without pants to put back or to buy. He charmed people so much they believed that their eyes were playing tricks on them.

As he grew up, he wanted to do much more than look up women's dresses. Women had caused him nothing but trouble. It was a woman who saw him take some fishing tackle at Cabella's, and he had to sit in a room for hours while his dad yelled at the female cop. She wasn't going to be bullied. Michael could've told him that charm works much better than yelling, but his dad wasn't about to take advice from his shoplifting son right then. The female judge made him go to juvenile hall because it was his third time he was caught. Michael wanted to tell the judge he may have been caught three times, but he'd done it hundreds of times. He was proud of himself. He could take what he wanted and only get caught once every hundred or so times he took something.

In college, Michael went through about six roommates. No one wanted to stay his roommate. He stole their girlfriends, stole money out of their wallets, stole their food, their beer, everything. He was charming, but he took what he wanted with no thought to anyone else. By the time his seventh roommate moved in,

Michael had figured out not to mess with his roommates because he needed them for more than twenty dollars or some Mac and Cheese. It'd be tough to keep his hands off their girlfriends, but he needed a roommate. He didn't have the cash to live on his own yet. He also needed his degree to make enough money to live how he wanted. He wouldn't be able to steal a house. He'd have to marry someone with a job, too. She would help pay the bills and be there for sex anytime he wanted. Plus, a wife would clean and cook for him. He could not imagine a better scenario. His mother sat around smoking all day while his dad screamed at everyone. Michael decided in his family, it'd be different.

Michael got his Bachelor's Degree in business in four years. He was qualified for whatever job in business that he wanted. The degree was so generalized these days. But that was good. It made him able to do what he chose. The job market was wide open for him, and with his charm and inability to feel guilt, he could do anything.

He saw Isabelle with her friends at the bar one night and sent them all a beer. He was in one of his brooding moods where he was introspective and wanted to be a deep thinker. The girl with Izzy looked mad at the world. She constantly stared at the DJ. Michael saw Izzy's shoulders were a little hunched over, and she looked shy. She was beautiful. But she wasn't bold about it. She was shy about it. That was the best kind. The shy ones could be more easily manipulated. He just wanted Izzy to like him. He thought she was the most beautiful woman he'd ever seen. He hoped she had potential. That meant she had to have a job, and she had to believe in traditional roles for women. She had to be willing to do what she's told and to keep things quiet. She can't be one of those women who tell their friends everything. She had to depend on him for her self-esteem. If she didn't, he couldn't date her no matter how beautiful she was. He'd definitely sleep with her, but he couldn't have a relationship with her. If he flat out asked any woman, whether she was traditional or not, he found out that he either got slapped or left holding the check. Women for some reason did not like that question although he couldn't figure out why. It was a simple enough question. Do you believe in a traditional household where the man is boss or not? What's so offensive about that? Some women like to have a real man around, but he didn't ask that question any more because he learned his lesson.

Now, he had to go out with the woman a few times to get a feel for what she's like. If she was some women's libber, he was out. If she was lazy, he was out. If she didn't have a job, not a chance. There was no way he was footing the whole bill for a piece of ass he could get anywhere. She had to have a job, and she had to take care of the house and kids. Plenty of women did that now days. If he couldn't find a woman willing to do that, he just wouldn't get married. Whatever. He didn't care. It wasn't like he had to try hard to get women into his bed. He just could not figure out what the big deal was about getting married, but apparently, the business world prefers people who are married. It shows they can commit is what he read in one of his business magazines. Fucking committing to his business wasn't enough? He worked his ass off. No one worked harder than he did. That was why any woman he dated couldn't be lazy. He worked hard and played hard. She would have to keep up. He was already divorced once, and he wasn't making the same mistakes again. That woman had an opinion about everything. She wanted everything to be equal. If she made dinner on Monday, he had to make it on Tuesday. If she did the laundry this week, he had to do it next week. The kids were pretty young when they split. She wanted full custody, but that was going to cost a fortune in child support. So, he fought for joint custody. After she testified about one of their fights, he lost that battle. She told of a fight they had so long ago that he forgot about it. He got home late. He actually worked late and the roads were slippery. He was supposed to stop and get diapers for Sophie, and he forgot. She was pissed when he got home. She tried to send him back out in the snowstorm for the diapers, and he tried to grab the baby out of her hands. He was just telling her to get the diapers herself. She was so fucking lazy.

She had Sophie five weeks prior. Pretty sure she was well enough to go get diapers. Well, when he grabbed the baby, she started to scream and cry. It freaked him out, so he let go of her. She fell to the floor. The kid was fine. She just had an egg on her head but his ex-wife made a huge deal out of it, and now, he was a "See ya on the weekend" dad. He lived in a shit apartment in a shittier neighborhood because he had to give that bitch four hundred dollars a month.

He didn't make much in his first job selling computers, so four hundred dollars was a lot of money. Just thinking about it pissed him off all over again. Thank God he didn't live in that rathole apartment any more. He was divorced by the time he was twenty-six. They only lasted four years, but it was the longest four years of his life, he thought. He was not going through that shit again. When he got married again, it couldn't be with someone who wanted him sorting clothes and buying diapers. His job was making money. Now that he was established in his computer business, he was making it, big time. He had a fish house, a truck, a house, a four-wheeler, and a boat. If he wanted something, he bought it. He made the money. He didn't want a free loader, but he wanted her to know that as the man, that was his job. She would make less, and so she could compensate by doing the housework.

He was getting close to thirty and kind of had to get a move on the married thing if he wanted to stick to his success plan. He always stuck to the plan. But the most important part of the plan was the type of woman he needed to compliment him in business and at home. He'd really like a woman who smoked, so she didn't piss and moan about his smoking, and a woman who knew how to drink so she wasn't pissed every time he went to the bar. He also wanted a woman he didn't have to be all buttoned up around. He didn't want to have to quit saying "fuck" or looking at nice pieces of ass because her feelings got hurt or whatever. He needed her to be chill, but he didn't want to bring Roseanne home to his mother either. Maybe a cross between June Cleaver and Murphy Brown with Roseanne's mouth and Jennifer Anniston's body. He didn't think that was too much to ask. If a woman wanted to be with him, she had to be the kind of woman he wanted.

This chick in the bar though, she was interesting. She was beautiful but not in a Pamela Anderson way. It was more like a hot librarian kind of way. She didn't know she was pretty though. He watched guys check her out, and she didn't even notice. She just talked to her friends, then dropped everything to go dance. He liked her attitude when she took the dance floor. She owned it. But when the song was over, she went back to the table and didn't look around until the beer came. He even sent one to her queer friend. What was she doing with that guy? That made him wonder if she wasn't too liberal to check off the boxes he needed checked.

He decided to overlook it because she had the right look. He was glad he did because when she got the beer, she looked around. We locked eyes, and she knew it was me who sent the beer. He thought this was going to be easy. She didn't look like she wanted to meet anyone. She didn't even look like she wanted to be there, but when they locked eyes, he knew he'd be sleeping with her within the week.

She walked over to him and thanked him for the beer. Michael asked her to sit down, and he poured on the charm. He almost made himself sick. He couldn't believe women fell for this shit. This chick was kind of different though. She was a high school English teacher.

She joked that she made people practice until they got it right. He liked that about her. She laughed at herself and could hold her own with guy humor. She was pretty relaxed after her third beer. She made it clear though that if he wanted to see her again, he would have to call her. He gave her his number anyway but thought it was a good sign that she wouldn't call. Job...check. Traditional... maybe check. He'd need to investigate further.

He dated her for a while, and she only freaked out once. He offended her bitch of a mother then drove too fast. He was kind of being a dick, he acknowledged, but she'd have to learn how to deal with that if she wanted to hang out with him full time.

After a year of dating, he decided to give her a trial run and live with her for a bit. His family was catholic, so it was not a popular decision with his mother. She kept asking him what his intentions were and if he planned to marry Izzy someday. Finally, he admitted that yes, he would marry her one day. His mom told him to ask her now then so they could quit living in sin. His mom was the only woman who could tell him to do something. She didn't tolerate sin although she smoked and ignored her kids when they were small.

Michael despised religion, but he'd never tell his mother

that. He had to save face with her. He couldn't be the guy who even his mom couldn't stand. Someone told him once that it sounded really bad when he yelled at his mom, so he didn't do it any more. For him to be successful, he couldn't do stupid things that would keep people out of his stores. He had to make up for his stint in juvenile hall and the divorce. So, he minded his manners in public most of the time and tried to keep his impulses in check. Thank God he learned how to read people young. He wasn't inhibited by what other people were. A therapist explained guilt as the thing that kept people from hurting each other. It made you behave because if you didn't, you'd get this huge pain in your chest and stomach that wouldn't go away until you apologized or made up for it somehow. He was so happy that he didn't have that. He could do what he wanted without feeling like that. He had to do bad things in secret, he knew. People who had the guilt thing didn't like people who didn't. They were jealous. So, he hid it, or he kept it in check.

37

As he got older, his impulses got stronger. He wanted sex all the time. There was never enough. He could leave Isabelle's and he'd have to pick up a hooker on the way home for one more quick one. He tried to stop this because he never wanted to get caught. He knew it wouldn't be good if he got caught. When he and Izzy got married, he'd have to stop.

Izzy and Michael got married July 3, 1995. His appetite for sex did not go down. He figured it would. He thought the ring on his finger would slow things down. But women like men with wedding rings. He couldn't help it. They'd see the ring and want to fuck. It wasn't his fault. Besides, if Izzy hadn't changed so much the minute that ring went on, he wouldn't have to seek it out with other women.

She used to be fun. Now she was like, "I'm tired. I don't want to go out." She promised she wouldn't change. She told him it was just a lot teaching full time and having to do all the housework. He told her she knew the deal when they got married. It shut her up. She never mentioned it again. But she quit going to the bar with him Like that was such a huge punishment. He acted like it was and made a huge production about it whenever he went out. He told her she used to be fun. But she wouldn't budge, and then he could pick up whoever he felt like. "So, no, Isabelle. You didn't punish me," he thought on more than one occasion.

When they moved out to Oak Creek, the choices were pretty

limited. There was only one bar in town. He supposed he could have gone to the one five miles down the road, but a DWI was the last thing he needed. So, he kept it close to home if he was drinking.

Sometimes, he'd go there first have a couple, then get busy drinking when he got back to town.

He'd never forget the first time he didn't try to keep his impulses under control. Isabelle was being a bitch about him drinking too much and not being home, the kids would rather be with their mom and her side of the family, that bitch, and work was tedious. It was all coming to a head. The pressure was so much. He was wound so tight. Why did he drink so much? He was trying to keep the demons away. He heard them in his head all the time. They told him to take it. Take what he wanted. He deserved it. He could do what he wanted. He was Michael fucking Lewis. No one could tell him what to do. He was a grown-ass man. He could make his own decisions.

It was a cold night in January. The kind of cold where it almost hurt to breathe. It was minus-forty before windchill. Nights like that didn't happen very often even in Minnesota. It got cold, but that was cold even by those standards. His pressure-cooker brain was ready to explode. He was at a different bar. He didn't want to see any of the regulars at the local taverns. So, he went the extra twenty miles to Floodwood.

This blonde came up to him and said, "Watch this." She started making weird movements with her mouth. He had no clue what she was doing. She said "See! I tied the cherry stem without my hands." Jesus. That was hot. He should have married a chick like that. Fuck that. She'd change the minute he put a ring on it, too. He left the bar, worked up, horny, and pissed. He'd have just done that chick, but she had meth teeth. He couldn't overlook that. He followed this girl a few days before back to her place from the bar. He saw her go in and turn the light on in the kitchen. She was his type. She was smart, but not too smart. She was pretty, but not too pretty. She was desperate for attention. She was perfect. He logged that information for later when he really needed it. Tonight, he really needed it. He'd talked to her, her name was Vicki or Nicki? He was pretty sure it was Vicki. He should have paid better attention. But he knew she'd let him in. She gave him the signals last week. He knocked on her door. She looked confused at first. Then it dawned on her who he was. "Michael, hi. What are you doing here?"

"Last week, you told me to stop by for a beer anytime, so here I am. It's anytime."

"I don't remember saying that," she said. "I must have been really drunk."

"You were a little toasty," Michael said.

That made her laugh, and she let him in. She went into the kitchen to get them each a beer.

"Do you want an IPA or something light?" she asked.

"I'll take the IPA," he said.

She gave it to him and they talked for a few minutes and then he started kissing her. At first, she kissed him back, but when he got a little forceful she pulled away.

"I'm really not that kind of girl," she said. "I don't have sex with people I'm not in love with."

Michael was in no mood for this shit. This woman shit. This lead the guy on until he's hard as a rock and walk away bullshit that women liked to pull all the time. "Oh no, I'm a virgin, I can't do it unless I'm in love." Well fuck that. There were times when a man just needed sex the way he needed it without all the constant chatter. He exploded.

"Do not fuck with me," he said. "You won't like the end result."

"Michael, I can't," she said.

He lost it. He grabbed her around the throat and squeezed. He squeezed and squeezed until he felt her life drain from her. He let go, and she came back.

"Can you do it now," he asked.

She was coughing and hacking and looking like a deer in caught in the headlights. Her eyes were so wide. But she managed to nod. He knew he had to kill her now. She would call the cops, and he was not going to prison for a piece of ass. But it was too late now. She didn't know that though.

When he finished, he started to strangle her again. He decided to make it quick for her. And broke her neck. He used a condom because during the OJ trial they were talking about DNA and they could tell if you did it by that. He found a Walmart bag and put the condom and his beer bottle in it. He finally felt the pressure lift. For the first time in his life, he felt a rush. The downside to having no guilt, was that he felt no excitement either. Sexual excitement, he felt. Regular excitement, he never felt. Everything felt boring and the same. Except that. Killing Vicki / Nicki was the single greatest thing he'd ever done. He couldn't do it again, he knew, but he wouldn't have to. The pressure in his head was gone. Vicki / Nicki was the ticket. She was all he needed to feel normal.

Of course, Vicki / Nicki wasn't a one off. He never did figure out her actual name. Every few weeks, the pressure built up again. He'd keep it at bay with porn or a willing girl from the bar, but eventually, it wouldn't be enough. He drove down to Minneapolis for his next one. He saw some young girl walking by herself in the dark and just grabbed her. That one was really exciting. She didn't know what hit her. Then there was the Bodega girl, there was one he didn't think they'd found the body yet. There were a few more. Two got away. The old lady he grabbed by mistake. She had kids for Christ's sake. He saw their pictures in her wallet. He would have to be more careful.

They were talking about him on the news a lot now. They were calling him the I35 killer. He didn't like that because wasn't there some guy with a similar name in California or Washington or whatever? They could do better than I35 killer. He'd like the "Minnesota Maniac or Sex Slayer, or the Close-up killer because his killings were up close and personal." He just knew they could do better than I35 killer. That was stupid.

He knew it wasn't good that they talked about him on the news, but he couldn't help but be a little proud of his work. He put so much into it and risked everything. He had to do it to relieve the pressure in his head. He kept thinking the next one would be his last, and it got worse. The pressure built back more quickly, and he had to do more to satisfy his need. A few days ago, another one got away.

He tried to grab her from a park by his house. He knew better than that. He would bring the cops to his neighborhood. Stupid. Why would he do that? He didn't even get anything off her.

He tried to get her to come back to his car to get his card so she could call him to set up a modeling gig. He stroked her ego.

At first, she bit. She blushed when he told her she was beautiful. He told her she needed an agent, she should model. She said she didn't want to be a model. She was studying to be an architect and was almost finished with her degree.

He pushed and said a little side gig to pay school loans wouldn't hurt. But she had this dog who kept growling at him. He was a mutt with black hair and white spots. He had hair coming out of his ears and a beard like a terrier. She called him Doug. He thought she was calling him Dog at first and thought she could get more creative than that. Doug was a creative name for a beast of a dog. He hated Michael. He growled, barked, and lunged for him. The girl kept telling Doug to stop and to sit. Finally, she told Michael that she wasn't interested, and she had to go. He told her to have a good day and walked to his car. He didn't see her look back, so she probably thought he was just a perv trying to pick her up. He hoped that's what she thought.

The pressure was almost too much. Isabelle wouldn't be home until after a play with Eva, so he decided to go home and watch porn to get rid of some of the pressure building within him.

38
Izzy

Michael was getting worse. He was crabby all the time. If they ever had sex, it was so rough that I told him to keep his hands off me for a while. I couldn't run forever, but he hadn't touched me since.

He wasn't home much. I saw evidence that he had been home during the day when I wasn't. The bed looked like it had been slept in while I was at my stupid college classes. I had to take classes to renew my license. I hated them, but they were free, so I couldn't pass them up. They were some special thing for teachers because no one wanted to be a teacher any more.

They had to offer us something. Extra classes meant extra money eventually, and I had to renew my license this year anyway. The Linguistics class was the worst. I got cocky. I had no business in that class. I'd never even taken a linguistics class, but it was approved by my boss to take for a lane change, and that was a raise. So, I thought, "How bad can it be?" It turns out that it can be really bad. It can be exceedingly bad. I wasn't even sure that I would pass. It was awful. The professor was nasty. She would not take questions. She said she was busy, and we could email her if we absolutely had to. What a bitch. So, I dealt with trying to teach linguistics to myself while helping Eva get ready to move to New York and trying to keep everyone safe from Michael's wrath.

He was so crabby that he needed a wide berth at home. We

stayed clear. Often, we stayed away. He didn't even look for us any more. He was so lost in his own little world that we did not matter. That was fine with me, but I wondered how this happened. How did the obsessive Michael, who even made me ride with him the mile and a half to the dump so he "didn't have to be without me." He was crazy obsessive since the day I met him. He never went anywhere but the bar without me. The last few weeks, I drove past the bar each night that he said he'd be there, and his truck wasn't there. His truck was a distinct blue. I couldn't miss it. It was one of those new colors for cars they kept coming out with, and I was shocked that he picked it. He always talked about how stupid it was to get any color but silver. Silver could go the longest without washing, and since we lived in the country on dirt roads, we usually drove silver vehicles. He wasn't at any of the bars near our house, and he wouldn't go further. He just wouldn't. He'd have to drive too far. He feared another DUI. He said he'd never go through that again. Thank God for that, anyway.

  Eva and I got home from a play a bunch of kids from different churches put on every summer. They'd do it for the community, and then they'd board the bus and set out for Utah or California or wherever the director booked them. It was a great opportunity for the kids, and they were incredibly talented. They performed Les Miserables this year. I couldn't figure out how this equated a religious play, but I wasn't complaining. I'd sat through Godspell about a million times, and this one was one of my favorites. It was really cool to see the kids who were so "cool" during school belt out One Day More. I couldn't believe the quarterback for the football team was Marius and had the most beautiful voice I'd ever heard. He was spectacular. I was still kind of floating when we got home. So was Eva. Gregg was in it. He actually had a huge part. He had a great voice and such charisma. He tried to get Eva to try out for the play, but she wasn't in a place for organized religion, she said. I think the two of us had prayed so hard that we didn't even know what an answered prayer looked like to us any more.

I flipped on the light when we got home. I assumed Michael was asleep because his car was home, but the lights were off.

I screamed when I turned on the lights. He scared the shit out of me.

"Honey, why are you sitting in the dark?"

"Why are you sleeping with your ex-boyfriend?"

I had no idea what in the hell he was talking about. I didn't even know which ex-boyfriend he meant. I hadn't kept in touch with anyone. I didn't want people to see my pathetic excuse for a life. So, I had very few friends, and I became an introvert in the last seven or eight years. It was easier than trying to explain why a song sent me into a panic attack or why I fixated on stupid little things like a class I didn't belong in. That was all I wanted to talk about. I needed everyone to know what a bitch that professor was. I fixated on that. It was so much easier than facing my truths. My life was out of control. I'd lost it to alcoholism and psychopathy.

I was a prisoner in my own home. He always needed to know where I was and what I was doing and said he was "checking in." Like that was a good thing. For most people, it was a good thing. But his checking in was sinister. He was spying on me, stalking me. He wasn't just checking in. He was making sure I was where I said I'd be. That's why this took her so aback.

"Michael, have you been drinking?" I asked. At that he leapt from the table like Spiderman. I'd never seen him move so fast. He even hurdled a dining room chair. Well, he jumped over the seat part of a dining room chair. He was on me in a second. Eva was filming the whole thing with her iPhone. Dang those things have come in handy. I wished I had one before. He slapped me so hard that I fell and hit my cheek on the dining room chair that he leapt.

Faces bleed a lot I've come to find. Mine had been bleeding a lot lately. This time, I wasn't all that worked up by it. I was getting used to it.

"Admit it," he said. "You still love Terry. Your big high school boyfriend who you bragged looked like a blonde version of Kirk Cameron. Do you think I don't listen when you talk? I hear everything you say. I know you're sleeping with him. Wanna know how I know? I heard you talking about him to your little friend Beth."

"First, we are fifty-year-old women. I do not have "little friends." Second, do you tap the phones now, you crazy fuck? He just shook he was so mad. I didn't care any more. Go ahead and kill me. I'm done. I talked about Terry one time when Beth and I were reminiscing about old flames. This happened months ago. You cheat on me all the time, you two-faced bastard. You want to hit me because I talked about Terry months ago with my best friend which I am entitled to do. What about all the women at the bar? The bar closes at two. Some nights you don't stroll in until it's light outside." I swallowed hard because I was early, but he'd hit me for the last time.

"I want a divorce," I said. "I can't be married to you for one more second."

I already had clothes, toiletries, food, television, everything set up at the new place. Eva stocked her dresser with clothes and make up too. We could pick up and go anytime we wanted. He shocked me when he got all calm.

"Fine, go," he said.

I kissed his cheek and wished him peace. And we left. Just like that. We left. It was so much easier than I thought it would be. I laugh cried all the way to the apartment. I got a garage so he couldn't creep around and find my car. The garages didn't have windows. He'd still find me if he really wanted to, but I was not going to make it easy on him. I had to remind myself not to be fooled by that easy departure. Michael would make me pay for leaving him. I knew he would. He just had to figure out his little revenge plots.

We walked up to our new place and locked the doors. Our apartment was on the fourth floor of a secure building. There was no way for him to shimmy the walls and break in through our sliding glass door like he did when we were first dating. I had a little pang of missing him right then. There was something seriously wrong with me. When he tried to break in through the patio, he'd driven so fast that I thought he was trying to kill me. He was having a temper tantrum and my roommate, and I called the police on him. Not a great memory, but I missed him already a little nonetheless. I was a freak show.

I wondered when I'd get over all of this. I doubted I ever would. He'd traumatized me too much to ever be myself again.

39

Eva said she was exhausted and wanted to call Gregg. She went to her room, and I poured myself a glass of the box of wine I had in the fridge. I didn't think a bottle would be enough when I was in the grocery store, so I bought a box. I was nothing if not classy. It tasted good to me, and I took a glass onto the patio. I hadn't felt that free in years.

I think the last time I felt this comfortable, I was in college. It definitely dated back to before I knew Michael. I can't believe I let myself go this far down the rabbit hole with him. Twenty years of my life was gone. Twenty years. I would never get that back. Still, I wouldn't change a thing. I got Eva out of this deal. If I would have made any other choice, I wouldn't have exactly Eva.

If I wouldn't have stayed as long as I did, I wouldn't be as close to Sophie and Oliver. They would have gone their own way, and I'd have been an ex-stepmom. When Michael remarried, because he is who he is, the new woman would be their stepmom. Since I stayed until they were both in college, we had a strong bond. That was worth everything. I would change nothing, but I wouldn't want to do it again. I had a feeling I would need a lot of therapy to help me get past everything I saw and all that was said and done to me. I'd have to get over my guilt and accept my part in the whole circus. I'd read a gazillion self-help books, so I had an idea of the work that lie ahead.

At that moment, I felt no stress. I wasn't worried about him finding us. I wasn't worried about tomorrow. I wasn't fixated on anything bizarre, so my anxiety was at bay for now. I just felt good. Finally, I could breathe.

Eva was in her room feeling pretty much the same way as her mom. She called Gregg and told him about her day. He listened and never interrupted. He didn't try to fix it or compare it to something he had been through. Her mom did that all the time. She hated it. She used that to show she understood what the other person was feeling. It was nice, though, to just be listened to. He asked how she was. He listened to her feelings. When she talked to him about it, it was about her, only her. With her parents, it was about her mom's guilt for picking him to be my dad, or about what my dad might pull next and how to avoid trouble.

With Gregg, she was just Eva. She was valued on her own merit, and her feelings were her own, and no one needed to feel guilty for them. When her mom said how bad she felt for what Eva went through, she knew her mom meant well, but it was like the story was about her then. Like Eva, herself, didn't matter. Eva knew that was a selfish way to look at things, but she heard the apologies so often that they were getting on her nerves and made her feel bad for feeling bad. She wasn't sure if that made any sense, but it was the only way she knew how to explain it. Gregg understood when she said it that way, anyway. She would never say these things to her mom, but she had to get her feelings out. Gregg was so sweet for listening.

When Eva got off the phone with him, she went for her phone. Then, she remembered that she couldn't have her phone on, so she went on WhatsApp with her iPad. She messaged the girls. Just Addie was online at that time, so the two of them messaged each other.

"Hey, Add," Eva said.

"I can't use my phone because we don't want my dad to know where we are. He can track our phones."

"I didn't realize you guys were that scared of him," Addie said. "I'm so sorry, Eva. I should have known."

"How would you know? I'd never have told you. It is embarrassing to have the your dad be the town perv and drunk."

"He's so mean to you guys. You deserve to be happy! We leave in thirteen days. Can you believe it?"

"Thank God. I will worry about my mom, though," Eva said.

"Do you want me to have my mom check up on her sometimes?" Addie asked.

"I'd love that, but I can't give this address to anyone. It's not safe."

"Okay. I hope you two can sleep tonight," she said.

"It'll be the first night that I've slept well in a long, long time," Eva said. "Good night, Addie. Love you!"

"Love you, too!"

Eva felt so lucky to be so loved. Her friends cared about each other like a family. She felt bad that her mom really only had Beth. But she and Beth had been best friends since they were little. So, she was just happy that endured. Eva knew her dad had something to do with why her mom didn't have a lot of friends and her grandparents were never around. Her dad didn't like to compete with anyone else for our affections. He also couldn't tolerate anyone who didn't fall for his line of bullshit. Eva's grandparents did not fall for it. Neither did her uncle. Her dad hated that side of her family with a passion. Once, Eva heard her grandpa tell her mom that a psychopath was born every forty-seven seconds, and he was convinced that her dad was one of them. He went into all the traits of a psychopath, and he was right. Her dad checked all the boxes. All Eva could do was hope that he didn't find them and be happy they were free if even just for today. She fell asleep without putting on her pyjamas or even brushing her teeth. She was exhausted.

    Every part of my body hurt. Today was harder on me than I wanted to admit. I wanted to cry, and I wanted to dance at the same time. It was the strangest feeling. I would flash often to things we did as a family or just the two of us that I remembered as fun for a split second. Then, I'd remember that he chose my clothes on that vacation or pinned me down on the bed and forced himself on me on that vacation. I think I was just overly tired. I put on my silk pyjamas that I bought just for this occasion, put lavender essential oil in my diffuser, and went to bed. I was asleep before I knew what hit me.

40

Eva and I slept until ten-thirty the next morning. I haven't done that since college. I could have slept the whole day away if I let myself. Instead, I put my swimsuit on and went down to the pool. I swam laps and felt so free in the water. I could get used to this every morning. What a great way to get a little exercise. I loved the pool. When I got back to the apartment, I took a shower and put on my robe. I grabbed a cup of coffee and sat on the patio. I wished I could turn on my phone, but I couldn't risk that.

 I had Eva's suitcases at the apartment because I knew she would have to pack up for NYC. When she got up, I made her a ham and cheese omelet and toast. She ate every last bite. We realized that we hadn't eaten much yesterday. I still couldn't eat much, but I did force down some toast. I couldn't risk getting sick right now. She had to be healthy and strong for Eva right now. This was so hard for her. We went to Target and bought a bunch of stuff for her to take to New York for school like toiletries and towels, school supplies and a coffee maker for their studio apartment. How exciting for them. Eva wanted to meet up with the girls, but I didn't want her out of my sight. I drove her to The Daily Grind coffee shop where she met up with Tasha, Addie, and Jenna. I sat in the car and listened to a podcast on my iPad. I bought the iPads last year and opened an account just for the iPads at Verizon. When I felt comfortable enough to be seen in public, I'd get our new phones. We'd have different accounts and different numbers. We were even using a different carrier. That should be safe. For now, the iPads worked, and I loved this podcast. It was about Ghislaine Maxwell and Jeffrey Epstein. Epstein was such a son of a bitch that I wondered if Michael really was a psychopath when there were people like Epstein in the world. He was dead now and deserved nothing less. I wondered when karma would catch up with Michael.

Did he care that they were gone? If he cared at all, it was because he lost something that he considered his. We were like possessions to him. We weren't people.

Eva, Tasha, Jenna, and Addie sat at the Daily Grind like they used to do before life got so complicated. She didn't mention that her mom was in the car listening to her podcast because it wasn't safe for her to be out alone. Her dad had no idea that The Daily Grind was their favorite coffee shop. It didn't pertain to him, so he didn't pay attention. I decided to be up front with the girls about just how bad it had become with him.

"Last weekend, I watched my mom practically run from him for the entire weekend."

"What do you mean?" Jenna asked.

"I mean he wanted her to be at his beck and call, and she wouldn't do it. So, he pursued her, big time. It was gross. She tried to walk by him Saturday morning, and he untied her robe. So, she tied it back up. He came up behind her and untied it again. This went on for ten minutes, and she finally got dressed. He barged through the door while she was getting dressed. He does that. He doesn't bother turning the knob. He just pushes, and it makes a big noise when the door opens. It makes me jump every time he does it. I have to lock the door when I go to the bathroom, or he'll barge in on me in there, too. It's a power thing."

"Ew. That's really gross," Addie said.

"I know," Eva said. "It's ridiculous what has become normal

to us. We don't even really think about this shit any more. It got to the point that I hated life. I walked on eggshells all the time."

"Love you, Eva. Everything is going to be better now that you guys are out of there."

"I couldn't believe my mom did it," Eva said.

"It was like all of a sudden, she could take not one more thing and told him that we were out."

"She's so strong," Tasha said.

"I know," Eva said. "She's my hero."

41
Michael

What the fuck? Michael wondered. Why in the hell would she leave him? She was nothing without him, he knew. She could barely keep a checking account, he thought. He pulled her out of poverty, put a roof over her head, food on her table, and clothes in her closet. He let her have a kid even though he didn't want another one. He already had Sophie and Ollie. He didn't need more kids, but she wanted one more. Michael had to agree to that for her to marry him. So, he said fine. In five years or so, another kid would be fine. She was pregnant in a year. She claimed she didn't do it on purpose, but Michael was pretty sure she did.

The kid was fine. Eva was quiet and basically did what she was told. But Izzy paid way too much attention to her. She used to make him lunches to take to work. She used to do a good job ironing his shirts. When he pointed out they were now half assed, she started bringing them to the dry cleaners. She never ironed for him again. Which was fine. At least they weren't half wrinkled any more, and she dropped them off and picked them up. But she used to take pride in taking care of him. She used to like to be with him. She used to like sex for Christ's sake. As soon as the kid came, everything changed. She was tired all the time, she gave the kid and her job everything, and Michael was left with whatever scraps she had left.

So, yeah. He drank too much. And about the time the kid was born, he started giving in to his violent fantasies and urges, but he never acted them with Izzy. She should be happy he still wanted her. He thought he was probably the only guy on the planet who still fantasized about his wife sometimes. But Izzy didn't care about that. Apparently, she didn't like to be fantasized about. Other women told him this was a great quality, and Isabelle was lucky. But she didn't think so. She fucking left him and took the kid with her.

Who did she think she was? Did she really think she could leave him that easily? Did she think she could take what was rightfully his and just leave? She had another thing coming. She did not know who she was dealing with. She and Eva turned off their cell phones, so he couldn't track them, but they would make a mistake. Sooner or later one of them would cave to habit, and he'd have them. All he did was work to make them happy and look how they dishonored him. Fuck them. He'd make them pay for this.

42
Addie

Addie was sure the police would want to know this about Mr. Lewis. He was creepy. There was a murderer running around free, killing women and girls, and she saw the composite of the guy on the news. It totally could have been Mr. Lewis. It was only a side view, but he had shoulder length hair, and a pointed nose. He was about six feet tall and wore Carhart Jeans. Mr. Lewis always wore those. He just got his hair cut short, but he always used to wear it longer and put it in a man bun. He cut it about the same time the composite drawing came out.

Eva said he left town for three or four days a week almost every week. She and her mom loved when he was gone. That would give him the opportunity to be the I35 killer or whatever they were calling him now. The latest was the Minnesota strangler or Minnesota Murderer. Addie liked the last one best. Anyway, he had the means and opportunity. His motive was just that he was a psychopath. He displayed everything she read about psychopaths. He was glib, grandiose, a pathological liar, he only cared about himself, it was impossible for him to feel guilt or shame, he was easily bored and craved excitement.

Eva said he went skydiving several times a year. He also drove really fast and acted like a teenaged boy. He drank like a fish. He rarely made sense when he was drinking. But he almost talked about killing people. He'd talk about the stuff he thought the killer did wrong. He's say, "I would've made sure it looked like there was forced entry." He was just creepy. Addie wanted to tell Detective Engen what she knew. She knew she could trust her to tell her bosses, but not tell them her name.

It wasn't fair that this asshole was intruding on what should be the most exciting time for them. They should be packing their rooms and labelling boxes not calling cops and looking over their shoulders all the time. Addie caught Michael spying on her sometimes. She'd see his car parked by her house. Sometimes someone was in the car. Sometimes, there wasn't. But she saw him. She knew he was there. Jenna and Tasha said the same thing. "He thinks one of them will lead him to Eva and Izzy," she thought. "How stupid did he think we were. We'd never do that."

Michael knew they'd have to be leaving town in a few days to get to New York. There were only three days until Labor Day weekend. Everyone moved into apartments or dorms the Saturday before Labor Day. He knew they had an apartment off campus, so they would want to move in on the first of September. It was August 23rd. The clock was ticking for him to get back at them. Finally, he figured out how to access them. He would find their most vulnerable. Their weakest link, and use her to entice Eva out of her corner. Her mother wouldn't be far behind. Izzy was really the one he wanted. She was the one he was really pissed at. She had no right to ditch him and take Eva with her. How dare she? The bitch hadn't even had an opinion in ten years. She was totally trained in. He didn't want to give that up to train a new one in.

43
Izzy

I was so happy. Eva was the happiest she'd been in, well, her whole life. Eva finally seemed to be the carefree teenager she should be. Precious girl. I was so proud of her. She hadn't seen Gregg in a while, but she knew they were messaging on WhatsApp. That way her dad couldn't track her.

We did get new phones the other day. The representative at Verizon assured them they'd be safe. He even put the bill in the name of JC Christianson and had the bill sent to my school address just in case he figured out the initials JC. He'd check Christianson but there were lots of Christianson's. Christianson was my maiden-name. J was for my brother Jared who died when he was a week old, and C was for Carrie, who was my mom's sister. She died when she was eighteen of cancer. He'd never figure that out. The rep. said I could just go by my regular name if I wanted. There was no way for him to track me. I just wanted this one more layer. If he was going to find me, it didn't hurt to know I did what I could to keep him away.

This morning, Eva told me that she and Gregg had their last date before we left for New York. He was taking her to dinner at a fancy restaurant that was at the very top of the Radisson hotel. It was a JJ Astor restaurant. It always made me think of the Titanic because the real JJ Astor was killed on it. His millions couldn't buy him a seat on a lifeboat. They were going there. The restaurant spun around so you could see all of Duluth's beauty at night. It didn't move fast, it wasn't like a carnival ride or anything, but it was cool. I was impressed. It wasn't cheap to go there. Eva made me promise not to follow her. It scared the hell out of me, but I promised. What good was leaving him if we couldn't live at least a little. They promised to be careful. They were going to yet another marvel movie after dinner. I wasn't sad to miss that movie. I didn't get their appeal. Of course, I was too old Eva informed me. She didn't mean it as a slam. She meant that only young people could accept the What if scenarios of Marvel movies. There was probably truth in that.

Eva and Gregg left the apartment about six o'clock. They walked to Gregg's car hand in hand. Eva looked a little bit sad to be leaving him. But they both knew she had to go. If it was meant to be, they'd make it work. If not, he was a great first love for Eva. She seemed to understand the significance of this night for their relationship. He didn't. He was totally confident that they'd be together forever. Distance didn't change a thing in his little optimistic heart.

My heart was full as they left on their date. I was so lucky. They were gone about twenty minutes, and I went to my bedroom to put my swimsuit on again. I thought another swim wouldn't hurt. Exercise kept my demons in my mind at bay. It however, could not fix the real demons that existed around me. As I was looking for my beach towel. My door kicked in. It was a huge bang, and it broke the chain lock. How had she forgotten to bolt the door? It automatically locks when it shuts, but I also had a chain and dead bolt installed. I had forgotten to turn the dead bolt.

I jumped and screamed, but I knew who it was. He followed Gregg. He knew that sooner or later Gregg would lead him here.

Michael tackled me on the floor of my bedroom and put a knife to my throat.

"If you move, I will kill you."

Having him breach the sanctity of my new apartment really pissed me off. This was my safe place. I decided to run anyway. I had to get out of here I already had my keys in my hand because I was planning to go to the pool. So, I pushed him off of me and rammed my keys into his eyes as hard as I could.

He stumbled back holding his eye. He screamed and called me a bitch. He told me that he would get me if it was the last thing he did. I ran as though my life depended on it.

I hit the stairwell and ran down them. I went as fast as my feet would carry me. I came out into the parking garage and ran to my stall. I jumped in my car and took off. He was not behind me that I could see, but I knew he was there. I could feel him.

44
Detective Engen

Neither Detective Engen nor Detective Townsend had slept in weeks. They worked this case from the time they woke up in the morning until they went to bed. They each generally worked a sixteen-hour day. They had to figure out who was killing these bright, beautiful, young women before he killed more of them. Engen took Addie's call and jotted all the information down. After Addie called, she compared Lewis's mug shot from a DWI a few years ago to the composite. It was exact. The nose, the hair, everything matched. Addie had no idea how important her tip was. Lewis had to give a DNA sample when he was arrested for DUI, so they had that on file. The question was, did it match the DNA collected in the skin samples under the fingernails of three victims. Neither Engen nor Townsend would go home while they waited for the lab results. They waited in the waiting room and paced. It took nearly thirty-six hours for the rushed samples to be analyzed. They had a match. They got him. He thought he was so clever using condoms in his sexual assaults that he didn't count on the quick thinking of his victims. They got him. The women he killed were the heroes of this story. The two of them and about eight cars of back up went to Lewis's house to arrest him.

    The son of a bitch wasn't home. Now what? Where would Lewis go if he wasn't home. The bar. The Detectives went to the local bar, but Lewis's truck wasn't there. They decided to go into the bar and see what people knew.

When Parker Engen walked into the Lost Tavern, Earl couldn't help but whistle. Parker was beautiful, but she didn't appreciate the cat calls. Earl, however, was talkative. He apologized for the whistle when Townsend walked in and gave him the eye. Earl gathered a couple of other regulars and they took the back corner table. They had to take what they heard with a grain of salt because you could have knocked half of them over with a feather. They were several drinks into their daily drunk. There was a blonde at the bar who was obviously avoiding eye contact. Those are always the ones with the real information. "Hi, I'm Detective Parker Engen, and I was wondering if you'd like to join us at the corner table."

"I'd really rather not," she said.

"Well, we could do it at the station," Parker said.

"I don't know nothing," the blonde said.

"I can judge that for you, even little things can be helpful."

"I ain't saying nothin' in front of all them," she said gesturing to the table Townsend was getting information from.

"That's okay," Parker said. "You can just talk to me."

"If people know I talked to you, and Mikey boy finds out, I'm in trouble," she said.

"Mikey boy? You mean Michael Lewis?"

"Of course. Ain't that who you're asking about?"

"Yes, it is. Could we just start with your name?" Parker asked.

"Fine. Name's Kaycee Carlson."

This woman was rough. She was missing a couple of teeth, her face was dirty, she was skin and bones, and she obviously had been hitting the meth lately. She would not make a good witness, but she could point me in the direction of someone who was.

"I'm going out for a smoke. In a minute, you can come out,

and I'll tell you what I know," Kaycee said.

"That works for me," Parker said.

She took that minute that Kaycee gave her to check the place out. She heard that there was a piece of driftwood in the bathroom with a bathrobe over it standing in the corner. It looked like a guy with a very big, very erect penis. She had to check this out for herself. Sure enough, there he was in all his glory, "Woody." The townspeople cleverly named this piece of driftwood Woody, and people would stop at this hole in the wall bar just to get a peek at that stupid piece of wood with a bathrobe on. It was really funny, if Parker was being honest.

She walked out of the Lost Tavern out to the smoking area in the grass. They had several tables set up out there with ash trays. They had signs saying not to take their drinks out there, but everyone did.

Kaycee was sitting at a table all by herself. There were only a couple people out there, and Kaycee didn't know them.

She suddenly appeared very sober and said to Detective Engen, "Lewis is evil. He is the devil. Be careful around that one."

"How do you mean, evil?"

"He gets off on causing pain," Kaycee said.

"How do you know?"

"I just know, all right?" Kaycee asked.

"Well, Ms. Carlson, I wish that was enough, but I really do need to know where you get your information."

"Well, I see stuff," she said. "My grandma could see stuff in people, too."

"Okay," said Parker who knew people in this neck of the woods. Everyone had a story. They either saw the future, could read palms, did Taro card readings, or they knew someone who did. This claim didn't surprise Parker all that much.

"See, one night, Lewis was talking to me, and I could see black all around him. Black means death. He has a black soul."

"Do you know any specifics? Like how Mr. Lewis's black soul shows itself?"

"You say you're a cop? Don't you know about all these killings up and down the freeway? Everybody knows about those."

"Yes, ma'am," Parker said. "I know about them. What do they have to do with Michael Lewis?"

"Lewis likes girls. He likes to have as many as he can. He can turn on the charm, or he can come down to my level and try to have sex with all of us. He doesn't care who we are or what we look like. He just wants sex. He wants sex with violence most of all. If he can kill someone and have sex with her, that's the best for him. He's sick. He can't help it. He has a black aura."

"His cheating is stuff of legend," Parker said.

"No, it's real," said Kaycee.

Parker tried not to laugh. "Kaycee, how old are you?" Parker asked.

"Thirty-two, why?"

"I was just wondering. You are an old soul." Kaycee looked about fifty-five not thirty-two.

"I've heard that," Kaycee said.

Parker gave her card. "Kaycee, if you ever want help cleaning up, let me know. I can help you get a great counselor."

"I ain't got no money for no counselor," said Kaycee.

"This is free for you."

"I'll think about it," Kaycee said. Parker hoped she meant it. Kaycee needed to clean up.

She was way too young to look like that.

That was when Townsend walked out of the bar.

"Why do you insist on wearing that trench coat every day," Parker asked Carl.

"I look like more of a cop in this," said Carl Townsend.

"Um, you look like you think you look like a cop in that. You look like you're playing a cop on TV. Not like you actually are a cop."

"Fuck you, Engen, Let's get in the car and get the hell out of here. It's like Deliverance in this town."

"I know, right? Guess how old the lady is that I was talking to, the one with the meth scars."

"I don't know sixty?" Townsend guessed.

"That's what I thought, or close to what I thought. She's thirty-two."

"Just say no to drugs," he said.

"No shit," said Parker. "That poor girl is a mess."

"Wait until you hear about the idiots I interviewed," Townsend said as he got into the car. "I can just imagine."

"Actually got a couple things we can use, but they were wasted already."

"It's five o'clock somewhere," said Parker.

"Nowhere around here! It's one-thirty in the afternoon, for Christ's sake," Townsend said.

"Well, we are lucky we are not alcoholics," she said.

"Avoided that one by the skin of my teeth," Carl said. And they both laughed. "Seriously, though, this guy is nasty. According to these guys, he does shit just to see what happens. They said he lit a cat on fire once when they first moved to town."

"Oh my God," Parker said. "That is disgusting."

"I know, right? Even these drunks are scared shitless of him. The first guy, Earl, he said Michael brags all the time. He caught the biggest fish, he has the most money, he drives the best truck, his business is the most successful."

"Who does that sound like?" Parker asked.

"Yeah, I know. Sounds just like Trump. I guess, he is ruthless when people don't listen to him or buy his line of bullshit."

"Did they say how they know this?"

"One time, Earl, asked him about his wife when he was trying to pick up a different girl. Earl said he harassed him for over a year. He called and left messages referencing his kids and where they went to school. Earl was afraid he'd get to his kids. He also slashed his tires and broke his windshield. Earl said he was scared shitless of him, but he got over it. Michael bought him drinks whenever he was in the bar now as kind of a peace-offering. Earl liked this kind of peace-offering. He thought that while Michael was scary at one point, he's a good guy now. His opinions were based completely on free beer."

This town was fucked up, Townsend thought.

45
Izzy

I didn't know where to go. Where was the last place he'd look for me? I found a parking garage in downtown Duluth and went into the Casino. He knew I didn't gamble, and he'd never think of the casino. Plus, it never closed. I'd be okay there. I played some quarter slots and lost all my extra cash in twenty minutes. So, I went to the bar and drank endless diet cokes.

When the sun came up, I went out to my car. I thought I'd be safe now that it was daylight. Eva hid at Tasha's sister's house. Michael didn't even know Tasha had a sister, so she was safe.

I went straight to the police station. They drew up a restraining order for me, but so far, he hadn't done anything they could arrest him for, they said. This pissed me off. I knew it would be the case, but seriously what good was the law if you had to wait until you were dead for it to help you. They'll "get justice," but they can't protect us. That's bullshit if you ask me.

I finally went back to my apartment. I parked under the building, and I went home. I couldn't run forever. Come and get me, asshole. I am done being afraid. I'm done running and pretending. I'm done feeding your ego and walking on eggshells waiting for the next bad thing to happen. I'm done wearing what you want me to wear and listening to your opinions as though they are facts. I'm done with my part of this fucked up union. I'm done putting my needs and those of my family last. I want to get to know my friends and my family again. I want Eva to spend time with her grandparents, whom she adores. I'm done camping in the wet grass and sleeping on rocky hillsides. I'm done looking for frogs in my free time. I'm done worrying if my activities will be Michael approved. I'm done with the nerves, the tears, the loneliness, and the craziness. Kill me if you have to, Michael. I'm done running.

Of course, those were words I said to myself, but frankly, I never felt stronger. Eva was safe, and death was better than the life I'd been living.

When I got home, there were four voicemails that I hadn't checked, and I decided to check them. They were all from the detectives I talked to earlier.

They begged me to come back to the station. They had new information for me. On the fourth message, Detective Engen told me to get the hell out of the apartment. He would kill me, and they were trying to find and arrest him for the murders of three young women in connection with the serial murders between Minneapolis and Duluth. They got the DNA back, and it was him. He killed those girls. I wondered why it took them so long to run the DNA. Engen said that they finally had a good enough test to get a profile from a couple of skin cells. They only had the tiniest of samples under the fingernails of three of the young women. They had his DNA on file from a DUI he got a couple years ago.

My knees gave out. I hadn't expected this. I knew he made our lives a living hell, but I didn't know he was out murdering people! How could I possibly reconcile this with the charismatic man I met in the bar all those years ago. The hot guy with the man bun. I loved him, and he was a fucking murderer. How stupid was I? I chose that guy to be Eva's father? That was the least of it, really. There still was an Eva. All those parents whose daughters would never come home because of him, my heart bled for them. I couldn't wrap my head around it completely. I was still scared of the jackass I was trying to get away from in my head. This wrench was not something I could comprehend.

Michael was a murderer. They thought he killed fourteen girls and young women in the span of three years. How did it come to this?

Three years ago was when he started staying away for a few days at a time. I thought he had a different family somewhere. I didn't think he was out murdering people. How could I not know? I lived with him. How did I not see the signs? I knew he was impossible to live with, he chose my clothes, he talked down to me, he decided what I could and could not do, he was abusive to both Eva and to me with his words and his fists a few times. I never thought he was physically abusive because it didn't happen very often. I blamed myself for those events, too. I egged him on, I said things that I knew I shouldn't have, I watched a movie instead of going camping or whatever reason he came up with. I bought it. I had so little self-esteem that I believed I deserved the abuse. I was going to have to figure this shit out in therapy, however. I had to get the hell out of this apartment. I reminded myself of the idiot teenagers in slasher films who didn't get out when they had the chance. Instead, they went to the basement or the attic where they were bound to be cornered by Jason Vorhees or Mike Meyers or the Nightmare on Elm Street guy. What could go wrong if I just take a last look around the apartment for old times' sake? The audience is yelling, "Get out!"

It was too late. He was here. I felt it. I could always feel when Michael was around. My anxiety went up and my heart beat out of my chest until I consciously calmed myself by breathing out slowly. I had to think of my counsellor who said when I got too upset to just focus on breathing and nothing else. I could remember how great it was to just breathe. How amazing my body was that the air would flow in and out without thinking about it. I should concentrate on how wonderful it felt to inhale all that oxygen and to exhale slowly. This was way past breathing exercises working, but I did slow my exhales so I could think. I grabbed a butcher knife out of the block on the counter and hid around the corner. He couldn't do anything half assed. He had to come in and taunt me.

"Isabelle... oh, Isabelle. Where for art thou, Isabelle?" I rolled my eyes. What a dick.

"I know you're here Izzy. Do you want to draw this whole thing out or should we just get it done now? Come on out."

"Hey, Izzy, I've got a surprise for..."

I didn't wait for him to finish the sentence. I lunged at him with the knife. I buried it as far as I could into his chest and ran. I ran like my hair was on fire.

I made it to the Liquor Store across the street from my apartment complex and had the owner call the police. He called the police for me, and hid me in the back room. His wife stayed in back with me, rubbed my back, and told me everything would be all right.

It seemed to take forever, but in reality, it was about five minutes.

As soon as the police arrived, I called Eva and told her it was over. She cried and cried. She assured me that they were tears of happiness. Finally, our lives were ours, and that bastard was going to prison where he belonged if he lived, that was. I didn't know if he was dead or alive. No one would tell me.

Finally, Detective Engen and Detective Townsend arrived. Engen told me that he was dead. She said it was obviously self-defense since he was in my apartment. However, we were married and technically, what was mine was his. I had to go make a statement, and the courts would decide if the stabbing was justified or not. Engen assured me it would not be a problem. Everyone knew he was just identified as the I35 killer, and that I knew it.

I told Engen about my apartment and that I was leaving him. So, it was known to law enforcement that I was leaving him. And his name was nowhere on the lease. He was evil. Still, I cried when I found out he was dead. He was the man I loved for all those years. My identity was wrapped up in him. Who was I if I wasn't the wife of that lying cheat? What would I do when I wasn't planning our escape or even how to survive each day? I didn't even know how to live like a normal person any more. I had one friend, and I had alienated my family. But Eva and I were alive. Like I said, we'd work that shit out in therapy. Right now, I had bigger fish to fry.

I went to Tasha's sister's house and hugged my daughter.

"Mom, I am so proud of you! You did it. We're free!"

"We did it," I said. We were happy to be rid of him so we could start our real lives, but we didn't celebrate. To some degree, we both loved him, and we knew the pain he caused so many people. There wasn't celebrating to do, but there was a lot of healing to do. That, we could start now.

A psychopath is born every forty-seven seconds. Never underestimate their evil.